A

Detective _____ ___ ___ __ catch his breath.
Audubon Park is New Orleans's largest, and Dino
had chased Lemoni through most of it. He found
cover and reloaded again, slipping six more magnums from another speed loader.

"The fucker must have a hundred clips with him,"
he told himself as he closed the cylinder. He looked
out in the direction from where the last shots had
come and could see nothing but blackness.

Dino rose and began to lope in long, deliberate
strides, straight for the shadow he prayed was
Lemoni. As he moved, Dino told himself, "Ice in the
veins. Ice in the veins." He knew that whoever gained
control of himself first would triumph. There would
be no more ducking or hiding, no more wild shots.

Dino lost sight of his quarry behind a tight row of
magnolia trees, but continued forward anyway,
fighting off the instinct to slow down.

Then he saw a sudden movement between the
magnolias as Lemoni's red, panting face gleamed
out at him. His gun pointed at Dino, who raised his
own gun, cupping it in both hands, aiming carefully
at the gleaming face. Lemoni's gun flashed as Dino's
own gun recoiled from firing.

Fire. Fire was burning on Dino's neck. He grabbed
the side of his neck with his left hand and felt wetness and knew he was hit. Gunshots burn.

THE Big KISS

O'NEIL DE NOUX

ZEBRA BOOKS
KENSINGTON PUBLISHING CORP.

ZEBRA BOOKS

are published by

Kensington Publishing Corp.
475 Park Avenue South
New York, NY 10016

Second printing: August, 1991

Printed in the United States of America

For Debbie, John, Andre, Vincent John,
and Little Joe De Noux

My father was a cop . . . so was my big brother . . . and so am I. . . . I have taken my rightful place at the end of the long blue line . . . but above all . . . I am Sicilian.

— Dino LaStanza

City Park Avenue

If there was one thing Dino LaStanza should have known, it was that in Homicide you were only as good as your last case. He should have known it did not matter how many mysteries you solved, did not matter how many killers you sent to Angola Penitentiary for that long wait for the electric chair. There would always be another body waiting. It did not even matter if you'd just solved the most sensational case in recent history. As soon as the next victim got himself killed, you were right back in the Homicide pressure cooker.

Dino LaStanza was beginning to think he was a pretty good detective, especially after solving the Slasher murders. That's how it went in Homicide: one minute you're on top, and the next minute a body is found somewhere and you have to start all over again.

At nine o'clock on a summer night so hot that the streets of New Orleans were still baking outside, Detective LaStanza was sitting at his desk in the Homicide Office when the telephone rang. Leaning back in his gray metal chair, hands cupped behind his head, he was thinking about the way his girlfriend had kissed him the night before, how she ran her fingers over his lips and then slowly opened her mouth to kiss him softly and then not so softly. He was thinking about Lizette's lips when the phone interrupted him.

"Homicide . . . LaStanza," Dino answered.

"This is Headquarters," announced the communications supervisor. "We've got a Signal 30 working at the St. Maurice Wharf . . . body found in the river . . . Harbor Police say he's got bullet wounds. . . . They're calling for Homicide."

"This better be a joke," Dino moaned.

"No, Detective LaStanza." The supervisor's cold voice almost slipped into laughter before she caught herself. "I'm not joking."

"All right," Dino began taking down the information. After securing the necessary details, he asked, "By the way, where the hell's the St. Maurice Wharf?"

"Lower Ninth Ward," advised the supervisor. "A couple blocks from St. Bernard Parish."

LaStanza hung up and looked over at his partner sitting across the desk. Paul Snowood, his feet up on his own gray metal desk, opened one eye and groaned, "Don't tell me . . ."

Dino nodded and tossed his pad and pen into his briefcase.

"Son-of-a-bitch!" Snowood yelled. He reached over and picked up his phone, punched out a number, and snapped into the receiver in disgust, "We just got nailed. I'll see ya tomorrow sometime." Hesitating a moment, he added impatiently, "What's there to be careful about? The bastard's dead!" Then he hung up. He looked back at Dino and shrugged. "She's always telling me to be careful. You'd think we did something dangerous for a living."

"I don't know what you're complaining about," Dino said as he stood up and stretched. "This is my case. I'm up for the next whodunit."

Paul reached into his briefcase for a can of smokeless tobacco and tucked a large pinch inside his lower lip. "What makes you think it's a whodunit?"

"Body in the river. You think the perpetrator's waiting on the dock?"

"You're right. It's all yours. But I think I'll mosey along and give you a hand." Snowood was the only policeman in New Orleans who ever moseyed anywhere. Dino was certain Paul's problem in that regard was that he read too many western novels. The previous night Snowood had a "hankering" for some barbecue jerky.

"Guess ya'll won't be seeing the Princess tonight, huh?" Paul asked as the two detectives picked up their briefcases and portable radios. Everyone on the platoon called Dino's girlfriend the "Princess," because she was an uptown girl who happened to live in a mansion overlooking Audubon Park.

"Actually," Dino advised as they stepped out of the office, "we don't have a date tonight."

"Yeah? Well, I hope this ain't no all-nighter. I'm taking my son to the zoo tomorrow morning."

The two rode the small "Police Only" elevator down to the first floor of Headquarters. It took almost three minutes. "Slowest fuckin' elevator on earth!"

"What's your hurry?" Paul needled. "Fucker ain't going nowhere."

Towering over LaStanza by half a foot, lanky Paul Snowood was the lone ranger of Homicide. Dino called him "Country Ass" because Paul always wore western shirts with rope ties and cowboy boots in a city of g-strings, sequins, and tight pants. On this

9

particular night, Paul was wearing a shirt with silver collarpoints and a bullhorn clip on the rope tie around his neck. Earlier Dino had asked him, "You ever dress like a normal person?"

"There's nothing wrong with these duds," Snowood argued. At which time Paul started in on Dino, chiding him about his penny loafers and baggy pants and pastel shirt with matching tie. "You look like you're still in high school."

Leaving their air-conditioned office for the sticky heat of New Orleans, Dino felt as far away from high school as he ever had. At thirty-one, LaStanza was the youngest and newest member of the Homicide Division. Usually he felt a lot younger than thirty. But tonight he felt his age as he climbed into their stripped-down, unmarked tan Chevrolet police unit.

Without another word, the pair made their way down to the Ninth Ward. Snowood drove, periodically spitting wads of brown saliva out the driver's window while LaStanza stared out the passenger side at the city. By the time they reached St. Claude Avenue, Dino had developed a stomach ache, a familiar queasiness brought on by the thought of what lay ahead. There was a body out there waiting for him. Suddenly he was no longer on top, no longer the hotshot detective with the perfect record. It was time to start all over again.

The St. Maurice Wharf rested along the dark Mississippi at the edge of the city. Beyond the small wooden pier lay nothing but weeds all the way to the Chalmette Battlefield, and it was dwarfed by the large concrete Alabo Street Wharf next door. St. Maurice must have seen better days before it was converted into a repair depot for barges and tugs. At least that's

10

what Dino figured when they parked their unit on the levee overlooking it.

The coroner's meat wagon was already there, sandwiched between a Fifth District unit and a Harbor Police car. Dino could see several uniforms assembled on the wharf, their flashlights helping illuminate the dark area that was lighted by a single, low powered, yellow street lamp.

As soon as the detectives stepped out on the wharf, Paul started gathering the names of all present. Dino moved directly to the body that lay at the edge of the pier under the golden glow of the antique street light.

"Jesus!" he said to himself when he saw the face.

"Nice duds, huh?" quipped one of the Harbor policemen, referring to the three-piece business suit on the victim. Dino ignored the Harbor cop. Kneeling next to the corpse, one word came to mind: the word *floater*. He had seen floaters as a patrolman, but always from a distance. This floater was his, and there was no distance anymore.

From the condition of the body, it was obvious it had been in the water for a while. The arms were stretched outward from the torso, the fingers curled grotesquely, like swollen white pretzels. It was as if the dead man was reaching for something he would never feel. The body was bloated to almost twice its normal size. But it was the face that was most startling: the eyes bulged obscenely from their sockets, a blue tongue protruded cruelly from the mouth, the cheeks were puffed, as if the victim was holding his breath.

Just above the bulging eyes were two small gunshot wounds. "Entry wounds," Dino noted on his pad, "small caliber." Even in the dull light he could clearly see scorching next to the wounds, the obvious signs of powder burns. Leaning closer with

11

his flashlight, he peered at the flakes of dark gunpowder embedded in the bleached white flesh. "Contact wounds," he jotted down, "or close range."

"That's one ugly motherfucker," Snowood exclaimed when he moved up behind his partner.

"He looks like a fuckin' gargoyle," Dino added.

"What's a gargoyle?" asked the same Harbor policeman, his flashlight also pointed at the dead man's face.

"A gargoyle's a monster looks just like that," Snowood pointed to the body and then patted Dino on the back. "That's a good name. The Gargoyle Murder . . . it's got a nice ring to it."

"He's been in the water at least forty-eight hours," Snowood explained to his junior partner, "time enough for bacteria in the gut to produce the gases that caused him to swell up and rise to the surface. That's why he's so bloated."

"How come they don't end up in the Gulf?" asked the Harbor cop.

"Swirling currents keep bodies right here until they pop up like turds."

Everyone in uniform laughed.

"Look here," Dino pointed to the jagged earlobes.

Paul nodded in recognition, "Crabs."

Snowood took a quick statement from the tugboat captain who had spotted the body in the river. Then he took an even quicker statement from the Harbor policemen who had fished it out of the water. Then they waited for the crime lab technician to arrive.

LaStanza walked the technician through the photos, full-lengths and then closeups and then closeups of the closeups, especially of the wound. The physical evidence was next, the little there was to collect.

A brief search of the body yielded a gold wedding band and a gold Rolex watch, still running smoothly, attached to the victim's wrist by a gold-nugget band. There was a wallet which contained a hundred and three dollars cash, three major credit cards, seven local credit cards, an Orleans Parish library card, and a Louisiana driver's license in the name of Thomas Jimson, white male, thirty-five years old, six feet tall, one hundred and eighty pounds, with brown eyes. When Dino saw Jimson's address, he blurted out, "Son-of-a-bitch was my neighbor!"

"You serious?" Paul asked.

"Yeah. He lived on City Park Avenue, a couple blocks from my house."

When the technician was finished with the body, Dino watched the coroner's assistants zip the Gargoyle into a black body bag and then load the bag into the meat wagon. He would see the body again, soon enough, at the postmortem early the next morning. The uniforms left when the meat wagon pulled away. Paul walked back to his unit and waited for his partner.

Dino moved to the edge of the pier and looked out at the ink-black water, at the reflections of the silver city lights dancing on the tips of the swift-flowing river. It felt cooler next to the water. But he was not thinking about coolness or water or silver lights or even his girlfriend's lips. He was thinking about his victim, his case, his mystery to solve. He was the case officer. He was now responsible for closing the final chapter in the life of one Thomas Jimson, late of City Park Avenue, also known as the Gargoyle. The knot in his stomach tightened again.

*　　　*　　　*

On their way to City Park Avenue, their sergeant called them on the radio. "What you got?"

"Floater," Dino answered. "We're going to his house now."

"Meet me at CDM first," Sergeant Mark Land told them. "The chaplain's tied up." Nothing more need be said. It was the police chaplain's job to notify relatives of deaths in the family. In Homicide, a detective's job was to catch killers, not comfort grieving families. Although they would be there to note the reaction of family members, it was the chaplain's job to tell them.

Snowood made a quick left off St. Claude Avenue at Elysian Fields and then an even quicker right on Decatur Street until they pulled up across from Jackson Square at the Café DuMonde. Their sergeant pulled up a second later in his own stripped-down, unmarked white Chevrolet, parking in front of them. Big and burly, with a handlebar moustache and a dark mass of unruly hair that was always too long, Mark Land lumbered out of his car. He looked like a bear coming out of hibernation.

The three detectives took an outside table at the edge of the café next to one of the green and white canopies. After ordering three coffees from a young black waiter, Mark asked, "So what do we have?"

Dino nodded. "A floater—he looked just like a gargoyle."

"A what?"

"Like one of those monsters on top Notre Fuckin' Dame Cathedral." Dino closed his eyes and rubbed his tired neck. "You know . . . like in *The Hunch-back of Notre Dame.*"

"He was a hunchback?"

"No," Paul roared, "he was just fuckin' ugly!"

Mark shook his head in disgust. "Ask a simple

14

question and you tell me the guy's a fuckin' monster."

"That's what he looked like." Dino leaned back in his chair and quickly described the body, which caused the young waiter's face to contort into a grimace when he returned with the coffee.

"Did I ever tell you boys how much you look like brothers?" Paul had told them at least twenty times, "especially when you wear the same suits."

It was a remark they both ignored. They knew they could easily pass for brothers. Both were dark, Italian, with moustaches and full heads of black hair, although LaStanza was much smaller and looked far less unruly. On this particular evening, Mark and Dino wore gray suits they had purchased from the same cut-rate store back when they were partners.

"Yep . . . brothers."

"Two wounds?" Mark asked Dino, getting back to the subject.

"That's right . . . contact wounds . . . stippling and flakes even after soaking in the river for God knows how long."

Mark sighed as the three detectives began mixing various amounts of sugar with the strong coffee-and-chicory mixture of café-au-lait. At that particular moment, an elderly oriental man wearing no shirt, a pair of baggy khaki shorts, and a black matador's cap sat at the table next to the detectives. Mark nodded toward the oriental and asked Dino, "What does that remind you of?"

For a second, Dino thought of Vietnam, until he saw the smirk on his sergeant's face. "The Buried Gook Case!" Dino laughed, and it became Paul's turn to shake his head.

"That ain't funny."

It was funny enough for a good two-minute laugh.

15

The Buried Gook Case was still a source of annoyance for Snowood, who had to handle it in the middle of the Slasher murders. While all of New Orleans was out chasing a mass murderer, he had to waste his time on a body found buried at a construction site. The body was of a middle-aged oriental who turned out to have died of natural causes . . . which enraged Snowood when he found out he'd wasted all that time on a natural death. What made it even funnier was how long it took Snowood to discover that the oriental construction workers had simply buried their companion where he fell, just like in Vietnam. The man died, so they buried him and went back to work. Only later, when the American foreman found the body and called the police, was this important caper assigned to Country-Ass.

Paul glared at the oriental and then turned to Dino. "You shoulda killed that bastard in Vietnam when you had a chance."

Mark picked up his coffee cup. "By the way, what's our victim's name?"

"Thomas Jimson," Dino answered.

"You kiddin'?"

"You know him?"

Mark put his coffee down and covered his face with his hands. "Did he live on City Park Avenue?"

"Yeah."

Mark looked up with an expression beyond disgust and announced, "Thomas Jimson just happens, happened, to be the son-in-law of Alphonso Badalamente."

There was a moment of absolute silence at the detectives' table before Dino ended it with a moan, "Jesus fuckin' Christ!"

All three men exchanged looks of dismay as the realization hit them. Snowood was the first to speak again. He leaned over and patted Dino on the shoulder. ''Well, pardner, there goes your perfect record.''

He knew exactly what Paul meant. Not only was this a whodunit, this was a gangland whodunit, organized crime. La Cosa Nostra.

''Could it have been a 64-30?'' Mark asked. Robbery-murder.

Dino shook his head. ''He had over a hundred bucks cash and a solid gold Rolex on his wrist.''

The three detectives drank the remainder of their coffee without another word. When they stood up to leave, Mark concluded the meeting with, ''Well, at least we won't have to go hunting for the killer tonight. He's probably back in Detroit or Chicago or fuckin' China by now.''

Stepping out of the cafe, the detectives passed several couples dressed in tuxedos and brightly colored evening gowns. The couples breezed into the café, laughing and giggling. Beautiful people having a good time, leaving scents of perfume in their wake. The somber detectives waited for them to pass before stepping out to their cars.

''Did you see that blonde?'' Paul asked as he reached for the car door.

''Did you see the limo they pulled up in?'' Mark asked.

''Yeah,'' Dino answered defiantly, ''but who'd *they* ever send to Angola?''

''Yeah,'' Paul replied. ''And how many floater autopsies did *they* ever handle?'' He smiled at Dino from the far side of their car and added, ''You're gonna love that autopsy in the morning. Wait'll they cut open his gut. It makes shit smell like perfume.''

City Park Avenue ran along the south side of City

Park. A narrow, palm-treed neutral ground divided its four lanes. On one side of the avenue lay still lagoons and towering oaks dripping Spanish moss in a park that remained green year round. On the other side stood well-groomed houses that rivaled the finest mansions of the Upper Garden District.

The Jimson place was a two-story Victorian built of cypress and knotty pine, with trellises, porticoes, and a wide gallery running the length of its front and sides. It was called a wedding-cake house because of the domed porticoes at the front which resembled the gazebo atop a wedding cake. White paint served to enhance the image.

When the two detective units pulled up in front of the house, Dino immediately recognized the police chaplain standing on the sidewalk next to a bald man in a black suit. Mark shook hands with the chaplain, who introduced Jules Rosenberg, a man who needed no introduction.

Rosenberg was best known as the attorney of record of the wealthiest families in the city, including the Badalamentes. He was also the most celebrated lawyer in New Orleans who had never run for public office. He was portly, with no hair on his pointed white head. Standing mute in his shiny black sharkskin suit, Rosenberg looked as sullen as the detectives.

Mrs. Jimson answered her own front door, and Dino could see immediately in her large brown eyes that she knew. The police chaplain introduced himself, but before he could go any further, Mrs. Jimson asked, ''He's dead, isn't he?''

As soon as the chaplain confirmed her suspicion, the tears came. Dino watched the priest help Mrs. Jimson to an easy chair in the living room as the detectives waited in the foyer. Rosenberg waddled to a telephone and started making phone calls, turning his back to the detectives.

Dino was surprised to discover, when the crying subsided, that Mrs. Jimson was alone in the house. The daughter of an LCN Boss was never left alone, except maybe in the Badalamente family. It was rumored they were the most powerful family outside the council in New York. Independent, loners; they did things differently. At least, that's what Dino had heard.

After the detectives settled in separate chairs in the living room, Mrs. Jimson returned from washing her face and sat back in the easy chair.

Mark handled the questions. As he started, Rosenberg hurried over to Mrs. Jimson, perching on the arm of her chair. He looked like an overweight vulture protecting fresh carrion. Dino took notes.

Mark's precise questions were answered even more precisely by Mrs. Jimson, who explained that her husband had been missing for four days. "But you should know that. I filed a police report."

"Ma'am, we haven't checked anything yet. We just found him."

Her eyes misted again as she fought back tears. Rosenberg injected a barbed question. "Why haven't you checked with Headquarters on your radio to see if he was missing?"

Mark paused a moment before answering, "We don't put victims' names on the radio." He spoke to Rosenberg as if he were talking to a child. "No telling who's listening."

The questioning continued when Mrs. Jimson was ready again. Thomas Jimson was an accountant with an office on Camp Street in the central business district. He was last seen by his wife leaving for work at eight o'clock in the morning. His car was found

19

parked and locked at his office, which was also locked. No one at the office saw Jimson because he worked alone . . . no secretary . . . not even an answering service. The Jimsons had been married fifteen years and had no children.

Gina Badalamente Jimson had a classic Italian face, fine Roman features set in a pale white complexion, a straight nose, full lips, and dark wavy hair. She was a thin woman with large eyes that looked vacant and stunned. She wore a dark blue dress with a high collar, and she reminded Dino of a schoolteacher.

"Did your husband keep a diary or a datebook of any sort?" Mark asked.

"A what?" Mrs. Jimson answered, moving her eyes from Dino back to Mark.

"Did Mr. Jimson keep any papers here at the house?" the sergeant asked softly.

Rosenberg had heard enough. Before the woman could answer, he put a friendly hand on her shoulder and stepped between her and the detectives. "You will be able to go through Mr. Jimson's papers later . . . at a time that is more convenient." As he said "convenient" he turned sympathetically to Mrs. Jimson and nodded like an altar boy seeking a blessing. Rosenberg looked like a frog when he smiled.

Mark's face was getting redder by the second. It was then that the new sergeant acted, for the first time since he'd acquired his stripes, like a sergeant. He said nothing. He just rose slowly and signaled to his men that it was time to leave. Dino had to force himself to keep quiet, force himself to keep from reminding the reptilian lawyer that murder was always inconvenient.

Rosenberg followed the detectives into the foyer. He pulled a notepad and pen from his coat pocket as he asked the sergeant for the name of the detective in charge of the investigation. Mark casually pointed to Dino. "Detective LaStanza is the case officer."

"How do you spell that?"

"Guess."

Dino glanced back at the attorney and saw Mrs. Jimson's Orphan Annie eyes staring back at him from behind Rosenberg. He looked twice because he was sure there was a slight smile on the widow Jimson's face. But in an instant the smile was gone.

The detectives assembled by their sergeant's car for a minute. Mark leaned against the fender and growled through gritted teeth. "When it's more convenient, huh? Fuckin' lawyer!" He turned to Dino and asked, "What did you call the victim again?"

"A gargoyle."

"Fuckin' victim's a gargoyle, and his lawyer's a fuckin' snake."

Mark pushed an index finger against Dino's chest. "Well, it'll be *convenient* first thing in the fuckin' morning. We're gonna get search warrants for that fuckin' house, *and* the Gargoyle's fuckin' office and we're gonna hit 'em both in the morning."

"A search warrant for a *victim's* house?" Snowood asked as he tucked a large dip of tobacco under his lower lip.

"Fuckin' A," Mark snapped. "They wanna have bigshot mouthpieces giving orders, then we'll play it by the book. All right?"

"Okay by me," the case officer answered.

"Good," Mark huffed loudly, letting out his frustration before changing the subject. "You got any cold beer?" he asked Dino.

"Sure. But first I got a question for our friendly police chaplain." Dino took a step toward the chaplain as the priest walked away from the front of the house.

"Excuse me, Father," Dino stepped in front of the priest, "mind if I ask a question?"

"Not at all Dino. It is Dino, isn't it?" answered the friendly chaplain.

"Yeah," Dino responded quickly, "who called the lawyer?"

The chaplain blinked twice before answering. "Well, I did." He smiled and quickly followed his answer with a question of his own, "And how's your father, Dino?"

"He's fine," Dino replied tersely as he made note of the chaplain's answer.

The chaplain spoke again in a fatherly voice. "I remember back when your father was a sergeant, Dino. He and I . . ."

"Just one more question," Dino interrupted. "Who told you the victim's name?"

"What?"

"Who told you the victim's name, Father? Nobody knew his name but us. All Headquarters gave you was an address."

The chaplain smiled. "I recognized the address," he said as he turned away.

Dino watched the priest leave and declared, "He just happened to recognize the address and just happened to know how to get ahold of Rosenberg in the middle of the night, huh?"

"Yeah," Paul agreed, "ain't that interesting?"

"What are you getting at?" Mark snapped. "You don't think the police chaplain is involved in any of this, do you?"

"Not really," Dino started for his car. "It just proves that Signore Badalamente has ears everywhere."

* * *

Dino's bungalow was three blocks from the Jimson place. Just off City Park Avenue on North Murat Street, Detective LaStanza lived in a green-stucco, one-story house built in the twenties. There was an old-fashioned narrow front door with a round top that gave the place the look of a dungeon. In fact, that was what Dino's mother nicknamed the bunga-low the only time she visited.

The three detectives settled in the living room with three cold beers as Mark laid out his plan for the search warrants in the morning. "Mason and I will get the warrants while you're at the autopsy," he told Dino. "Then we'll hit the Gargoyle's office the same time you and Paul hit the house."

"Sounds good to me," Dino kicked off his penny loafers and plopped down on his sofa. He looked over at Paul. "Guess you won't be going to the zoo tomorrow after all."

"I wouldn't miss this search for all the tumbleweed in Tombstone," Paul replied. "But I'm gonna miss that autopsy. There's nothin' like a floater autopsy . . . to open up your sinuses."

Before Dino could think of anything to say in response, his phone started ringing. He answered it after the third ring, and it was Lizette. He asked her to hold on a second and then proceeded to get rid of his company.

"I don't mean to be inhospitable, but why don't ya'll get the fuck outta here?"

Mark stood up and smiled for the first time that night. "Call me on the radio as soon as you leave the autopsy. We'll get the warrants."

They each took another beer for the road and left Dino alone in his dungeon with his princess on the phone.

*   *   *

Dino's voice sounded tired to Lizette. She waited patiently for him to come back on the line, relieved that he was home. She was having another bad night, lying awake and fighting off thoughts of her sister . . . again. She needed to talk to Dino, needed to hear his voice, as she had every night since their ritual of late-night calls had begun, not long after the murder of her sister. He had handled the case. He told her from the start he would catch the Slasher, and he had. That was how it started. Now the two were seeing each other as often as his schedule allowed.

When Dino came back on the line, Lizette asked sympathetically, "You've been busy tonight, haven't you?"

"You heard?" Dino sat back on his sofa and kicked his feet up on the coffee table.

"It was on the news. I'm surprised you're home," Lizette leaned back on her bed.

Dino listened closely. Her voice had that soft, sad quality that told him she was feeling down. After a moment of silence he explained, "It looks like a gangland killing."

"Gangland?"

"Mafia." As an afterthought, he added in a mock Italian accent, "Who killa da chief?"

"Now, Detective LaStanza," Lizette sighed as she smiled to herself, "you're going to have to explain that last remark."

"Who killa da chief?" Dino repeated. "You never heard that expression?"

"Not exactly," she was pleased to have the conversation move along. "Tell me about it."

"Well, a long time ago, the first Chief of Police in New Orleans was murdered by the Mafia. He was an Irishman named Hennessey, and he was gunned down by Sicilians outside his house one night. The last thing he said was the word *dagos*."

"Did they catch the killers?"

"Yeah, but the trial was fixed and the killers were acquitted."

"They got away?" Lizette's voice rose.

"Not exactly. The mayor of New Orleans started a riot, and a crowd stormed Parish Prison and lynched the killers."

"Wait, I heard about that. I remember hearing something about the lynchings in a history class."

"Well, it wasn't long before the fine white citizens of New Orleans began using 'Who killa da chief?' when addressing citizens of the Italian persuasion, like my grandfather. He was a fruit peddler. He used to sell fruit from a hand-drawn wagon, and every time he went into the Irish Channel he would hear it." Dino's voice became higher as he mimicked the hecklers, "Hey Joe, who killa da chief? Joe, who killa da chief?" Dino's voice returned to normal. "My father must have told me that story a hundred times."

"I didn't know your grandfather sold fruit from a wagon."

"Oh. Yeah, his name was Joe . . . Joe the Wop. He pulled his wagon all around the city, peddling fruit from the French Market to Carrollton Avenue. In fact, my father tells me his favorite place to sell fruit was Audubon Park. He probably sold fruit to your family a long time ago."

"Now wouldn't that be a coincidence." Lizette began twirling a strand of her long hair between her fingers.

"Sure. He probably pulled his cart up Exposition Boulevard and stopped right in front of your house. Your grandmother probably went out and bought bananas or tomatoes or maybe a watermelon."

"Watermelons, huh?"

Again Dino's voice changed as he mimicked the voice of his very Sicilian grandfather, "I got ba . . na . . na. I got tan . . ge . . rine. I got water . . melon!" Dino cleared his throat. "That's what my father said he sounded like."

"What did he look like? Did he have green eyes, like you?" Lizette's voice became deeper, giving it a sexy quality that told Dino she was feeling better already. Sometimes, just a little time on the phone worked wonders with her.

"I don't know what his eyes looked like. He died when my Dad was a little boy. But he must have been a character. My father never lets a day go by without telling some story about his old man."

"Who killa da chief, huh?" Lizette repeated and then added with concern, "I hope this case won't keep you from our date Saturday night?"

"Not this case. The killer's probably back in Detroit or Chicago by now. Anyway," he wanted to change the subject, "how did it go with the dean today?"

"Well, he offered me an assistantship."

"Which means?"

"I'll be teaching and working on my PhD at the same time."

"Wow, those college guys get all the luck." He could picture Lizette standing in front of a class, automatically receiving the undivided attention of all the male students. Dino closed his eyes and thought of Lizette's fragile, pretty face, her gold-brown eyes and long wavy hair.

"You know something?" Dino began again, "I don't have a picture of you."

"Next time you come, take your choice. Take any one from the library."

"All those are you?" Dino remembered all the

glamorous pictures in her father's library. He figured some of them had been Lizette's twin sister. He knew that the painting above the fireplace in the library had been of Lynette. There was something different in the eyes. But he had never met Lynette before he saw her lying in a pool of her own blood in the grass of Audubon Park. Lizette and Lynette were identical twins . . . until that night.

"I'll have to drop in on one of your lectures," Dino announced in a challenging voice.

"I don't know if I'd like that."

"Will you toss me out?"

"I'll call Security on you," she teased.

"Yeah? And I'll introduce them to a real police-man!"

Lizette started laughing. When she let herself go and laughed that way, she reminded Dino of a little girl.

Lizette felt better after hanging up her Princess phone. She picked up a novel from her nightstand and continued reading a South Sea adventure about a land far, far away. When her steady breathing lulled her into drowsiness, she returned the novel to the stand and turned off her light. She closed her eyes and thought of Dino LaStanza, of his light green eyes, the shy way he smiled at her.

When sleep came to Lizette she had another vision . . . a vision of Lynette sitting in the big easy chair in their father's library. Lynette was laughing . . . at Lizette . . . in that twin-sister-teasing-laugh that had been with the girls since their earliest days. It was a laugh that always caused Lizette to laugh along.

But her sleep was a fitful one because of Lynette . . . because of the sadness that they had grown so far

27

apart so quickly at the end. Identical twins that were separated by more than the miles between colleges, separated by a dark chasm that neither would cross. In the back of Lizette's mind she felt there would be time to cross it. They were still young. That was before the night Lynette Ann Louvier came upon the man known as the Slasher. She was twenty years old.

Dino went to bed with thoughts of his dark-haired girlfriend and her pouting lips that had kissed him goodnight the night before. But it was not long before he was visited by a vision of the Gargoyle lying on the dock, the silver water reflecting in the distance. And Dino wondered, as he lay awake, why *he* had to catch a no-good, rotten, mother-fuckin' Mafia whodunit.

"Where's your tie?" was the first question Lieutenant Rob Mason asked when LaStanza walked into the Detective Bureau the following morning.

"It's with my suit and socks and underwear . . . at the fuckin' cleaners." Dino dropped his briefcase on his desk. Clad in a sport coat, dress shirt, and blue jeans tossed on after a hasty visit to the dungeon at the conclusion of the autopsy, he was in no mood for questions.

Snowood almost choked on the wad of tobacco juice in his mouth. "Floater autopsy! I told you! The stink sticks to you like glue!" He leaned forward and spit a large wad of brown juice into the ever-present styrofoam cup cradled in his left hand.

LaStanza plopped down in his desk chair and tried to ignore his laughing partner. Gathering his notes together, he waited until Mark came out of the small sergeant's office to join the three men in the squad room. Mason lit up a cigarette as Mark asked, "What about the autopsy?"

Dino did not look up from his notes. He spoke in a tired, serious voice. "He was in the water three or four days. Two entry wounds in the forehead, contact wounds. We got two pellets, twenty-two's. One's in good shape, one isn't. The trajectory was downward." He put an index finger against his forehead and pointed downward. "About thirty degrees down."

"He was probably kneeling," Mark injected.

"Probably," Mason agreed.

"Or our perpetrator is *very* tall," Paul added. No one laughed except Paul.

"How long does it usually take for the toxicology report?" Dino asked aloud.

"Couple weeks to three months," Mason answered, "depending on the breaks." The lieutenant exhaled a large cloud of smoke which caused Snowood to fan frantically. Mason shot a mischievous grin and puffed again. The newly promoted lieutenant commanding the Homicide Division was still one of the fellas. He never acted any other way especially with Land, LaStanza, and Snowood. Those men had been his platoon when he was a sergeant.

At forty-five, Mason was a lean man, with a thin, angular jaw that usually supported a lit cigarette. He always kept his stringy hair cut short, his pants cut long and his socks white . . . even in penny loafers. He wore penny loafers because he always wore them, since grammar school, even when they were out of style.

After taking another drag on his cigarette, Mason exhaled once again and announced, "We've got the warrants signed. And the uniform men will meet us as soon as we go 10-8. So, let's go get 'em."

*   *   *

Snowood took his partially filled styrofoam cup with him as LaStanza drove their Chevrolet to the corner of City Park Avenue and Bienville Street. A Third District unit was already there, waiting for the Homicide team. Paul recognized the driver and introduced Dino to Patrolman Patrick Tooney, a huge Irishman with a pink face, a prematurely balding head, and deep, narrow eyes that made him look angry all the time. Tooney was the perfect example of what a street cop should be: big, mean, and Irish.

Snowood gave Tooney a brief run down of the situation. The patrolman knew he was there only for show. He would follow the detectives to the front door and remain in the doorway during the search. He was there to protect them and keep any pain-in-the-ass bystanders from interfering.

Dino led the way to the Jimson house on City Park Avenue. He also led the way to the front door, which was answered by Jules Rosenberg himself, this time wearing a green sharkskin suit that made him look even more like a frog. "We've come to see Mr. Jimson's papers," Dino announced.

Rosenberg's face took on an annoyed look. "I told you, when it's more *convenient.*"

Dino placed the search warrant against Rosenberg's long nose, "It's *convenient* right now, counselor. That's a search warrant." He brushed by the lawyer and stepped into the foyer with Snowood right behind.

Rosenberg was not about to let the two detectives muscle their way in without further discussion. He followed, insisting, "Now, there's no need for this."

Dino continued walking and asked over his shoulder, "Where's Jimson's study?"

Rosenberg protested. "There's no *need* for this! I'll

provide the court with anything you request."

Dino nodded to his partner as Paul turned into a downstairs library and began searching. Then he asked the lawyer again if Jimson had an office in the house.

"Now, you just wait a minute," argued Rosenberg, placing a hand on LaStanza's shoulder. Dino grabbed Rosenberg's hand, leaned close to the lawyer, and shouted, "If you don't get the fuck outta my face, you gonna end up in Central Lockup in about *two seconds!*"

Patrolman Tooney started forward from his position at the front door. His face revealed how much he hoped he would be able to arrest a lawyer. But Rosenberg knew when to stop. He pulled his hand away from LaStanza's grip, wheeled around, and moved to the nearest telephone. With a copy of the search warrant in hand, the lawyer asked directory assistance for the judge's phone number.

Dino turned away and started up the stairs, smiling to himself, because no matter how much clout Rosenberg thought he had, there was no way he was going to talk Judge LeBeau into anything concerning the warrants. LeBeau was an old Cajun who went by the book, and a search warrant was in effect until executed.

Mrs. Jimson was waiting at the top of the stairs. Standing in a heavy yellow robe, her hair pulled back, her face pale and gray, she stared anxiously at the detective slowly ascending the stairs.

"I'm uh, sorry," Dino apologized. "But we have to look through your husband's papers."

The widow's face remained expressionless. She stepped back and pointed to an upstairs room. "His office is in there." Her voice was low and controlled.

Dino left the door open, placing his portable radio

31

and notepad on the cypress desk in the center of the room as he took a moment to look around. The furniture was expensive, made of dark wood and marble. There were large John James Audubon prints on the walls and French doors that opened to a balcony facing City Park. There were three filing cabinets in a closet next to the cypress desk and more files in the desk.

Dino sat in the leather captain's chair behind the desk and began going through the drawers. He found an appointment book in the center drawer. There were business notations and personal notations in the book, from bank meetings to birthdays to golf dates. Dino thumbed through the week prior to the Gargoyle's "disappearance." The pages were almost blank, except for some names jotted on various days. Dino put the appointment book next to his radio.

Rosenberg had no luck with Judge LeBeau or with the two councilmen he called, so he tried the Chief of Police. Dino could hear the lawyer's booming voice as it echoed from downstairs. At first it was obvious that Rosenberg wanted the detectives to hear who he was calling, but as the calls continued to frustrate the angry attorney, his temper got the best of him.

"What do you mean the Chief doesn't wish to speak to me at the moment?" Rosenberg shouted. "Did you tell him who it was? *No!* I'm not leaving a number for him." He slammed down the telephone.

Dino continued going through Jimson's desk drawers as Rosenberg called Police Headquarters again, this time asking for the commander of Homicide. After a while, he figured he would not be able to talk to the commander. "What do you mean?" Rosenberg asked loudly. "He's on a search warrant?"

"Yeah," Snowood shouted from the room he was searching. "The lieutenant's at Jimson's office on

Camp Street." To which Rosenberg did not reply.

It was not long before car doors could be heard slamming outside. Dino listened to loud voices at the front door and heard Officer Tooney announce sternly, *"Nobody enters during the search . . . period!"* To which there was no reply and no further disturbance downstairs.

Jimson's address book was in a side drawer. Dino placed it next to the appointment book before moving to the file cabinets. When he heard something behind him, he turned suddenly to see Mrs. Jimson standing in the doorway. She was dressed in a black suit dress, her hair down and brushed out, her face still pale, although she had put on makeup, even a hint of lipstick. Her face remained expressionless as she asked, "What are you looking for?"

"A reason. We're looking for a reason."

The woman's eyes narrowed momentarily as the detective's answer registered. She leaned her weight on one leg, pursed her lips, and asked, "Do you think you'll find it in here?"

"I don't know. But there's got to be a reason why it happened. And we've got to start somewhere."

Mrs. Jimson nodded as she looked around the room. "Please don't make a mess," she added and started to turn away.

"I won't."

The widow hesitated in the doorway and asked over her shoulder, "Would you like some coffee?"

"No. But thanks for asking."

By the time Dino started in on the second file cabinet, Mrs. Jimson returned with a tray carrying a small silver coffeepot and two fine china coffee cups, saucers, cream and sugar. "I've never heard of a policeman who didn't want coffee," announced the widow as she placed the tray on the desk. "How do you take it?"

"Cream and sugar."

Mrs. Jimson served LaStanza in silence. After he nodded his approval, she had one question for him. "Your name, what was it again?"

"LaStanza. Dino LaStanza."

"That's Sicilian, isn't it?"

"Yes, ma'am."

"Good," and with that Mrs. Jimson's pallid face almost smiled. She nodded at the coffeepot before leaving. "Help yourself, Detective LaStanza." Then she turned and walked out.

When Snowood joined LaStanza upstairs, Dino was finishing the last of the coffee. Paul, still carrying his styrofoam cup in hand, asked, "Where did you get coffee?"

"Mrs. Jimson. You didn't get any?"

"No."

Dino picked up the small coffeepot and shook it. "No more left."

Paul stood open mouthed before the desk as his partner finished the last sip of coffee before announcing, "That's what you get for being a redneck, country ass, tobacco-spitting peckerwood . . . instead of a devilishly good-looking Sicilian . . . like me."

Paul leaned close. "Fuck you, you little Wop. And I'll bet that's just what the good widow has in mind for you."

Dino was certain Mrs. Jimson had a reason, but it was not what his partner thought. "You are so wrong, Tobacco Breath." He gathered up his radio and notepad, along with the Gargoyle's appointment book and address book.

"Is that all you're taking?"

"Nope. Can you take that?" Dino nodded to a cardboard box full of files he had removed from

Jimson's file cabinets.

"What are these?"

"Records," answered Dino as he led the way down the stairs. He found the widow sitting in the living room. She was staring out her front window, her Roman profile outlined against the bright light. Rosenberg was still on the phone. As soon as he saw the detectives, he hung up and started over to them. Dino walked past the lawyer and gave Mrs. Jimson a receipt, which Rosenberg snatched out of the widow's hand.

"Good-bye," Dino nodded to Mrs. Jimson and started to leave.

"Wait just a minute!" Rosenberg ordered the detectives. "I want to inventory what you've taken."

"Get lost," Dino answered as he continued out the front door. He turned to Tooney and added, "If that son-of-a-bitch comes after us . . ."

"I'll take care of him," Tooney answered, a wicked smile creeping across his large red face.

As LaStanza and Snowood left the Jimson house, they walked past two long black cars parked directly in front. Each car had tinted windows, tightly shut, and their engines ran as their air-conditioners worked hard in the early morning heat. When the detectives passed, a door opened in the second car and a man stepped out. The man was tall and muscular, with long black hair combed straight back and slicked down. He wore a blue suit that had to have been tailor made for his huge frame, but was still too short for him. The man leaned against the car's fender and watched the detectives pass.

As Dino walked closer, he took a long look at the man's face, at the eyes hidden behind dark mirrored sunglasses. Although the eyes were unseen, Dino felt the man's stare. He reciprocated with his own hard,

Sicilian stare. It was a stare that came naturally to a man named LaStanza. And as he passed, neither man blinked.

Lieutenant Mason was a good leader because he led by example and worked as hard as his men. But more important, he was a good leader because he had been there before and had never forgotten it. He never gave orders. He just made suggestions, and everyone took the suggestions and ran with them.

That was why the lieutenant commanding the Homicide Division typed up the two Gargoyle warrants, took them personally to the judge, and led the search of the victim's office. Mason led by example.

When LaStanza and Snowood arrived back at the Detective Bureau from the house, their lieutenant and sergeant were waiting in the lieutenant's office. Mason was sitting behind his desk, sucking hard on a cigarette, when the detectives entered. Mark was sipping coffee, sitting on a folding chair in the corner.

On Mason's desk sat two large boxes filled with files secured from the Gargoyle's office. Paul put the box from the house next to them. Mason spoke in a low voice. "I'll go through the files. I got the time."

"Thanks," Dino said, "I've got enough with his appointment book and address book."

"There's just one thing I want to add," Mason advised as Dino and Paul started to sit in the two empty chairs before his desk. "I want to enlighten you men with some statistics I looked up this morning." He was always one for statistics. After another drag on his cigarette, the lieutenant said, "In the last five years there have been five hundred and twenty gangland murders in the U.S. . . . of which thirteen were solved."

Dino and Mark both sighed aloud as Paul shook his head.

"Of the thirteen solved," Mason added a postscript, "there were no convictions."

Coliseum Square

To a Homicide man, there are three types of murders. The first and most important type is the whodunit, which involves a mystery. Sometimes not only is the identity of the perpetrator in question, but also the identity of the victim, as in the case of a dumped body. A whodunit requires thinking, investigative technique, and a great deal of legwork. Whodunits are the only murders that count.

The second type is called a misdemeanor murder, which is any murder involving a husband and wife, boyfriend and girlfriend, or other instances where the victim and perpetrator are closely related. A misdemeanor murder is handled like any other misdemeanor investigation. It is strictly paperwork. There is no investigating, no thinking, just paperwork.

The third type of murder is not a murder at all . . . it's a killin'. It is similar to a misdemeanor murder, except a killin' usually occurs in a bar or like establishment, requiring either the victim or perpetrator to have consumed a substantial amount of intoxicant. A killin' usually results in a manslaughter conviction at best and requires even less paperwork than a suicide. A killin' is also the correct name for any murder that occurs in a housing project.

On the evening following the search of the Gargoyle's house, LaStanza and Snowood caught a killin'. Dino had just settled at his desk with a fresh cup of coffee, his Gargoyle notes spread in front of him, when Mark stepped out of the tiny sergeant's office rubbing his temples with both hands. "You guys gotta roll."

"Aw, *fuck!*"

"You gotta be fuckin' me!"

He told them there was an aggravated battery at the Calliope Housing Project and the victim probably would not make it. Dino immediately scooped up his Gargoyle notes and tossed them into his open briefcase.

"What about the other squads?" Snowood complained.

Mark almost laughed. For years that was his line when Mason piled another case on him. "What about the other guys?"

The sergeant smiled as he reminded Paul, "I got two guys out sick and two on vacation. And M and M are already at Charity, working a barroom killin'."

"What about you? You got crippled since you got stripes?" Snowood argued as he began to pack up his own briefcase.

"I'm already up to my ass in fuckin' paperwork. Remember, I handled the last two misdemeanor murders." Their sergeant started back toward his office and added, "Your victim's at Charity. His name is Richard Lionel. Let me know about it."

*　　*　　*

"This city never runs out of fuckin' murders," Snowood complained as they took the short ride from Headquarters to Charity Hospital.

"What are you griping about?" Dino goaded him. "It's just a killin'. You always catch easy cases."

"Yeah? Well remember I caught the last Slasher murder!"

"Yeah?" Dino could not resist, "and who solved it?"

"You sure are an irritating little wop."

"I know. But I'm good."

"Yeah?" Paul wasn't finished. "When you solve the Gargoyle Murder, then come back and brag."

The ritual of verbal sparring ended as soon as the detectives arrived at Charity's emergency room, a room which always reminded Dino of Vietnam. Charity resembled a war zone, perpetually filled with people bleeding from various wounds, coughing and wheezing as they sat around on metal folding chairs or on the floor, waiting to be helped. Charity was a large public hospital, built during the Huey Long years, when government believed people had a right to free medical care. It is said that a resident physician really earned his mettle when he worked Charity. It was like being a rookie in the Sixth Police District of New Orleans. The only part of the city that saw more red than the Bloody Sixth was Charity's emergency room.

The detectives had to squeeze through a horde of moaning people lined up in uneven rows of tired chairs in the waiting area. Without bothering to stop at the desk, they made their way to a bored security guard positioned at the entrance to the trauma rooms. Snowood asked about Lionel and was waved to the second cubicle.

Richard Lionel was a middle-aged black man with

a thick moustache and a large butcher knife imbedded to its handle in the center of his forehead. As soon as LaStanza stepped into the cubicle, he turned to his partner. "Now that's something you don't see every day."

At that moment a nurse with short red hair rushed into the room and began working on Lionel. Dino moved closer and watched the victim's eyes blink as the nurse began sticking tubes in his arms. "Hey," he called out to his partner, "he's still alive!"

Paul looked up from his notepad and began to chuckle as a doctor walked in. The frantic nurse told the doctor, "He's slipping!"

"I know," the doctor answered in a weary voice as he moved to Lionel and looked down at the victim who blinked up at him. Then the doctor turned away, picked up a clipboard and began writing his own notes.

"Excuse me Doc," Paul said after a moment, "but we're gonna need that butcher knife after you take it out."

The doctor answered in a voice that revealed the extent of his weariness. "You can get it at the autopsy."

At that point Lionel's eyes stopped blinking.

"I think he heard you Doc," Dino said.

It wasn't long before the nurse confirmed the obvious, "he's gone." At which time the doctor walked out.

Snowood secured details from the patrolmen and ambulance attendants who had accompanied Lionel to Charity while Dino called their sergeant.

"What you got?"

"A unicorn," Dino said.

"A what?"

"You gotta come see this. This guy's got a butcher knife in his forehead, sunk to the hilt. He looks like a fuckin' unicorn." LaStanza had done it again. Henceforth the case would be known as the Unicorn Killin'.

When Mark arrived, squeezing through the crowd in the waiting area, Dino was waiting with a big smile. "Go take a look."

Even Mark was awed by the sight of the large man with the butcher knife in his forehead.

"Who the fuck did it?"

"Girlfriend," Paul answered. "I'm gonna need some help with statements." He pointed toward the waiting area. "We got witnesses."

Dino took a statement from a thirteen-year-old black girl who, despite her tattered and desperate appearance, was an honors student with an excellent vocabulary. Her statement was concise and pertinent. She had watched her big sister and live-in boyfriend, the future unicorn man, argue over supper until her sister got up from the table, grabbed the nearest weapon, and implanted the butcher knife into the center of her boyfriend's forehead.

Dino was just finishing the statement when Detective Millie Suzanne approached from the rear of the emergency room. Millie was a mousy girl in her late twenties with tan hair, a pudgy figure, and thin lips. She was a Yankee, transplanted from Indiana to New Orleans as a teenager, and was the only female officer in Homicide. Although she was well liked, she had problems. The word on Millie was that she did not have the killer instinct, the drive to go for the jugular when it was offered.

Once, during a crucial interview of a killer, Millie had tried to go for the jugular. She'd raised her voice and actually yelled at the killer as she dug into her purse for a cigarette and lighter. But when she pulled out a tampon instead of her lighter, the killer laughed . . . until Mark kicked the chair out from under him.

"So, what are you doing here?" Millie was always cheerful, too cheerful for LaStanza's liking. There was something eerie about a Homicide cop who was cheerful.

"We got a killin'," he said as he tucked away the statement. "Mark's in trauma room 2. Go take a look."

"We're working a killin' too," Millie advised as her partner, Maurice Ferdinand, approached. Maurice was a native Orleanian, a tall, impeccably religious man with drooped shoulders and short, sandy hair. He was even more friendly than Millie and infinitely more irritating; he constantly referred to the scriptures.

Mark had labeled the team of Millie and Maurice the M and M team. Paul had another label for Maurice Ferdinand: he called Maurice by his initials "M.F.," and Maurice never complained, at least not to Paul. Once he mentioned it to Mark, who told him to take it up with Snowood, but M.F. never did.

When M.F. arrived, Paul stepped up and told Dino, "Let's go. Our killer's waiting at Central Lockup."

Before leaving, Dino turned back to Millie and repeated, "Go look in trauma 2. There's something in there you don't see every day. Only watch out for Mark. I think he's charging admission."

It has been said that New Orleanians understand death better than most people because their dead

44

are never far away. Because the city was built on a swamp, the water table was too high for anyone to be buried underground. Dig a couple feet and you hit water. Therefore the city's fathers were forced to stick the remains of their loved ones in tombs that were above ground.

They are called "little cities of the dead" . . . the cemeteries in New Orleans, where generations are buried in concrete sepulchers, marble crypts, or in the "oven" tombs in the long walls that line the edges of the cemeteries.

The Gargoyle was buried in a red marble sepulcher in a cemetery that was once a racetrack. On a bright Saturday morning filled with roses and assorted sprays of multicolored flowers assembled in wreaths, Thomas Jimson was laid to rest. Along with the hundreds of mourners, lingering in the background were Detectives LaStanza and Snowood, their portable radios turned down, their eyes scanning the large gathering crowded between the crypts and sepulchers of Metairie Cemetery.

The detectives were obvious in their presence. They wanted to be obvious. They were there as a show of force, to let grieving families know that Homicide was interested enough to be there . . . just in case someone stood up in a fit of anguished guilt and screamed, "I did it!"

"It sure is a pretty day for a funeral," Snowood said as he leaned on a crypt.

"Have you seen Baddie yet?" Dino scanned the crowd for the familiar figure of Alphonso Badalamente.

"Nope." Paul stuck a fresh dip under his lip.

Dino looked at his partner with disgust. "You're not gonna spit brown shit on these tombs, are you?"

"Why not? I don't think the tenants will complain."

45

When Dino looked back at the crowd, his eyes caught sight of a woman standing beside a nearby crypt. She had her back to the detectives as she peeked out at the crowd. She was tall, with long blond hair and a shapely figure that could not be concealed even by the plain black dress she wore.

LaStanza nodded toward the woman

"Nice ass," Paul said.

"Wonder why she's hiding like that?"

"Maybe she don't like Wops."

At that moment a man approached the woman from the other side of the crypt. He was a stocky man of medium height, with short, wiry hair that had a white streak down its center. He wore a shiny black suit and mirrored sunglasses.

Dino nodded toward the man. "Standard gangster-issue sunglasses."

Paul agreed as he spat a large wad of brown saliva on the ground between two sepulchers.

The man with the white streak in his hair moved next to the blonde woman, put his arm around her waist, and began to speak to her. Dino was too far away to hear, so he moved closer, his partner tagging behind.

As the detectives inched forward, the woman pulled away from the man, turned around, and walked directly toward them. The man followed right behind her. Dino stepped to the side of a nearby crypt and watched the two pass without even noticing him.

As they passed, Dino got a good look at their faces, at the harsh, acne-scarred face of the man with the gangster glasses and at the smooth, pretty face of the blonde woman. The woman was gorgeous. She had a Hollywood face, bright blue eyes and a body by Playboy. She was one good-looking woman.

"There's no accounting for taste," Paul said after the couple passed.

"Did you see her face?"

"She's a looker all right," Paul acknowledged.

"And did you see his face?"

"Fuckin' ugly."

"That's the ugliest face I've ever seen on a live person," Paul spat again. "Fuckin' ugly!"

After the couple left, the detectives went back to standing around and watching as the final prayers were solemnly spoken and the crowd began to dissolve.

"I wonder why she was hiding?" Dino asked again.

"You'd hide if you had a boyfriend that ugly."

Dino continued scanning the crowd. "Have you seen Baddie yet?"

"Nope."

Mrs. Jimson walked by, barely recognizable in her long black dress, hat, and heavy veil. The detectives moved closer to the tomb and waited until only the gravediggers were left to seal the sepulcher with a marble headstone that bore the fresh name of Thomas Jimson.

"That was one good-looking woman," Paul added as the detectives walked back to their cars. "Just my M.O. You know how partial I am to blondes."

"But she sure had one gruesome looking boyfriend."

"Fuckin' UGLY!"

Lizette Marie Louvier lived on Exposition Boulevard in a large house surrounded by a six-foot black wrought-iron fence. Exposition was a unique boulevard in New Orleans because it was not even a street. It was a promenade, a double-wide sidewalk on the east side of Audubon Park, where mansions stood in white splendor, bearing exclusive addresses. Built during the Louisiana Cotton Exposition of 1884, the double-wide sidewalk was put in place so ladies could stroll from St. Charles Avenue to the Cotton Exposition in their fine dresses without getting mud on their petticoats.

The Louvier house was a three-story, immaculately white southern veranda home with a wide gallery surrounding the entire first floor. There was a double swing on the front gallery where Dino and Lizette first began to notice each other as more than detective and victim's sister.

Its front gate opened to the wide expanse of Audubon Park. Its front door was made of cut glass and also faced the park. It was a sad house, where death had visited earlier that year. Not more than a hundred yards from its front gate, in the darkness of Audubon Park, Lynette Ann Louvier had died at the hands of a mass murderer. The house, once a well-lit mansion, was now dark most of the time.

When Dino arrived at the Louvier Mansion later that Saturday night, he was still thinking about the Gargoyle and about the ugly man and the blonde woman at the funeral earlier that day. But as soon as he saw Lizette descending the long spiral staircase of the mansion, he forgot about the ugly man and the pretty blonde and even the Gargoyle.

Lizette smiled broadly as she walked down to Dino. With a jerk of her head, her long dark hair moved to one side as she eased up and kissed him gently on the lips. Then she leaned back and checked his lips for lipstick. Finding none, she smiled again at her handsome detective.

"You look nice," she whispered to him in that deep, sexy voice of hers. "You look good in black and white," she added, "with that dark complexion." Lizette examined Dino as he stood smiling back at her. "Nice coat," she ran her fingers along the sleeve of his new jacket.

Dino had just bought everything he wore that night, from the European-cut, white sport coat to the gray dress shirt and pleated black pants and black penny loafers. Cut-rate suits were for fooling with dead bodies.

"I like your hair like that," Dino told her. Lizette had done something different with it, and it took him a couple seconds to realize she had simply put barrettes in it, pinning up the sides. It made her look even younger than her twenty-one years.

Dino took his time ogling Lizette, who obliged with a slow turn. She was dolled up in a black mesh halter top that had no back and a snug red skirt with a long slit up its rear. In her spiked high heels she was slightly taller than Dino.

"Come on," Lizette grabbed his hand, "let's go." On her way out she picked up a black mesh purse from the table in the foyer.

"You sure about this?" he asked on their way to the garage behind the house.

"Of course I am. I insist."

Dino just shrugged and went along with Lizette to her car. He even let her open the passenger door for him. When she climbed into the driver's seat, he watched her pull her tight skirt up in order to sit.

"That's a good way to get out of speeding tickets," he told her as he stared at her legs.

"I've never gotten one," she smiled and rolled her eyes at him. Dino laughed as Lizette backed her black Alfa-Romeo Milano sedan out of the garage.

"So, where are we going?"

"You'll see," she teased, turning down Calhoun toward Magazine Street. She wasn't going to tell him until they arrived. This was her night. She had asked him out and insisted on planning the entire evening.

They had dinner at Commander's Palace on Washington Avenue, one of the finest restaurants in a city of great restaurants. They dined on gulf shrimp, blackened redfish, and white Bordeaux.

Later, when Dino tried to pay the bill, waiting until Lizette went to the ladies' room, he was told by the prim waiter that the bill had been taken care of. Lizette laughed when she returned. "We have an account here. They send a bill to the house."

"Oh," Dino shrugged as he put his arm around her waist on their way out. "Excuse my mid-city manners."

Lizette snuggled close. "You know how I adore my little peasant."

Dino got a good laugh at that one. He had initiated the "peasant" description of himself a few weeks earlier when Lizette's father had found him staring at the Louvier family crest in the library. After Mr. Louvier explained the meanings of the symbols in the crest, Dino said that his father had tried to find a LaStanza family crest but failed because all his ancestors had been serfs.

Waiting outside Commander's for their car to be returned by the valet parking attendant, Dino looked across the street at a cemetery. There was a little city of the dead directly across narrow Washington Avenue from the restaurant. Dino thought of the Gargoyle, wondering what the Gargoyle had been doing that night. As a Catholic, he was supposed to believe Jimson was either in Heaven, Hell, or Purgatory. But standing under the canopy of the restaurant, his arm around his beautiful girlfriend, he wondered if the Gargoyle was watching him. He knew one thing for certain, that if the Gargoyle could speak, he would have one question for Dino and it would be, "Why haven't you caught my killer yet?"

Lizette took him to a St. Charles Avenue nightclub called Slow Dancin'. It occupied a Greek Revival mansion that once housed one of the families of old money of New Orleans. There was a restaurant at the front of the mansion and an intimate club in back where dressed-up Orleanians could sip their liquor and dance slowly in the dim light.

There was a Forties Room that played only soft music from that era, the same slow music that accompanied all the old movies from World War II. There was also a modern room where Beatles' love songs were mixed in with Barbra Streisand and Johnny Mathis and all the other softies. Slow Dancin' catered to an older crowd, friendly people who actually introduced themselves to strangers sitting nearby. There were huge chandeliers and soft sofas and no pushy waitresses asking, "You ready for another yet?"

Dino and Lizette settled on a comfortable sofa in a corner of the Forties Room. After Dino retrieved a Scotch rocks for himself and a Sazerac for Lizette, he asked her to dance.

Barely moving to the soft music, his fingers roamed up and down Lizette's bare back, beneath the tips of her long hair.

"Oh," Lizette purred in his ear, "that feels so good."

"You telling me?" He pulled her close, feeling her full breasts against his chest as she nestled the side of her face next to his. By the time they returned to their drinks, the ice had melted in Dino's Scotch.

Lizette watched Dino without him realizing how much she was watching. She liked the way this detective looked from the first moment she saw him dozing in the big easy chair in her father's library. She liked the way his soft wavy hair remained untouched by hairsprays and mousse. She liked his full moustache, taut cheeks, and pointed chin. But most of all she liked the way he was with her, the way he spoke to her, the way he touched her and smiled at her.

Dino had eyelashes any girl would envy and light green eyes that darted around when he scanned a room. But when he focused those greens on her, they did not dart. They were gentle, almost childlike.

Although she could tell he was very attracted to her, he was not aggressive. In that regard, Dino was almost shy. If she had not seen him in his pursuit of the Slasher, it would be hard to picture him fiery, his Sicilian temper pushing him hard.

"Come on, Short-Dark-and-Handsome," Lizette pulled him onto the dance floor when Fred Astaire began singing, "let's snuggle on the floor."

She wrapped herself in Dino's arms. His hands circled around her back, his fingertips slipping under her halter to brush the sides of her breasts. Lizette kissed him softly on the neck and whispered, "That feels great."

He had thought this girl was beyond reach when he first met her, not because she was so pretty and wealthy, but because of the way they had met. But it was not long before he realized how much they were attracted to one another. And now, as he held her close, he wondered about this girl and those golden eyes and full lips, wondered where they were headed.

It was after midnight when they left Slow Dancin'. Lizette drove in silence all the way to the dungeon, parking her Alfa in the driveway behind Dino's old Volkswagen, leaning on her boyfriend's shoulder as he unlocked the front door.

Stepping inside, Dino flipped on the living room light switch next to the front door. He turned back, wrapped his arms around her and kissed her long and hard. She kissed him back just as hard.

Slowly the two moved as they kissed until Lizette had her back to the living room wall, Dino pressing against her. His hands reached down to her thighs and pulled up her skirt. Her legs parted to allow him between them as the kiss continued. It wasn't long before they were moving in unison, his pelvis pumping against hers, until she pulled her mouth away and gasped, "You want to close the door?"

Dino shrugged, stopped moving, and stepped away to shut the front door. Lizette ran her hands through her hair, removing the two barrettes, dropping them on an end table on her way across the living room. She stepped through the open door of the bedroom, kicked off her high heels, and turned to face Dino, who had moved up behind her.

"Let me," he whispered as he reached around and unbuttoned the rear button of Lizette's skirt, slowly unzipping it. He leaned close to kiss her and she stepped back, whispering, "Just strip me."

Dino was very excited, yet he took his time. He pulled her skirt down and then traced the tips of his fingers up the back of her legs, over her silky panty hose, and then up the small of her back to the button at the rear of her halter, which he undid. His fingers then moved to the button at the top of the halter, which he also undid, causing the top to fall. He looked down at Lizette's full breasts and pointed nipples. His breath fell on her neck and then on down between her breasts as he slowly knelt in front of her.

Dino cupped his fingers into the top of her pantyhose and pulled the hose down her legs, moving his face close enough for his breath to be felt against her navel and down the front of her thin white panties.

Lizette put a hand on Dino's shoulder as she stepped out of her pantyhose. Still kneeling in front of her, he tucked his fingers into the top of her panties and slowly pulled them down, his face remaining an inch from the silky, dark hair between her legs as his breath continued to be the only part of him which touched her.

In the light from the living room, Lizette stood naked in front of him. For so petite a girl, her breasts were large, with small, tan nipples. Her waist looked extra narrow above her round feminine hips, her skin smelled fresh and sweet in that perfume she always wore.

"My turn now," Lizette said as she took a step back. Dino rose and stood motionless in front of the naked girl. She removed his white jacket, tossing it on the floor next to her clothes. Then she unbuttoned his shirt to do the same. Lizette took her time removing the belt as she went to her knees in front of him to slowly pull down his pants. When her right hand brushed against the ankle holster on his left leg, she stopped momentarily and looked down at the large silver handgun strapped to Dino's inner calf. She left his pants down at his ankles, raising up to put her hands into his jockey shorts, and pulled them down slowly. Then she helped him step out of his pants and shorts, all the time letting her breath fall between his legs.

When she stood, she brushed the tip of his excited penis with her fingers and said, "Join me, big boy." At which time she turned and stepped out of the bright light from the living room into dimness and climbed on the bed, lying on her back, her legs slightly parted.

When Dino started toward her, she snapped, "Aren't you going to take off your gun?"

"I might need it," he smiled, then turned and moved back to his desk chair to remove his ankle holster, socks, and shoes. He took his time and when finished, he asked, "You want something to drink, or read?"

"Get over here," answered a deep, sexy voice. "Now!"

There was no way Dino could do it slowly, although he tried to slow it down and stretch it out. He was far too excited for it to be anything but hard and hot the first time. He tried holding back, but there was no holding anything back from the passionate woman beneath him, her body moving hard against his, her hips pumping wet and strong. But he held back as long as he could, until Lizette, through heavy breathing, rasped, "Come on, Babe— Come on."

After, as their bodies tried to return to a more normal state, Lizette and Dino lay entwined on the bed. At first their eyes were closed, but it was not long before she opened her eyes and said, "How about something to drink?"

Dino forced his eyes open and looked at her as she lay half atop him, her right leg wrapped between his legs. "A drink?"

"Do you have any hot chocolate?"

"Sure." It took a few seconds for him to get up. He brushed his lips against hers before going into the bathroom to get the robe that hung inside the door. When he turned back, she was picking up his shirt from the floor and putting it on. He watched her button up his shirt and move over to kiss him again.

He took her hand and led her to his kitchen. As soon as he flipped on the lights, he knew he should have warned her.

"Oh, wow!" Lizette covered her eyes as the bright light bulbs flashed on in the very white kitchen of Dino's dungeon.

"I'm sorry." He flipped off the lights. "I should have warned you. It's kind of bright in here."

"You telling me?"

It took awhile for their eyes to adjust. "I keep meaning to change those bulbs, but sometimes it's the only thing that can wake me up when I got to roll in the middle of the night."

Lizette moved around the kitchen as he fixed her chocolate and his coffee. He watched the easy way she moved, the form of her figure beneath his shirt as she turned and walked to the table. He really like the way she smiled at him from across the table, sitting there naked in his dress gray shirt.

Lizette stared back and had to smile at him as he sipped his coffee. Even Dino's moustache was messed up, but not as much as his hair. He looked so much younger under the bright lights, his hair messed, his light eyes staring at her with a confidence she had never seen in him.

"How long have you lived here?" she asked between sips.

"Since I got out of the academy. My mother calls this place 'the dungeon.'"

"I think it's cozy."

She asked a few more questions and let Dino talk. Without much prompting he told her how he had grown up a few blocks away in a two-story shotgun double house on North Bernadotte Street. He told her about his father and mother but said nothing about his brother. He had spoken about his brother in the past, as she had spoken of her sister. But this was not a night to speak of such things.

The second time around Dino took his time. He began by making love to her breasts, letting his tongue roam over each, back and forth, caressing her nipples and then kissing them, and then gently sucking them as Lizette's breath grew deeper and harder. The second time around was always better.

She let Dino make love to her, let him do the touching, let his mouth do the probing as she lay back and let her body react.

They fell asleep after the second time and did not wake up until it was almost four o'clock in the morning. And still they took their time getting out of the snug bed and getting dressed. Lizette didn't bother putting on her underclothes, just tucking them in her purse.

As Dino drove the Alfa through the dark streets, Lizette rolled her window down and let the air blow over her. She closed her eyes, leaned back, and rested one hand on the back of Dino's neck, gently toying with his hair.

Dino looked at her, the night air rushing through the Alfa, her face still sleepy, its makeup worn off, her hair in disarray in the wind, one long strand of dark hair flying across her face. She never looked better to him.

Later, when he kissed her goodnight at the door of the mansion, she had one question, "Tomorrow night?"

"You know it."

He climbed into the unmarked Chevrolet he had left parked next to the mansion at the dead end of Garfield Street, cranked up the engine, and waited for it to warm up, his mind at ease, his entire body relaxed and loose. Then he sailed home.

He felt good, better by the moment, as he thought about the night and the nights to come. He smiled to himself realizing he would start the day shift the following Monday. There would be plenty of evenings to spend with Lizette Marie Louvier.

On his way home, Dino flipped on his portable radio and caught the tail end of a conversation between two Homicide detectives from the other watch. They were working a murder at Coliseum Square. One of the voices was that of Cal Boudreaux, the biggest fuck-up in Homicide.

Dino was feeling so good, he picked up his radio and actually asked Cal if he needed any help.

"What are you doing out at this time?" Boudreaux asked, incredulous.

"Cruising," Dino answered, realizing he was in no condition to work and was relieved when Boudreaux declined his offer in the next sentence. He felt dumb for asking in the first place, but he was feeling so good he forgot himself.

Later, when he returned home to that same bed

that still smelled of Lizette, he slept a deep and restful sleep.

The monthly shift changed the following Monday. LaStanza's squad took its turn working the hot day shift of summer in subtropical New Orleans. It was not a pleasant experience, yet Dino was feeling so good he went in early Monday morning. On his way in, he stopped by Café DuMonde and picked up some coffee.

Settling at his desk with his coffee, he scanned the Homicide daily reports compiled over the last week. His daily on the Gargoyle was on top, initialed by each of the detectives and sergeants who had read it. Near the bottom of the stack was Boudreaux's daily on Coliseum Square.

Boudreaux's dailies were must reading because of their ineptness. Dino glanced at the brief report until his eyes caught something that caused him to pause and reread. The victim was a black female in her twenties wearing a yellow minidress and no panties. But that wasn't what caught Dino's attention, it was the description of the wounds that caused him to nearly spill hot coffee on his hand. The victim had been shot twice in the forehead with a small caliber weapon, at close range.

"It couldn't be," he told himself. But if there was one thing LaStanza did not believe in, it was coincidence.

He put down his coffee and quickly dialed the number to the crime lab and luckily an old academy classmate answered the phone.

"Hammond . . . this is LaStanza. How've you been?"

"Fine, man, what's happening?" Fat Frank Hammond sounded as if he had a mouthful of apple fritter.

"I need some help."

"I'm your man," Hammond answered cheerfully.

Dino took less than a minute asking Hammond to compare the bullets from the Gargoyle to the ones from Coliseum. "Call me right away, okay?"

"Sure."

"If I'm not here," Dino went on, "I'll be up in Intelligence."

"I'll track you down."

"Thanks." Dino hung up and then sat up straight in his chair to reread Boudreaux's daily. Except for the brief description of the wounds, there was nothing of any value in the report, which was usual for anything written by the fuck-up.

Dino was too excited to keep still, so he went early to the Intelligence Division, hoping Detective Felicity Jones would be in. Fel Jones was there all right, sitting behind his own gray metal desk, greeting LaStanza with a large grin on his face.

A thin black with a sharp wit and an ever-present smile, Felicity was also the bravest man LaStanza knew. One night an armed robber filled his chest with bullets. Felicity had the courage to draw his revolver, pursue the robber, and shoot him dead. Dino had transported Fel to Charity Hospital, holding his hand in the trauma room until he passed out.

Like LaStanza, Fel was a veteran of the Sixth District. In fact, he and LaStanza had been partners briefly after Fel recovered from his gunshot wounds. The partnership was short-lived, though, broken up after one controversial night when several armed robbers were gunned down outside a liquor store on

60

Dryades Street, a shooting that ended the careers of several policemen, put more gray hair on the chief's head, and almost killed Jones and LaStanza.

Born in a house on Felicity Street a few blocks from the Sixth District Station, Fel grew up next door to the Melpomene Projects. Yet an inquisitive mind and a natural curiosity helped him through Catholic school and the police academy. Being bright and black made him a natural for the Intelligence Division.

"Say, man, what it is?" Fel beamed in the old familiar project lingo.

"I'm up to my ass in dead people," Dino answered as he sat in the chair next to Fel's desk.

The black detective smiled broadly and slapped LaStanza on the shoulder. "And how's your Paw?"

"Fine. Drinks too much—the usual." Dino was in a hurry, and it showed in his voice. "You got my information?"

Fel reached into a tray on his desk and said, "You ready to copy?"

"Shoot."

Fel smiled at that. "Now that's a nasty word around you and me."

Dino had to smile as he remembered that night on Dryades Street, the exploding bottles, the shattering plate glass storefront, the fluorescent lights raining down on them as police bullets cut down the robbers.

"Here." Fel handed Dino a thick file folder. "I took the liberty of copying this for you. Don't lose it. We're not supposed to give it out."

As Dino opened the folder, he added, "I've put a biography of Thomas Jimson in there, along with a history of the Badalamente Family, a flowchart that'll show you its business dealings, as well as a hierarchy

61

of members and criminal associates of the family, including pictures."

"Thanks, man." Dino examined the thick file. When he came across one picture, he stopped and pointed the face out to Fel. "He was outside Jimson's house when we searched it." It was the large man who had been leaning on the limousine when the detectives had left.

"That's Frank Porta. He's Baddie's bodyguard. He's a soldier, a button man. There's a bio on him in there too."

"Soldati," Dino said under his breath, but loud enough for Fel to hear.

"That's right, you know all about this Sicilian shit, huh?"

LaStanza continued through the file until he came upon the harsh face of the ugly man from the funeral.

"That's Pus Face." Fel explained.

"Who?"

"Pus Face, Harry Lemoni. He's Baddie's nephew. He owns a strip joint in the Quarter. There's a bio on him in there."

"He's called Pus Face?" Dino stared at the face.

"That's because of his acne. Disgusting, ain't he?"

Dino nodded as he continued through the file. When he came to a picture of Mrs. Jimson, he stopped. The picture had obviously been taken some time ago. In it, she was walking across a parking lot, the wind blowing through her hair as she looked past the camera with a broad smile on her face. Her fine, dark features stood out in the black-and-white photo. In the photo her Italian face reminded Dino of his mother.

"Gina Badalamente Jimson," Fel advised. "Doesn't she look like the girl on the tomato paste can?"

62

"Who?"

"The picture of the Italian girl on the tomato paste can. At the grocery," Fel poked LaStanza's side. "Doesn't she look like her?"

Dino flinched. "I guess all Sicilians look alike to you?"

"Yeah, you all look like Spicks." Fel laughed heartily, and when Dino did not, the Intelligence detective added, "Lighten up, man."

"Not funny." Dino gave Fel a hard look, and the black detective laughed even harder.

"I love that hard-ass wop stare!" There was no acting with Fel, he knew LaStanza too well.

The next photo was of Baddie himself, Signore Alphonso Badalamente, businessman, entrepreneur, contributor to every imaginable charity, supporter of politicians, defender of Holy Mother the Church, and boss of La Cosa Nostra in New Orleans.

The photograph was of a man in late middle age, with a full head of white hair and a full white moustache against his dark Sicilian skin. It was a craggy face, a strong face. Alphonso Badalamente looked like Ernest Hemingway without a beard, except Baddie had shark eyes, lifeless and black.

There was no picture of the pretty blonde from the cemetery, so Dino asked about her.

"It sounds like Minky. There's a bio on her in there, but no picture. Her real name's Karen Koski. She used to be Baddie's main girlfriend."

"Oh."

"That file should have everything you need to know about the Mafia in New Orleans," Fel declared. "If there's anything more I can do, just call."

"Thanks." Dino got up to leave.

"Just one more thing," Fel added. "When do I get

to see the shit you got on the search warrants from Jimson?"

"Lieutenant Mason's going through the records. I'll Xerox you a copy of Jimson's appointment and address books right away."

"Good," Fel said, "and let me know if you guys start tailing any of these fellas. We don't wanna both be tailing the same people."

Dino hesitated a moment and asked, "You guys weren't by any chance tailing Jimson lately?"

"Nope, wish I could help you. We've been busy with a motorcycle gang. We haven't tailed any of these characters for over a month."

Dino nodded and turned to leave. Fel called out behind him, "Ya'll be careful. Watch out for exploding glass." Fel was still laughing when the door closed behind LaStanza.

As soon as he got back to his desk, Dino called the crime lab, "Got anything?"

"Bingo!" Hammond declared. "It's a match."

"Jesus fuckin' Christ!" Dino jumped up from his chair, "I'm coming right down!"

Fat Frank was eating a moon pie when LaStanza rushed in and said, "Show me."

Frank pointed a piece of moon pie at a microscope across the narrow firearms examination room. Dino pressed his eyes against the dual eyepieces and could see two images below, two projectiles with their markings magnified so the grooves looked like canyons.

"Okay, what am I looking at?"

"Two projectiles from the same gun." Frank moved up behind the detective and continued, "One was from your body and one from Coliseum." Frank

64

twisted a dial which caused the images to move slightly. "The comparison microscope lets us look at two pellets at the same time, and as you can see, there are six identical lands and grooves. Your killer's using a Colt .22 magnum. The bullets are copper-jacketed magnums, left twists, six lands and grooves. It's a Colt, all right." Hammond sounded proud of himself.

"Can you write me up something on this?" Dino asked.

"Sure, right away."

"Thanks," Dino said. "Thanks a lot."

"Anytime, my man. Anytime."

Dino slapped Frank's shoulder. "That's good work."

"We aim to please. Want a moon pie?"

"No thanks."

He did not wait for the elevator but bounded up the rear stairs and rushed into the squad room. The sergeant's office was empty. He noticed the soles of Mason's penny loafers on the desk in the lieutenant's office. Dino scooped up Boudreaux's daily and his own notes and hurried in to see Mason.

It took less than five minutes to convince Mason to assign the Coliseum Square Murder to him. LaStanza laid out the facts, pointing out that the same follow-up was required on both cases and there was no way two different squads could work it without fucking up the trail. The more he talked, the more excited he became. "I've already linked the two murders. Now I'm gonna link the victims and the fuckin' killer too."

"All right. All right." Mason held up both hands in surrender. "Boudreaux's got enough unsolved murders to work on." The lieutenant picked up Boudreaux's daily, read it, and shook his head. "He

65

couldn't solve a whodunit if the killer turned himself in." Exhaling one large cloud of smoke before sucking in another, he added, "I'm probably gonna have to suspend him anyway." Mason handed the daily back to Dino. "He didn't even conduct a canvass on this case."

"I gotta tell Mark." Dino gathered up his notes.

"Mark's off today," Mason said. "You know he never comes in the first day of day watch." Mark hated the day watch more than any of them.

Dino hurried out to his desk just as his partner strolled in wearing a pair of mirrored sunglasses, gangster shades. Paul did a jig and a quick spin as he fell into his desk chair across from Dino. "How you like my new glasses?"

Dino put his notes down, moved over to his partner, removed the glasses, and tried them on. He grinned at Paul and said, "Guess who isn't in Chicago or Detroit?"

"Huh?"

"Our killer. Our hit man. He's still here!"

Coliseum Square was built as a pleasant urban park in the center of the lower Garden District. Elegant nineteenth-century mansions surround the square. Children used to frolic in the park on fine china grass. But that was before someone built the Melpomene and St. Thomas Housing Projects.

Coliseum Square was no longer pleasant. Children still played there, but now they had to keep out of the way of drug dealers and pimps and skid-row bums who had set up permanent residence in the square.

When LaStanza worked the Sixth District, he used to prowl around the park in his unit, shining his spotlight on the scum that settled there nightly. He would roust them with his public address system: "What are you doing there, scumbag?"

On the rare night when things were quiet in the Bloody Sixth, a favorite sport of patrolmen was to start at each end of the park and take a walk across the dirt and scumbags where fine china grass once grew.

Dino explained about the bullets to Paul on their way to Coliseum Square later that day. "Damn Boudreaux didn't even canvass," he concluded as he parked their Chevy at the intersection of Terpsichore and Coliseum Streets. "The body was dumped there," he pointed in the direction of one of the large oaks along the perimeter of the square. Paul followed him to a muddy knoll next to an oak.

For a full minute the two detectives stood in the mud, staring at the ground. Finally Snowood said, "What the fuck are we doing?"

"I knew I should have come here Sunday morning," Dino muttered as he looked up and around the square. "I was on the radio the other morning when Boudreaux was here. I should have come."

"Well, pardner . . . no use crying. Let's canvass. I've a hankering to knock on some skid-row doors." Snowood moseyed off in the direction of Camp Street. He was wearing a tan corduroy suit, cowboy boots, and his gangster glasses.

Dino remained by the spot where the body had been found, scratching at the ground with the toe of his shoe. Then he looked around the square, at the empty, black wrought-iron benches before turning around and walking up to a large house across Coliseum Street to knock on its front door.

Although Coliseum Square was only a block wide, it ran several blocks between Coliseum and Camp

Streets, from Melpomene to Race Street. There was a children's play area at the center of the park, a few feet from where the body had been found. Built of untreated logs and steel, the play area was surrounded by a sand pit that was muddy most of the time. There was a central grassy area in the square with small knolls crisscrossed by concrete walkways. Near the Race Street side there was a large water fountain that never worked.

Dino canvassed Coliseum Street while Paul took the houses along Camp. The two linked up at the front door of a huge mansion with white columns on Race Street. This mansion was the only one on the square that was still owned by its original owners. At least that was what the other people had said, the ones who even bothered to talk to the detectives. All the other houses had been converted into tenements or were simply unoccupied. Around the square Dino counted sixteen "For Sale" signs.

An ancient woman with cotton-candy white hair answered the door of the last mansion on Race Street.

"Heh?" she responded to LaStanza's first question. To his second question, she repeated, "Heh?"

"She can't hear," Paul said.

"What?" the woman shouted. When the detectives turned away she added, "I didn't order no groceries," before slamming her door.

"This canvass is useless," Paul complained after the woman slammed the door on them.

"We'll have to come back at night."

"What time was she found?"

"Four in the morning."

"Fuck, I'm too tired for tonight."

"Me too," Dino agreed as they started to their unit. On their way across the square, they spoke to a black man with a wine bottle in a paper sack, a bag lady munching on a piece of bread, and three black kids playing in the muddy sandpit next to the monkey bars. No one knew anything.

"I'm hungry," Paul said. "Let's get some grub."

Back in their unit, Dino told his partner, "We'll have to come back tomorrow and spend the night out here." He went on, talking more to himself, "Check the park and the houses again, see if anyone just happened to see someone toss a fuckin' body out." He began to rub his tired eyes. "Gotta check the Sixth to see if any cops were around here. Gotta check the buses and cab drivers and fuckin' ambulances. . . ."

A familiar feeling returned to Dino's stomach. It was a piercing sensation of muscles contracting tighter and tighter. He closed his eyes and tried to fight off the knot growing in his gut. He knew what was happening to him; it had happened before. During the long weeks when the Slasher was wreaking havoc, his stomach twisted into wicked knots that ate at him day and night.

"I won't let it happen to me again," he told himself. Leaning back, he thought about Lizette, about her deep voice, her full lips. She had eyes the color of autumn leaves. He remembered how sad those eyes were when they had first met. But recently the sadness had been replaced by a sharpness, an intelligence that went beyond her education. Lizette had smart eyes that revealed an inner beauty far beyond her obvious good looks. She had sexy eyes, alluring eyes, eyes he could daydream about when he needed to.

By the time LaStanza and Snowood returned to the Bureau, it was already dark. To their surprise they found Mark parking his unit in the police garage. He was unshaven, wearing a T-shirt and jeans. As soon as he spotted them he shouted, "What's this about another whodunit?"

Dino reached over, removed the gangster glasses from Snowood's front coat pocket, put them on, and grinned. "Guess who's still in town?"

"Who?" Mark yelled.

"Our hit man killed a whore the other night. He's still here!"

Soraparu Street

According to the autopsy record, the Coliseum Square victim ate red beans and rice shortly before she was murdered. She was described as a black female, estimated to be between twenty and twenty-five years of age, weighing approximately one hundred pounds, and measuring approximately five feet, five inches in length. Cadavers on autopsy tables were measured in length, not height.

An external examination of the cadaver revealed a tattoo of the words "Sweet Meat" on the inner right thigh one inch below the vagina and a tattoo of the name "Sondra" on the left wrist. The body had recent needle marks on both arms and an appendectomy scar. She had two gold teeth and wore gold pierced earrings. She had borne at least one child. There was no physical evidence of sexual assault.

The cause of death was listed as two penetrating gunshot wounds of the forehead. The trajectory of the bullets was downward at about forty-five degrees. The manner of death was listed as homicide. The time of death was approximated as at least three hours before discovery. A quick examination at the scene revealed telltale purple marks of postmortem

71

lividity, but in the wrong places. The body had been moved after the murder.

According to a press release, the cadaver was identified the same day Detectives LaStanza and Snowood were canvassing Coliseum Square. The victim's mother, Sandra Joseph, appeared at the Orleans Parish Coroner's Office and identified the body of her daughter, Lutisha Marie Joseph. Lutisha's street name was Sondra. She was twenty-one.

A check of fingerprints confirmed the victim was indeed Lutisha Joseph. Her criminal record included three prostitution arrests, a "B drinking" charge, and two narcotics charges. There were no convictions.

At eight o'clock on Tuesday morning, LaStanza parked his tan Chevrolet on Soraparu Street, directly across from the house where Lutisha Marie Joseph had lived. The house was a skinny, wood-frame shotgun covered by gray slate. The rooms were built one after the other from the front room to the rear kitchen. If you opened all the doors and fired a shotgun from the front yard, you would have a clear shot to the back yard.

The rusted page fence was riddled with gaps, and its front gate was missing. The tiny front yard was overgrown and cluttered with tire tools, a bent tire rim, and the remains of an aluminum lawn chair. The front stoop had holes in each of its four steps. Dino's knock at the front door was answered by an old black woman wearing a pink robe and baby blue slippers.

"Police." Dino showed his badge and identification. "I'm looking for Sandra Joseph."

"I Sandra," said the woman, who turned slowly

and retreated into the house, leaving the door open for him to follow.

"I'm Detective LaStanza, Homicide. I need to talk to you about Lutisha."

The woman sat heavily on a lime green sofa a few feet inside the front door. Dino stepped in and was greeted immediately by the insufferable heat of a house that was closed up in summer with no air conditioning. He remained by the doorway, quickly glancing around the living room, at the worn carpet and the pink walls and the black velvet paintings of Mexican bullfighters that hung on the wall above the sofa. There was a bedroom beyond the living room. A little boy was sleeping in a double bed. The woman stared blankly at the wall across from her and waited.

"Is that a picture of Lutisha?" Dino asked, stepping over to an end table next to the sofa, where an eight-by-ten picture stood in an orange plastic frame. The picture was of a young woman with wicked eyes, wearing a red blouse and smiling at the camera.

"Yeah, dat bees Sondra. She be known as Sondra." The woman's voice sounded scratchy and tired.

Sondra was a pretty girl whose wicked eyes looked Egyptian, like those on King Tut's mask, long and narrow eyes, black eyes. Sondra was dark skinned, with fine African features and face that was smooth and clear, like brown velvet.

Dino stepped back to the doorway and took out his pen and pad to begin the slow process of questioning the woman. He remained in the doorway, in the only area of the room where the air was not a hundred degrees.

The heat pressed in on him as the old woman answered his questions about her daughter. Born at Charity Hospital, Sondra went to public school until

73

she was fourteen when she dropped out to have her baby, who was now a seven-year-old boy living with his grandmother. The boy's father had been killed in a motorcycle accident when the child was two.

"What did Sondra do for a living?"

"I don't know," answered the woman, who continued to stare at the far wall.

"Did you know Sondra had been arrested for prostitution and narcotics?"

The woman shook her head "no."

"When did you last see Sondra?"

"De night she died. She get dressed up. She go out."

"Was she with anyone?"

"No," answered the scratchy voice.

"Did anybody pick her up?"

"No, she walk."

"Which way?"

"I don't know." The woman's face remained expressionless.

"Who did Sondra hang out with?" Dino asked as he wiped sweat from his brow.

Sondra's mother had no idea. She knew none of Sondra's friends or where Sondra went or anything about her daughter's activities once the girl left the front door.

The heat became almost unbearable. Dino put one foot out on the front stoop and paused to suck in air from outside. "Can I borrow a picture of Sondra?" he asked when he turned back into the hot room.

The woman rose slowly and moved to the bedroom, where she dug into a drawer in an old fashioned chest that rested atop several telephone books. She returned with a smaller copy of the photo from the living room and handed it to the detective without looking at him.

"I'll see that you get this back." He gave her his card and asked her to please call if she heard anything about Sondra that could help. Turning to leave, he asked, "When is the funeral?"

"Ain't no funeral," the woman answered as she sat back on the sofa. "City gonna bury her."

Dino remained in the doorway for a moment, looking back at the bed and at the little boy still sleeping on it. He had one more question. "Did Sondra eat red beans and rice before she left Saturday night?"

The woman turned her tired eyes to the detective for the first time since he stepped into her house. "How you know dat?"

Dino looked back at the boy once again before stepping out on the stoop and leaving the house.

There was a slight breeze drifting up Soraparu Street from the river when LaStanza stepped out onto the brick sidewalk. He looked up and down the narrow street at the mixture of parked cars crowding both sides of it. Soraparu ran only four blocks from Tchoupitoulas to Annunciation Street. It was a lower class street populated by lower class people. It was a familiar street to Detective LaStanza, who had passed over Soraparu many times as a Sixth District patrolman, but never stopped.

There was always an abundance of litter on Soraparu Street, where the houses looked alike in their tired paint and dilapidated fences. The sidewalks were made of old red bricks, overgrown with grass and fungi that caused Dino to watch his step as he walked from door to door.

The Soraparu canvass produced nothing of value. Most of the people had never heard of Sondra, although Dino was certain many recognized the photo he showed them. Near Tchoupitoulas Street, he found two boys who were curious enough to talk to the plainclothesman carrying a small black radio and a picture of a black girl. Both boys knew Sondra as "that pretty girl" who lived down the street.

"She a whore," one boy said.

"How do you know that?" Dino asked.

The boy was about six years old, wearing a soiled Spider-Man T-shirt and tattered jeans. He answered, "Everybody know she a whore."

"Ask a stupid question," Dino told himself as he gave each child one of his cards. Maybe one of his cards would find its way into the hands of someone who knew something beyond the fact that Lutisha Marie Joseph, better known as Sondra, was a whore.

"Do you know who Sondra hung out with?" he asked.

"No," the boys answered simultaneously, and then quickly ran away with the detective's cards, as if they had made off with something of value. Returning to his car, he made a mental note to return to Soraparu. In time, maybe he'd have better luck.

It was almost one in the afternoon by the time Dino left the litter of Soraparu behind and headed toward Audubon Park and the fine manicured lawn of Lizette's house on Exposition Boulevard. He passed a playground a couple blocks from Soraparu, on Annunciation Street. He made another mental note to return to that playground to canvass.

"Sorry I'm late," he told Lizette when she answered her door.

She grabbed his hand to pull him in. "You're just in time. I just finished fixing everything." She started to lead him through the foyer.

Dino pulled his hand away and lowered his voice.

"You got a minute?"

Lizette turned back with a "What?"

"Come here," he narrowed his eyes and pulled her back. Lizette wrapped her arms around his neck as he French-kissed her in the doorway, holding her tight.

"Now," he said when they parted, "that's better."

"You know it," she sighed, pausing a moment to catch her breath before grabbing his hand again. She led him through the foyer and hallway, back to the kitchen. The Louvier kitchen was at the rear corner of the house, airy and well lit, with windows running the entire length of its two outer walls.

Lizette sat Dino at the tile counter in the center of the kitchen and busied herself with their lunch. He turned the volume down on his portable radio, placed it on the counter, and watched her move around the kitchen, noticed the easy way she tossed her long hair aside when reaching for utensils, her hips when she bent over to retrieve whatever was in the oven. She looked nice and casual that day, with only a hint of makeup on her face. She was wearing a pale yellow LaCoste tennis shirt and baggy yellow shorts, which made her waist seem extra small. She looked different from that dressed up, glamor girl from the other night. She looked fresh and young and happy.

It wasn't long before Lizette laid out a meal of hot croissants, cool chicken salad, fresh fruit, and iced tea. Dino picked up a croissant and made a chicken salad sandwich as Lizette climbed on the stool across from him. "Now," she said as she smiled at him, "what have you been up to, Detective LaStanza? You look beat."

"I've been sweating all morning in a hothouse. Remember I told you they found a body the other night, after I brought you home?"

"Uh-huh. Coliseum Square." Lizette nodded, and began to prepare her own sandwich.

"Well, the same gun that killed the Gargoyle killed her."

Lizette paused as she reached for the poppy-seed dressing. "You mean, the same killer . . ."

"That's right. Somebody's going around putting twenty-twos in people's foreheads."

She shuddered a moment before prodding him for more. "And so . . ."

"So I got another whodunit on my hands. I just took over the Coliseum Murder, too."

A look of concern came over Lizette's face as she stated the obvious. "You'll be putting in a lot of hours now."

Dino nodded as he took a bite of sandwich. Lizette took a bite herself, her large eyes never leaving him. After a sip of tea, a curious grin came over her face. She cupped her chin in her hand, her elbow on the counter, and asked, "So how are you going to solve this one?"

"You got me," he answered between bites, then started listing the initial steps that had to be done before any solution was in sight: He would canvass until there was nothing more to canvass, search for the dead girl's prostitute friends or maybe even a pimp, and dig into the Gargoyle's background until he brought Jimson and Sondra together. "There's got to be a link between the Gargoyle and Coliseum, beyond the bullets."

When Lizette asked about the hothouse, he told her about Soraparu Street and the gray-haired woman whose daughter was a whore and about the whore's son sleeping in the bed and about the telephone books beneath the chest of drawers.

78

"What do you suppose will become of the boy?" Lizette asked when he finished.

"Probably go to Harvard, become a neurosurgeon." Dino's retort was automatic. He caught himself, shrugged, and added quietly, "The kid doesn't have a chance. Do you know what's the leading cause of death of young black men in America?"

Before she could think, he answered his own question: "Gunshot wounds."

Lizette leaned forward with a curious look in her eyes. "Sometimes, when you're talking about crime scenes and autopsies, you sound so aloof, then you tell me about poor little boys and chests of drawers with no legs. You don't fool me one bit. There's a southern liberal inside you just struggling to get out."

Dino almost laughed. "Yeah?" He finished off his sandwich and thought about it. A southern liberal. Never. He knew that given half a chance, he would personally pull the switch on that little boy if the boy lived up to his heritage.

"You want to see a picture of her?" pulling Sondra's picture from his coat pocket, he handed it to Lizette.

"She was pretty." There was an element of surprise in Lizette's voice.

"She's got Egyptian eyes."

When he finished his third glass of iced tea, Lizette moved over and put her arms around his neck. She kissed him softly on the ear and whispered, "Easy chair?"

"Easy chair," Dino agreed, returning the picture to his pocket and following her to the dark coolness of the library at the front of the house. With its long silken drapes closed, the library looked smaller than it was. Crowded with books that ran to the ceiling, two desks, several small tables, and a big easy chair in front of a real fireplace, the library was the quietest room in the house. It was a room made for thinking or resting.

Dino and Lizette curled up together in the big easy chair in front of the fireplace and leaned back beneath the large portrait of Lynette that hung above the marble mantel. The portrait was in oil, a face identical to Lizette's, alabaster skin against a dark blue background, red lips, and eyes that followed you around the room.

Dino stared at the eyes in the portrait as Lizette snuggled in his arms. Soon his eyes closed, and it did not take long for the easy breathing to lull them both to sleep in the comfortable chair in front of the fireplace.

When he woke with a start, it made Lizette jump. "I'm sorry," he apologized, stretching the kinks from his legs. He looked at his watch and found that they had slept for over two hours. Lizette closed her eyes and snuggled her face against his neck.

After a minute, he shook her gently. "I've got to go. I'm meeting the fellas at the bureau. I've got to work tonight."

Reluctantly Lizette opened her eyes, reached up, and kissed his lips before disentangling herself from him. Dino stood up and stretched. He looked around the room, at the other portraits, pictures in assorted frames atop the tables and desks.

"Since I'm collecting pictures today, can I have one of you?"

"Take your choice." Lizette arched her back and stretched. He took that opportunity to pull her to him and bury his face between her breasts.

"You really *have* to work tonight?" she sighed as

Dino's mouth rose to kiss her neck.

"Uh-huh." His mouth moved over to her ear.

"Call me," she added before his mouth reached hers. When the kiss ended, Lizette ran a finger over Dino's lips, asking, "Tomorrow. Supper at the dungeon?"

"Oh, yeah."

"Good."

On his way out of the library, he grabbed an eight-by-ten portrait of Lizette in a black lacquer frame. It was a close-up of her face smiling at the camera, her large eyes dark and golden, the strands of her hair flowing in an invisible breeze.

On his way to pick up his partner, Dino stopped at a large drugstore on Carrollton Avenue and bought a pair of gangster glasses. Snowood was waiting outside his small Lakeview home on Chapelle Street when LaStanza pulled up in their Chevy.

"So where you been all morning, boy? I been calling you," Paul asked as he climbed into the unit.

"Canvassing Soraparu Street. I was on the radio. Anyway, I thought you took the morning off."

"Find anything?" Paul tossed his briefcase into the backseat.

"Nope."

For the remainder of the trip, Dino never got another word in as Paul gave a blow-by-blow description of his little boy's latest escapade. Apparently the boy had stolen his mother's engagement ring from her jewelry box and given it to a neighbor girl. Paul's son was an eight-year-old redheaded terror. The neighbor was seven. The Snowoods found out when the girl's indignant mother returned the ring. The woman, described by Snowood as a "self-righteous, dried up old hag" gave Paul a ten-minute lecture on how his son was a menace to the neighborhood and would probably grow up to be a child molester.

"I felt like punching her fuckin' lights out, but I didn't. I just took back my wife's ring and said I'd talk to the boy. But that wasn't good enough for the old bitch. She asked if I was gonna punish him.

"'Sure,' I told her, 'gotta teach that boy his priorities.'

"'And what does that mean?' she asked.

"'It means you don't give a woman diamonds *before* you go to bed with her,' I told the bitch."

Paul roared and slapped his leg. "You shoulda seen her face. I thought she was gonna faint."

"You didn't really say that," Dino finally got a line in as he parked the Chevy in the police garage.

"I sure the fuck did. And that ain't all. Before the old broad left she told me she was gonna call the police on me." Paul got a real charge out of that. "Fuck! I been living there six years and my neighbors still don't know I'm the fuckin' police!"

"So," Dino asked as another interesting Snowood story concluded, "what did you tell your boy?"

"I didn't tell him anything. Just beat the shit outta him for stealing his mama's ring. The little bastard's punished until he's seventeen!"

Mason called LaStanza and Snowood into his office as soon as they entered Homicide.

"You wanna see us, boss?" Dino asked as the two entered wearing their gangster glasses.

Mason's face remained expressionless, but Mark snapped at them, "Cute. Real cute."

"You want me to get you a pair, *sarge?*" Paul

82

smiled at Mark, dragging out the word *sarge*.

Mark ignored the remark, asking Dino, "How did your canvass turn out?"

"I found out she was a whore."

"Hell, I coulda told you that," Paul cut in.

"So what's up for tonight?" The sergeant was not distracted.

"Coliseum Square canvass," said Dino. Mark nodded approval as he curled his mouth in a frown.

Mason occupied himself with lighting another cigarette as the detectives settled in the three chairs crowded in the tiny office. Dino watched his lieutenant meticulously light the cigarette and take a deep puff before leaning back in his chair to announce, "We just got served with two subpoenas for all the shit we took from Jimson's office." Mason waved his hand over his desk at the pile of accounting files that lay scattered there.

"Two subpoenas?" Dino asked.

"Yeah. One from Jimson's mouthpiece, Rosenberg," Mason said as he took a drag on his cigarette, "and one from the FBI." He smiled as he said, "Seems the Feds wanna see this as much as the family wants it back."

Dino looked down at the files. "Is there anything in these?"

Mason shrugged. "I think the Badalamente family's too smart to have anything here that will hurt 'em. It's got some intelligence information on some legitimate businesses they got investments in, but nothing that'll help in the murder case."

"Speaking of Intelligence," Dino injected. "I promised Fel Jones he could look through this before we gave it back."

"He already did," Mason advised. "But that ain't the issue here. You're the case officer, which subpoena you wanna honor?"

"I got a choice?"

"Why not? They both arrived at the same time. Depends on who you'd rather piss off, Rosenberg or the Feds."

"Can't we just throw them away and piss 'em both off?" Paul asked. No one answered him.

Dino thought about it a second, looked over at Mark, and shrugged. "I guess we'll give it to the Feds."

"I agree," Mark said. "I hate that fuckhead Rosenberg." Nobody had to say how much they all hated the FBI.

"Did they subpoena the stuff from Jimson's house too?" Dino asked.

"No," Mason advised. "But you better photocopy that stuff just in case."

"Okay."

The only other comment of any consequence at that particular meeting occurred when Mason played devil's advocate again. "You know, we may just have a nut with a twenty-two on our hands. There may be no reason for any of this. It may have nothing to do with the Mafia." But even Mason's voice gave away his true belief that the Gargoyle and Coliseum had to be connected.

When the meeting ended, Dino went straight to the copy machine and made three copies of the Gargoyle's address book and appointment book. He gave one to Mason to lock away, sent one to Fel Jones, and kept the third.

Mark went with them to Coliseum Square that evening, but had to leave early to help M and M with an unclassified death in the French Quarter. "I'll

84

meet you at CDM later," he told them, leaving the two detectives to continue from door to door, asking the same questions over and over and getting the same answer. The only excitement of the night came when a trampy white girl wearing a bikini top and ratty jeans asked Snowood if he wanted to come in for a hamburger.

"I can't," Paul answered, "I'm impotent."

"I don't mind," the girl replied with a yellow smile.

"Morons!" Paul complained to Dino when they linked up after finishing the canvass. "Nothing around here but whores, bums, and fuckin' morons!"

Mark was already at Café DuMonde, waiting alone at an outside table, when LaStanza and Snowood pulled up. "If you'd a brought M and M here, we was gonna breeze on by," Paul told him as the two sat heavily in the small chairs.

"Nothing, huh?" Mark asked Dino. Dino nodded as he flashed three fingers at the oncoming waiter, who turned around and went back inside for their coffee.

"So, what'd you have in the Quarter?" Dino asked.

"A prostitute fell off a building." Mark ran his fingers through his thick hair and added, "Looks like she jumped. She's still alive, but there's no brain activity."

"How can you tell?" Paul asked. He quickly held up a hand and answered himself, "I know, she don't charge anything now."

Even Mark smiled. "You exhaust me," Mark admitted.

Dino had been feeling good earlier that day, especially after leaving Lizette's, but as the day wore on, as the second canvass produced the same negative results, he became increasingly weary.

"You've put in a long day," Lizette told him on the phone later. "Sixteen-hour days will wear anyone down."

"Eighteen hours," he responded in a tired voice.

Lizette paused a moment before adding, "If you were here, I'd make you lie down, and I'd rub your back and neck. . . ."

"Keep that up and you'll get me all hot over here," Dino cut in.

She listened to her boyfriend's tired breathing on the other end and asked, "What time do you get off tomorrow?"

"I'm not sure."

"Call me. I'm bringing supper."

"Including dessert?"

Lizette laughed a deep, naughty laugh. "Including dessert."

LaStanza rubbed his drowsy eyes as he focused on the little green letters on the computer screen in front of him. He punched up the last name on his list, Karen Koski, and watched the screen blink and then flash: *No Record on File.* He would have been relieved if he was not so tired. Koski was the only name he had run all day that had no criminal record.

Wearily, he punched up another series of commands, and Koski's driver's license information came on the screen. She was listed as Karen Elizabeth Koski, white female, twenty-two years old, five feet seven inches tall, one hundred and ten pounds, blonde hair, blue eyes.

Dino punched up the print command, and in an instant the information was printed on the rolled paper at the next desk. When he tore off the printed sheet, he noted Koski's address was listed as 676 Robert E. Lee Boulevard, Apartment 22, New Orleans. On his way back to his desk, he took a quick look in the city directory and discovered Koski's address came back to the King Louis XV Court Condominiums.

Back at his desk, he looked up at the electric clock on the wall. It was already eight o'clock. The evening watch had already come and gone. Dino rubbed his eyes and waited until they could focus again. The clock now read eight-o-five. Beneath the clock hung a gaudy etching, a grotesque piece of pop art. It was the unofficial emblem of the Homicide Division, a drawing of a vulture perched atop a New Orleans Police star-and-crescent badge. Mark had a tie tack made of the emblem. So did Mason and most everyone else in the division. Even Paul had the emblem forged into a large western belt buckle. Dino wondered what Lizette would think of the emblem.

He closed his eyes a moment and recalled how Lizette had looked when she'd arrived at the dungeon the previous evening with a hot supper and eager eyes, and how she felt against him later after they had disposed of dinner and retired for two helpings of dessert in the bedroom. Before Dino could even start in on her, Lizette climbed on top and whispered, "Let me." And he let her take control, let her make the moves, the touches. He laid back and let her make love to him.

"I'm not going anywhere," he told Mark that morning, still wiped out from the long hours the day before and the extra dessert. "I'm staying here and hitting the computer and the record room." So Dino worked on the computer and ran back and forth to the record room to gather all the available police information on the vital players of the Gargoyle case and the Coliseum case.

By eight in the evening he found himself sitting at his desk with a vast assortment of police reports, arrest records, driver's license records, rap sheets, computer printouts, and mug shots. After five more minutes of staring blankly at the papers on his desk and remembering nothing of what he had just read, Dino packed it in. He gathered what information was available from police records and tossed it into his briefcase before turning out the lights on his way out. When he got home, he went to sleep in his clothes without even kicking off his penny loafers.

On his way to the office the following morning, he stopped by Lizette's for coffee and to feel the best moment of the day when she answered the door and put her arms around his neck, opening her mouth to kiss him.

Over coffee she told him how her research had been going for her classes at Loyola. She was excited about one particular project involving several of Shakespeare's plays. Dino watched her, but heard little of what she said. He was thinking about how smart Lizette was. He had taken some college classes before getting drafted, but she was working on her PhD and was smarter than any teacher he had ever known.

A familiar feeling crept into Dino as she spoke. It was the same out-of-place, insecure feeling he had felt when he'd first gone to the Louviers'. He felt like a peasant visiting a royal house. But it was a temporary feeling . . . it went away as quickly as it came. Yet Dino was glad it came. It reminded him of who he was and who she was and how good it made him feel knowing the girl sitting next to him with the golden eyes had chosen him.

Back at the office, Dino went over the information he had secured from the police files the previous day. He learned that Lutisha Marie Joseph, alias Sondra, had been arrested twice on Decatur Street for prostitution in Vice-Squad roundups. Although many prostitutes were arrested at the same time, the police reports listed no one arrested with Sondra. Dino made a note to check the newspaper clippings for those arrests to get the names of others rounded up. Sondra had to have associates, especially in the whore business.

Sondra was arrested for prostitution a third time after she picked up an undercover officer and took him to a seedy motel. After money was exchanged, the undercover officer waited until Sondra stripped before whipping out his badge, handcuffing her to the bed frame, and calling his Vice Squad buddies to come and take away this dangerous criminal. A search of Sondra's purse, subsequent to arrest, surfaced several bottles of controlled substances. She was therefore additionally charged with possession of narcotics.

Sondra was also arrested for possession of marijuana after she was stopped and questioned as a suspected shoplifter at a Canal Street department store. The security guard searched her purse and found a bag of marijuana, and she was booked. She was never charged with shoplifting, which made the narcotics charge worthless.

Sondra was arrested for B drinking at the Nutcracker Bar on North Claiborne when she tried to put the muscle on a truck driver who was too smart to fall for a B girl. He watched as the bartender fed Sondra drink after drink. She continued to come on to the driver, who was getting real drinks instead of the tea Sondra was getting. The trucker paid his exorbitant bill and did not even object when Sondra refused to leave with him. The driver just left alone and called the police. The Fifth District officers had listed Sondra's occupation as "tramp."

Any idea of going to the Nutcracker was quickly extinguished when Dino discovered it had burned down a year earlier. "You sure?" he asked Fel Jones.

"Fuckin' A, I was still on the road and seen it myself."

"Thanks."

"Call me anytime."

Frank Porta, listed by the Intelligence Division as a driver/bodyguard of Alphonso Badalamente, was listed in the police computer under his real name, Franco Guiseppe Porta, white male, forty-two years old, born in New Orleans, six feet six inches tall, two hundred and eighty pounds, black hair and brown eyes, no visible tattoos or scars. Porta's last known address was a box at the New Orleans Lakefront Marina. Frank was arrested once for aggravated battery when he was eighteen and twice for extortion. In the arrest for aggravated battery he put a man's eye out with a letter opener, but the man subsequently dropped the charge. There weren't even any arrest reports on file on the extortion charges. And there were, of course, no convictions.

Harold Eugene Lemoni, alias Harry Lemon, alias Harry Lee, alias Pus Face, white male, five feet eight inches tall, one hundred and seventy pounds, salt-and-pepper hair, hazel eyes, was born in New Orleans. No visible tattoos or scars were listed, although under "distinguishing marks" a police-man with an accurate sense of humor had listed *real ugly*.

Lemoni's criminal career wasn't as distinguished as Frank Porta's. He had two Peeping Tom arrests, no convictions. The last known address for Lemoni was in the four hundred block of Bourbon Street. His occupation was listed as bar owner of Club Morocco, which bore the same Bourbon Street address.

Under the name of Alphonso Badalamente, the police computer had one word: expunged. Whatever record Baddie once had had, a sympathetic judge had ordered it eradicated. Alphonso Badalamente did have a driver's license which revealed him to be a white male, sixty-one years old, six feet tall, two hundred pounds, white hair and brown eyes, last known address his well-known house on Lakeshore Drive. Dino had seen the house many times in passing, re-membering it to be a gaudy, Spanish hacienda-villa surrounded by a ten-foot white wall. Actually he had never seen anything but the second story of the house beyond the wall.

Over a second cup of coffee, he separated the data into sections and then put it all, along with the Intelligence Division report, in a large folder in his briefcase marked "Gargoyle/Coliseum." Then he took out a pad and pen and listed the steps he would take in his follow-up of both murders. When he finished, he realized just how much legwork had to be done.

When Paul returned to the bureau from handling a suicide, he handed his partner a copy of the newspaper article about the Coliseum Murder. "Here, my wife cut this out for you."

Dino read over the small article. "Exact same M.O. as the Gargoyle, and the papers haven't even

91

connected them."

"Reporters only report what people tell them," Paul said. "If nobody tells them, how are they gonna know?"

That was a relief, after the way the papers handled the Slasher murders, with lurid headlines and sensational stories chronicling the return of Jack the Ripper. "I guess it's easy connecting murders of innocent young girls slashed to death instead of a floater and a whore with the same wounds."

"Yeah," Paul agreed as he retrieved a styrofoam cup from the coffee area before putting a particularly large wad of smokeless tobacco between his lips. "So, what's your next move on your whodunits?"

"I have no fuckin' idea." Dino kicked his feet up on his desk.

"If I were you," Paul kicked his feet up on his own desk, "I'd go interview blondie, the girl from the cemetery."

"Her name's Karen Koski."

"Yeah? Well I been thinking about that woman. I think I met her once, a long time ago."

Dino sighed, "All right, I'll play along. Where'd you meet her?"

"In a wet dream I had back in the seventh grade. Fucked the piss outta her and she loved every minute."

"You've been swallowing too much of that brown shit," Dino told his partner.

"Naw. I just figure a woman like that's got to have the prettiest little pussy this side of Amarillo."

Dino was sure that Snowood didn't know Amarillo from an armadillo.

"Can I come over?" Lizette asked. She sounded as if

she had been crying.

"I'll come get you."

"But it's so late."

"I don't want you driving here alone. I'm on my way."

"But you sound so tired."

"I'm never that tired."

When Lizette answered the door, Dino could see she had been crying. Her eyes were puffy, and there was no makeup on her face whatsoever. He hesitated in the doorway as she wrapped her arms around his neck and squeezed him very hard. When her grip slackened, he reached down, pulled her chin up, and kissed her gently on the lips and then harder. He kissed each of her eyes, her cheeks, her chin, and her neck, and then her lips again.

They drove straight back to the dungeon, and Dino thought it would be a silent ride until Lizette choked back a sob. "My brother's therapy isn't working." She struggled to keep from crying. "He was very close to Lynette, especially after I went away to college."

Dino reached over and began to stroke the back of her neck as she continued, "He doesn't say anything for days at a time."

He had not seen much of Lizette's eight-year-old brother lately. He remembered how small and frail the boy looked and how interested the boy had been in his gun and the ankle holster which carried his .357 magnum.

"My parents are also in therapy. They want me to go, but I won't. I don't need it. I don't want to share my sadness with any therapist." Lizette's voice almost broke. "I cry a lot. I don't need a therapist to get it out."

She paused a second, almost losing it. "I knew Lynette better than anyone. I know how she thought and how she'd feel about me now. She'd want me to live for the both of us." Lizette started crying.

Dino continued to rub her neck as she leaned forward and cried and then dried her eyes with a tissue. Looking up with red eyes, she asked, "Did you cry when your brother was killed?"

"I still do," Dino admitted, "sometimes."

"I remember what you told me about him, how close you were. Probably closer than Lynette and me. You must have been destroyed."

Dino nodded in response, thinking about what she said. How could he and Joe be closer than twins? She meant something by that, and he'd have to find out . . . later.

"Does it ever get better?" she asked.

Dino shrugged. "You just got to face it. You can't be afraid. It's always going to hurt. You just have to let it out, and crying is the best way.

"Sometimes I tell myself he isn't dead. He's still living in me, in my mind. It isn't the same but it's all I got left."

Although neither said it, they both knew that was not true. Lynette was gone and so was Dino's brother, and nothing would ever be the same again.

When they made love that night, Dino took his time, slowing down when he was close to coming, pushing in and out of Lizette in long, slow strokes, and then pushing hard when she curled her back beneath him and cried, "Oh Babe . . . ohhh Babe."

Dino felt a power in him, an inner strength that helped him from exploding as he continued pumping in and out of her wetness. He felt a power that made him hold up so she could feel it, all of it.

When she began to cry again, he stopped. She squeezed her arms around his back and said, "Stay in me. Stay inside me."

Lizette was the first to start pumping again after her crying subsided. She was unrelenting, reaching hard for it, taking control. Dino reared up on his hands and pushed back into her as she gasped and shoved her open mouth against his. When he could hold it back no longer, he wrapped his hands beneath her rear and let himself explode as her gasping movements matched his in depth and strength until they lay exhausted on the wet sheets.

Neither had ever said anything about their feelings for one another, but Lizette felt a need for words as she lay beneath him. Dino was not one for words. She knew that, just as she knew how much he cared for her by the way he looked at her, and the way he touched her and kissed her. But she wished he would surprise her and come out and say it. She wanted to hear it as much as she wanted to say it. She wanted it put into words.

Lying in the darkness of the dungeon, Lizette thought about how Dino had surprised her before, the first time he kissed her. She knew he was interested but was not expecting him to grab her in her doorway, pull her to him, and kiss her. He had surprised her again, later when she told him how many men she had been to bed with. He was quiet at first as she explained how she had started early, how she was never a wallflower. He was curious, but accepted it without the usual bruised male ego. He just shrugged.

He was more interested in the boys she had cared

95

about than in the number of men that had been to bed with her. "The sign of a mature man," she told herself.

Lizette looked at his tranquil face resting on her shoulder. Softly she began to stroke his hair, whispering in his ear, "I love you, Babe. I really do." Dino was asleep.

She sighed and continued whispering to him, telling him things she had never told anyone, secrets she had locked inside, about her twin, and her father's newfound concern that she was seeing too much of this detective too quickly. Then she told him about the men she had known.

When he woke an hour later, she was still awake. He tried to get up, but she held him in place. "But I gotta bring you home."

"No, you don't. I'm a big girl now. I sleep wherever I want."

"Oh," Dino sank back on his pillow and rubbed his eyes.

"Besides, my parents are out of town."

"Oh."

Lizette leaned up on an elbow. "Tell me something about you I don't know."

His eyes blinked at her. She ran her fingers over his bare chest. "I want to know all about you, Dino LaStanza. Tell me something about you I don't know."

"Um," he blinked up at the ceiling, "I . . . I um . . . I went to Loyola for two years."

"Really? I didn't know that. Why didn't you stay?"

"I got drafted."

"Oh."

"Yeah. My Uncle Sam needed me to kill Vietnamese."

"What was it like?"

"I was a combat photographer. It was bad."

She waited.

Dino was quiet for a while, then continued, "I took a picture once of a half sunken sanpan with the sun setting behind it. It was a peaceful picture, the sun was huge and orange and the water was brown, and the sanpan was black. It was a quiet picture, except in a corner of the sun, in the distance, there was a helicopter flying with yellow fire streaming from its guns. The chopper was shooting at another sanpan out of the camera's range. I watched the second sanpan blow up and scatter on the water like sawdust." Dino went silent after that.

Lizette waited for a while before asking, "Did you have a girlfriend over there, a Vietnamese?"

"No. I went to bed with a few, but no girlfriends." He looked over and nudged her. "Like somebody else we know." Dino leaned over and kissed her lips gently, and in his green eyes she saw all the affection she needed to see.

The list of leads LaStanza had compiled left him feeling cold and impotent. He had no idea where to start. His initial elation at still being in the hunt, at still having a shot at a phantom killer, was buried beneath a long list of leads.

He had gone to work early to formulate a plan, but it had been a fruitless half hour.

"So, what you got there?" It was Mason, cigarette dangling from his mouth, straight hair hanging like strings from his square head. He sat in Snowood's

97

chair and tapped ashes in Paul's leftover styrofoam cup.

"I was just looking over my list of follow-up leads from Gargoyle/Coliseum."

"Looks like you got a shitload there."

"Sure do."

"What did you get from Jimson's appointment book?"

Dino had to think a moment before replying. "Mostly useless shit: haircut appointments, golf dates, reminders for the cleaners, birthdays." He reached over for the appointment book. "There's only one real lead to follow." Thumbing through the book, he stopped at the desired page and handed it to Mason.

"There," he pointed, "on the day before he disappeared he had a name written in. See it."

"Minky?"

"Minky. That's the alias of Karen Koski. According to Intelligence, she was Baddie's girlfriend. Paul and I saw her at the Gargoyle's funeral."

The lieutenant studied the page for a moment before tossing the book back to LaStanza. "So when are you gonna talk to this Minky?"

"Soon."

"What's wrong with now? I'm bored." Mason yawned and looked at his watch. "I'm tired of sitting around here all the time. Mind if I tag along?"

"No, not at all," Dino answered as he began to pick up his notes.

"Do you know where she lives?"

"Sure."

"Good. Sometimes you should just do something, make a move just to get going and who knows, you might get lucky and stumble onto something." Mason got up and stretched.

"I know," Dino began to quote one of his lieutenant's most often repeated lines, "the solution's out there . . ."

". . . you just gotta find it," Mason finished the quote himself.

"Right."

Dino drove the lieutenant's car while Mason leaned back and shut his eyes.

"What does this broad look like?" the lieutenant asked.

"A schoolboy's dream. Good-looking blonde with a great figure. Snowood fell in love."

Mason yawned.

"When Paul and I saw her at Gargoyle's funeral, she was watching from behind a tomb, hiding."

"Really?" Mason opened one eye.

"Really."

Karen Elizabeth Koski lived in a townhouse in the front section of the King Louis XV Court Condominiums. Her apartment's front door faced Robert E. Lee Boulevard. Dino knocked twice on the door.

"Who is it?" a woman's voice answered.

"Police." He held his credentials up to the peephole.

After a moment the woman's voice asked, "So what do you want?"

"We want to talk to Karen Koski."

"What about?"

LaStanza hated talking to doors. "A Gargoyle," he told her, "we wanna talk to you about a Gargoyle you used to know."

The door opened, and the blonde from the cemetery stood in the doorway, one hand resting high on the doorframe, the other hand on her hip as if she was posing. Winded, still breathing hard, she stood there in a red Danskin, matching leg warmers,

99

a blue headband around her forehead, half hidden by her white-blonde hair. There was a hint of sweat on her upper lip on a face made up to perfection. "You want to talk to me about a what?" asked the perfect face.

"Thomas Jimson."

"Oh." She hesitated a moment before turning and walking back into her apartment. "Mind closing the door behind you?" she asked over her shoulder. She pointed to the living room as she started up the stairs of the townhouse. "Make yourselves at home. I'll be back in a minute."

Dino glanced around at an art deco apartment of futuristic colors, a coffee table in the shape of a red cube, and a white leather sofa. On the one wall there were several large pictures of . . . Karen Koski. The pictures looked like fashion magazine covers. Mason sat on the white leather sofa and put his feet up on the red cube.

Upstairs the sound of a shower could be heard. Dino shifted his weight from one foot to the other before turning and walking back through the living room to the kitchen that was actually whiter than his without the one-hundred-and-fifty-watt bulbs. He nosed around the hallway that led to a room on the far side of the stairs. When he stepped into the room, he stopped immediately as several more photos of the girl from the cemetery stared back at him.

"Mason!"

"What?"

"Come here. You gotta see this."

Mason stopped as soon as he saw the photos.

"I wanted you to see these, because Paul's not gonna believe me."

"Jesus," Mason whispered as both detectives stared at a series of large nude photos of Karen Koski hanging on the walls of the room. Several of the pictures were in black and white, avant-garde shots with limited light. But several others were in bright color, taken on a sunny day, full frontal nude shots of Karen standing between two columns of a colonnade. She was natural blonde.

"Jesus," Mason repeated as both men returned to the living room. He took a long look at LaStanza and concluded, "that's the first time I've ever seen you struck speechless."

The lieutenant sat back on the couch. Dino remained standing, thinking about the photos. There was something familiar about the colonnade where the photos had been taken, but he could not yet place it.

Karen Koski came down in a yellow cut off T-shirt and baby blue jogging shorts. Her face was still made up to perfection. She sat in the loveseat across from the sofa where Dino joined Mason. The obvious outline of her nipples were clearly visible through the T-shirt.

"So," she said as she crossed her legs. "How can I help you?"

Dino sat up and introduced himself and Mason as he took out his pad and pen. Koski asked him to repeat his name.

"Italian, isn't it?" she asked with a hint of a smile.

"Sicilian," Dino answered as the hint of a smile grew on her face.

"And what nationality is Koski?"

"Finnish."

"Where do you come from, originally?" Dino asked.

"What makes you think I'm not from here?"

"Your accent. No Brooklynese flat "A"s like me. You sound like a Yankee . . . maybe New England."

"That's good," she flashed a broad smile. "I'm from Maine."

"So how long had you known Thomas Jimson?" Dino's eyes moved to his notepad for a second before looking back at her.

The smile was still there, only it was not so broad. "About five years."

"And what was your relationship with him?"

"There was no relationship," she answered quickly. "He was the relative of a friend."

"Alphonso Badalamente?"

"I refuse to say anything about him, so don't bother asking."

"Why?"

The girl narrowed her light blue eyes and leaned forward, "You really are Sicilian, aren't you?" Dino said nothing as he focused his Sicilian eyes back at her. She was the first to blink. "I think maybe you'd better go." She tried to make her face look tough, but it did not work. Her shaky voice gave away how nervous she had become.

He was going to just sit there and stare back at her, see what she would do next, until he heard a snore next to him. Looking over automatically, he had to stop himself from laughing aloud as Mason snored again. The lieutenant was in deep slumber, his head leaning to one side, his mouth open as he snored.

"Son-of-a-gun can fall asleep anywhere."

"Is he really?" Koski sounded relieved. Whatever tension Dino had placed in her was already gone. Her brow slowly lost its wrinkle. She leaned back and put her arms up on the back of the sofa, revealing the round bottom of her breasts as her cut-off T-shirt rose. "All right," she smiled, "what do we do now?"

Several sharp retorts came to mind, but he resisted. Koski broke the silence with a question. "Would you

102

like something to drink? Juice or Perrier?"

Dino thought a second before asking, "What kind of juice?"

When she returned with two glasses of "freshly squeezed orange juice."

Dino sighed again. "I wish I had a tape recorder."

"What for?"

"To show the guys how alert our lieutenant is."

Koski rose and walked in the direction of the rear room where the nude photos hung, returning with a cassette recorder that she placed in front of Mason and turned on. Then she sank back on her loveseat as she and the detective drank the juice to Mason's steady snoring.

When Dino finished his juice, she was quick to ask, "Would you like some more?"

"No," he pulled out his pad again, "I've only a couple more questions." He held up his hand and added, "And nothing about you-know-who."

"Okay. Go ahead."

Dino watched her face closely as he asked, "Why was your name the last thing in Jimson's appointment book?"

"I don't know," she was cool. "He's probably the only one who knows that."

"When was the last time you saw him?"

"Must have been months."

"What was the occasion?"

"No occasion," she winked, "I just ran into him. He was with his wife."

"You didn't have an appointment with him right before he disappeared?"

"No." Her icy blue eyes did not even blink. She had made a good recovery.

"No idea why 'Minky' was the last thing he wrote in his appointment book?"

103

Koski smiled broadly as she leaned back again, putting her arms on the back of the sofa, revealing even more of her breasts. She shook her long hair and said, "Maybe he was just doodling."

"Thinking of you?"

"Why not? Men have been known to . . ."

She was too cool, so Dino let fly his last shot. "Why were you hiding at Jimson's funeral?" As soon as he asked it, he knew the shot was a blank.

"If you were Karen Koski, you'd stay away from the family too."

Dino closed his notebook and looked back into her icy Scandinavian eyes. "Do you have any idea who would want to hurt Jimson?"

"No," Koski rose in an obvious signal that the interview had ended. "I hope you're not going to leave him here."

It was at that precise moment that Dino's mind recognized the colonnade from the nude photos. It was Pop's Fountain in City Park. This brazen woman had posed stark naked in the middle of City Park.

Dino reached over and shook Mason who woke slowly and stretched. "What happened?" he asked.

"You fell asleep."

"I did not," the lieutenant argued. "I was resting my eyes."

"You were snoring."

"I never snore."

"Wanna bet?" Dino reached over, turned off the recorder and removed the cassette tape before standing up.

When she opened the door for them to leave, Koski had a question. "What did you call Thomas earlier when you knocked?"

"A Gargoyle. That's what he looked like when we

fished him out of the river. He looked like a Gargoyle."

Koski's small nose wrinkled as if she was smelling something bad.

"I owe you one cassette tape," Dino added on his way out.

"Forget it."

"That girl likes you," Mason told him on the way back to the bureau.

"Like she likes the plague."

"No, Dino my boy. She *likes* you."

LaStanza laughed. But Mason added confidently, "It was in her eyes. The way she was looking at you. That girl likes you." Yawning, he added, "That could be useful."

"When did you notice the look in her eyes?"

"When I was snoring."

Snowood was sitting at his desk wearing his gangster glasses, styrofoam cup in hand. "Where you been?" he asked his partner.

"We were interviewing the blonde from the cemetery."

"You shittin' me?"

"I never shit you."

"Come on, man," Paul jerked off his gangster glasses, "You really interviewed her without me!?"

"Sure did." Dino sat at his desk and took out his growing Gargoyle/Coliseum folder.

After a half minute of huffing and snarling, Paul snapped at his partner, "Well, at least tell me about it." He put his gangster glasses back on and leaned back in his chair. "Tell me everything that happened. I'm gonna close my eyes and think about her with no clothes on." He leaned back, adding, "Ah, there's no doubt in my mind that woman's got to have a beautiful little pussy."

"As a matter of fact she does."

Paul slowly removed the glasses, "What was that?"

"I said she does have a beautiful pussy. A natural blonde." Dino turned around and called out to Mason, "Lieutenant, doesn't that girl have a beautiful little pussy?"

"She sure does," Mason answered from his cubicle.

"You guys are fuckin' with me."

"No way," Mason came out into the squad room. "You shoulda seen it. She had large nude photos of herself, stark naked, hanging in her apartment."

Paul jumped up from his chair, spilling his cup all over his desk. He screamed at his partner, "AND YOU DIDN'T BRING ME!"

The solution was out there. Dino just had to find it. He found part of it a few days later at the playground near Soraparu Street.

Burke Playground was a newly renovated park on Annunciation Street, two blocks from Soraparu. Lined with live oaks and new concrete picnic tables and with a black wrought-iron fence around it, Burke had two large grassy knolls on either side of the park. Atop the knoll on the Second Street side LaStanza found a witness.

"Yeah, I seen her before," Rawanda Jones said after glancing at Sondra's picture. "She be a whore." Rawanda was nine years old, small for her age, with braided hair, an inquisitive black face, and the eyes of someone much older.

Dino held his breath and showed Rawanda the picture of Thomas Jimson he'd pulled from the Intelligence file. "Yeah," Rawanda said, "dat be de man she meets.

"Right over dere," the girl added pointing to Second Street. "Dey sit in his car and do it."

"Do what?"

Rawanda looked at him as if he was retarded. "Screw," she said. "He come in his big car and she get naked and sit on his lap and dey screw right dere."

Bywater

"Well if it ain't the princess and the pauper," the loud voice of Sergeant Stan Smith boomed as he alighted from his Sixth District patrol car and made his way across the grass to where Dino and Lizette were picnicking.

Dino closed his eyes and moaned, "Oh no!"

Lizette recognized the tall, blond sergeant and smiled because she knew Dino's expartner was about to put on another show. She was grateful they had finished their picnic lunch before the patrol car arrived.

"Hey! Hey!" Stan shouted as he stepped on their blanket.

"Don't you ever stay in the Sixth?" Dino asked.

"Why change?" Stan slapping Dino hard on the back before plopping down between them. "Did he ever tell you how we handled that airplane crash at Moisant because we were in Metairie instead of the Sixth?"

Lizette shook her head no as Stan reached over, grabbed a pickle, and popped it into his mouth. "Help yourself, why don't you." Dino said.

"No thanks. I just had lunch, and you shoulda

seen the waitress." Stan slapped Dino on the shoulder, looked at Lizette, and continued. "This waitress sees me taking my time with the menu so she asks, 'What are you looking for?' So I tell her, 'I'm looking for a little pussy.' And she says, 'Yeah? Well so am I. Mine's as big as a bucket!'" Stan roared.

Dino moaned again, placing one hand over his mouth, patting down his moustache as he shook his head. Lizette struggled to keep from laughing. After a brief respite, Stan continued, as she knew he would. "You breakin' her in right?" he nodded toward Lizette. "He breakin' you in right?"

She tried to stop from giggling, knowing it would only encourage him. "I like her," Stan declared. "She's rich and pretty and rich." Looking back at his old partner, he added, "But you gotta break her in right. Just like I broke my wife in."

Stan shifted back to Lizette and explained, "My wife's got three duties: Feed me. Fuck me. And wash my dirty clothes. What else is a woman good for?"

Lizette stopped giggling, but almost started again when she saw the pain on Dino's face. When Stan did not get the expected roar of laughter, he asked, "Doesn't talk much, does she?"

"Only to homo sapiens," Dino answered.

"I'm no homo," Stan complained.

"What planet *are* you from?"

"And he oughta know I'm no homo," Stan was talking to Lizette again. "One time we picked up a couple redheads after a Mardi Gras parade and took 'em home and played hide the hockey puck with 'em." Stan pointed to Dino and explained, "He fucky his and then he fucky mine and we swapped around. He ever tell you about that?"

Lizette bit her lower lip to keep from laughing.

110

Dino sighed in disgust, "This man is not of this world."

Stan poked Lizette on the knee of her blue jeans. "Ask me about my wife," he urged. Lizette remained silent, but that did not deter him. "Okay then, don't ask. She's a sack-a-roaches anyway. I think she's pregnant. If we have a boy I'm gonna name him Shank. Shank Smith. It's got a nice ring to it."

Stan continued in the same breath, "So, Mister Bigshot Dick, how come we never hear from you anymore? Solve *one* case and you got no time for your old friends."

Dino focused apathetic eyes on his old partner. "I've been busy."

"Yeah? Well when you ain't so busy, drop by the station. You remember where it's at, don't you? Just hang a left at the Melpomene Projects until you hit Felicity Street. We ain't moved an inch."

Stan suddenly rose, signaling the end of another show was at hand. "Well, it sure is a lovely day for a picnic in Audubon Park." With that last remark, Sergeant Stan Smith walked back to his patrol car and climbed in. Over the public address system Stan added, "Catch ya later, Candy-Ass!"

"Whew," Lizette sighed in relief.

"Years of psychoanalysis wouldn't help him one bit." Dino was still shaking his head.

"How long did you ride with him?"

"Every night for over two years."

"My God." She began picking up the picnic utensils as Dino lent a hand. When he moved close to her, she looked up into his green eyes and asked, "Two redheads?"

"Do you think I'd go to bed with any woman who would go to bed with him?"

111

Lizette shrugged, "Did you ever talk like him in front of other girls?"

"I don't even talk like that in front of the guys. I mean, I curse like everybody else," Dino admitted, "but not in public."

"I wonder what his wife's like."

"She's very pretty and don't believe a word he says about her. He treats her like gold. He'd never admit it. That would ruin his image. The boy's sick."

As the two started back toward the Louvier house, Lizette began to wonder. She had seen three of Dino's partners up close now. Stan and Mark were both big and tough, harsh and often gross. Paul wasn't quite as bad, yet he did complain about his marriage a lot. Lizette wondered about Dino. She felt he was different than the others. She hoped she was right.

Tucking her free hand into Dino's, she asked, "Does shank mean what I think it means?"

"It sure does."

As LaStanza and Snowood were pulling into the police garage, an impatient patrolman got on the radio and asked headquarters, "You got a Reaper team enroute?" Headquarters responded in the affirmative just before Mark's voice cut in, advising he would be there in two minutes.

"Damn Mason," Paul complained. "You know he's the one give us that title Grim Reapers."

"Yeah?" Dino answered as he turned up his radio, trying to listen to the commotion at New Orleans' latest homicide scene.

"He sure did. You never heard that story?"

"No. But I'm about to."

Snowood spat a large wad of brown juice against the side of the garage as he drove in. "Mason done it back when he was a rookie dick." The country accent was in fine tune that morning.

"Have you been reading westerns again?" Dino interrupted.

"Huh?" Paul glanced over at his partner, acting as if he had no idea what Dino meant. "Anyway," Snowood continued his story, "back when Mason was a rookie dick, there was this murder out in New Orleans East, by the Rigolets. Ole Mason was having a time gettin' through traffic, and some goddamn uniform sergeant kept gettin' on the radio asking where Homicide was."

Mark advised headquarters he had arrived on Piety Street.

Paul spat another wad before going on. "After that dad-burn sergeant asked one time too many, Mason picked up his radio and said he was late 'cause he had to pick up the Grim Reaper on the way, the Reaper needed a ride." Snowood slapped his knee and started laughing as he eased the car into a parking slot, "Damn Mason!"

Millie Suzanne's voice was heard advising headquarters she was also on Piety Street.

"Did you hear what I said?" Paul asked his partner.

"Yeah! Mason started the Grim Reaper thing."

"You got to pay more attention when your senior partner is talking."

They both climbed out of the car. Before they reached the elevator, Mark got back on the radio and called for LaStanza.

"Go ahead, Sarge," Dino responded.

"You better get over here. This one may be connected to yours."

*   *   *

Dino drove. Paul held on, barely able to jot down the address on Piety Street. "Slow down, Boy! If the sum-bitch is dead, it ain't going nowhere!" But the Chevrolet did not slow down until it skidded to a halt behind Mark's Chevrolet in the six hundred block of Piety, just off Royal Street.

Dino rushed past two Fifth District units parked in front of the Chevys. One of the units had its blue lights still flashing. Paul reached in and flipped off the lights as Dino approached Millie, who was standing in the center of Piety Street next to a thin black man. She was trying to hold onto her radio, her purse, and one hand of the black man, who was wailing hysterically.

"Who's he?" Dino asked.

"Boyfriend. He found her."

"Oh no!" screamed the black man. "Please Lord, no!"

When Snowood arrived, the black man added, "I don't *want* to live!"

Paul made a circling motion with his finger alongside his head and rolled his eyes at the man dangling from Millie's hand.

"Where's Mark?" Dino asked Millie.

"Please," howled the black man, "give me a gun. I want to kill myself!"

"Mark's in there with Maurice," Millie pointed with the antenna of her radio at a two-story wooden house, half hidden behind a huge magnolia tree whose branches hung out over the street.

Dino started for the house, leaving Millie with her hands full of police radio, purse, and screaming boyfriend. From the corner of his eye, Dino spotted Paul taking out his gun.

"You want a gun?" Paul handed it to the boyfriend, "Here, take mine."

114

Millie had to fend Paul off with her hip. "Get away from here!"

The old house, once a single-family dwelling until someone carved it into eleven apartments, was half hidden by the magnolia. The homicide scene was at the rear of the house in a small efficiency apartment on the second floor. Dino walked past two disinterested patrolmen at the rear of the house and found Mark leaning in a doorway at the top of the rear stairs. Inside the room, Maurice Ferdinand was standing over the body of a black woman lying on a bed. M.F.'s head was bowed in prayer.

"What's he doing in there?" Paul asked when he stepped up behind Dino, "besides fuckin' up the scene?"

Mark turned to Dino, placed two fingers against his own forehead and said, "two small calibers right here."

"Fuck me!" Dino groaned.

M.F. assisted Dino in processing the scene when the crime lab technician arrived. Paul and Mark gathered witnesses from the other apartments in the house while Millie babysat the crying boyfriend. The efficiency apartment was smaller than Dino's bedroom. In one corner there was a plywood door that partitioned off a tiny bathroom with a commode and shower but no sink. There were several folding chairs in the room, stacks of books in each corner, one end table with a lamp, and a double bed upon which rested the body of Angela Italiano.

"That's a funny name for a Negro," M.F. exclaimed when he found her passport. Dino snatched the passport from Maurice's hand and read it over before tucking it in his coat pocket.

115

"She's probably part Italian," Maurice declared. "It fits."

Dino said nothing until the crime lab man asked if there was anything else. "I want the place dusted, and I want a neutron activation test on her hands."

"Why, you think she killed herself?"

"Just fuckin' *do it!* And swab the boyfriend on your way out." Dino was not going to miss anything. If either had fired a handgun recently, he wanted evidence.

He did not say another word until the body was removed. He followed the coroner's men down the stairs to where Mark and Paul were waiting at the bottom. But before Dino could say anything, M.F. began pontificating as he came down the stairs, sharing his divine revelation on the current series of murders.

"As I see it," M.F. announced to the world, "it has to do with water. We found the first body in the river, the second lived on Soraparu, a couple blocks from the river and now, here in Bywater, we find another body not three blocks from what? The river."

Besides being a pain-in-the-ass, born-again religious-fanatic whose primary mission in life was to convert people to the chosen way, M.F. had another annoying trait that caused Dino to grit his teeth and seriously consider unloading his gun before getting near him. That trait was Maurice's penchant for never looking anyone in the eye, ever. When conversing, M.F. would stare past his fellow man, as if he was looking to a faraway land. What especially annoyed LaStanza was that Maurice, who was over six feet three inches tall, always looked over Dino's head when speaking to him.

"Did you know," M.F. continued, his eyes moving directly over Dino's head, "not one hundred yards

116

from here was the site of the Corbett-Sullivan fight? Right on the river."

Paul tapped Dino on the shoulder and held out his gun. "Here. Do it now. Please!"

Dino thanked God a minute later when a suicide was reported in Gentilly. Mark, growling like an angry grizzly, quickly sent M and M. The boyfriend, who was still crying, was turned over to LaStanza. Dino found a cracked concrete bench in the front yard of the apartment house beneath the magnolia. He sat the boyfriend on the bench and waited until the crying subsided.

"We'll canvass the neighborhood," Mark advised as he and Paul went off in opposite directions on Piety Street. Eventually the boyfriend's crying slowed enough for Dino to interview him, although he continued sniffling as he sat with his hands in his lap, his shoulders still bouncing up and down. His name was Juba Dishu, and when he was not screaming he spoke with a distinct accent. Like the dead girl in the room, Juba bore a Somalian passport. "I exchange student from Somalia," Juba explained. "I go Tulane. Engineering."

Juba was dark skinned and very thin, taller than LaStanza and slightly effeminate in the way he crossed his legs while sitting on the bench and the way he patted his eyes with his long, skinny fingers. His hair was cut so short he looked bald.

He had met Angela Italiano at Tulane the previous year. It was not long before they set up housekeeping in the tiny apartment on Piety Street. According to Juba, there's was a perfect romance until that very morning. When he left the apartment, Angela was still sleeping. "But I forget book. So I go

117

back and find my Angela," his eyes began to water again as his shoulders bounced up and down. "I saw a man, a white man, running that way." He pointed down Piety toward the river.

He was still crying when Mark and Paul returned from their canvass.

"Nothing," Paul told Dino. "You got an unoccupied junkyard on one side of this place, an abandoned house on the other, and empty warehouses across the street."

"He says he saw a white man running toward the river."

"What?" Both Mark and Paul automatically looked down Piety Street.

"I don't think he's still there," Dino said, standing up, his feet crunching on the dead magnolia leaves that covered the yard.

"No one heard a damn thing in the house," Mark said.

Paul added, "A girl's shot twice in the head and no one hears a fuckin' thing."

"Nobody saw anything, except the boyfriend getting in and out of his car." Paul nodded toward the front of the house. "Front apartment lady saw the boyfriend leave and come back. That's all, 'cept I'm hungry. Why don't we rustle up some grub and you can take his statement back at the bureau."

Dino agreed. Paul volunteered Mark to pick it up, gave the sergeant his order. "And what you want, pardner?"

"Coffee," Dino answered, "just a shitload of coffee."

Seated in a hardwood folding chair behind the lone table in a small, colorless interview room, Juba

Dishu looked pale, even for a dark-skinned black man. LaStanza settled across the table in the only other chair in the little room.

"I told you I only wanted coffee," Dino objected when Snowood barged in with a Po-boy for his partner.

"I know, but you know I don't hear well since Wounded Knee." Paul put the sandwich on the table.

"He wound his knee?" Juba asked Dino.

"Get out of here," LaStanza told his partner, pushing the Po-boy to the side of the table and picking up his pen. When he looked back at Juba, the black man's large eyes were focused hungrily on the Po-boy sandwich.

"You want it?" Dino asked after Snowood left.

Juba nodded, grabbed the sandwich, and quickly unwrapped it before biting off large chunks of French bread loaded with roast beef, mayonnaise, pickles, lettuce, and tomatoes. Dino stepped out into the squad room and took his first cup of coffee of the afternoon.

"Want something to drink with that?" he asked Juba when he stepped back into the interview room.

"No. It is juicy." The African swallowed the last of the Po-boy and then sat back, wiping his lips with his long fingers.

Dino took a formal statement detailing Juba's entire relationship with Angela Italiano before concentrating on that morning, getting exact times and actions.

"What time did you get up?"

"Six-thirty."

"What time did you leave?"

"Seven o'clock."

"What time did you return?"

119

"I come right back. Ten minutes. And I see white man."

"Where was he when you first saw him?"

"Coming around side of house, running away."

"Describe the man," Dino instructed.

"He tall. Dark hair."

"What was he wearing?"

"Clothes was dark. Suit. Coat and tie."

"You saw his tie?" Dino asked, looking into Juba's dark eyes.

"Oh yes."

"If you saw him again, would you recognize him?"

"Most sure."

"When you left," Dino asked, "was the door locked?"

"No. We have one key. Angela got key."

Juba had no idea why anyone would harm his Angela. When his statement was finished, Dino showed Juba several photographic lineups compiled from the Mafia pictures supplied by Intelligence. "I never see any of these people," Juba concluded.

"What about these?" Dino showed Juba a lineup that included Lutisha "Sondra" Joseph and every prostitute who had been arrested on Decatur Street. Nothing.

Then Dino showed Juba driver's license pictures of Karen Koski and Gina Badalamente Jimson. "Have you ever seen these women anywhere?" Nothing.

"Okay. Now we're gonna make a face." Dino took out the composite kit and handed Juba a book of drawings with pages of noses, mouths, chins, ears . . . different drawings of different parts of human faces. Juba picked out the proper hair, then the forehead, then the eyes and nose and mouth and

120

chin of the mystery white man.

Dino pulled the appropriate plastic slides from the composite kit and then superimposed the slides together until the face of the mystery man took shape. After a few minor adjustments, the Somali looked up in amazement. "This is the man!"

Juba was then asked to look through the mug books, just in case the face they had just made matched someone with a criminal record. He obediently sat in the squad room and began the long task of perusing the mugs.

Dino made several photocopies of the composite face before returning to his desk to log the code numbers from the plastic composite sheets into his report.

"That him?" Paul asked, reaching for a photocopy of the mystery man. Dino waited for the inevitable smart-ass remark.

"Looks like one of the Clanton boys," Paul declared. "The older one that got killed at the OK Corral by ol' Wyatt Earp hisself."

Dino refused to comment as he tugged on his moustache and looked over at Juba, who was dutifully thumbing through the first book. There were over twenty volumes of mug books, with pictures of every white male arrested in New Orleans in the past five years. Dino was grateful Juba did not have to look through the black male mug books. They took up an entire wall.

Dino started in on his fifth cup of coffee. Paul placed a fresh pinch under his lip and handed Dino the statements from the Piety House occupants.

"Did you run them through the computer?" Dino asked of the witnesses.

Paul nodded. "Nothing much. Just a couple traffic arrests. One disturbing the peace and one criminal neglect of family."

Dino dropped the statements on his desk and began to rub his eyes as he leaned back in his chair.

Paul broke the quiet with, "I just don't fuckin' get it."

"What's there to get?" Dino continued rubbing. "We don't even know if it's the same gun yet."

"Same MO," Paul reminded his partner, "and the girl's got an Italian name."

"Gotta go with the facts," Dino argued, quoting Mason once again. "We won't know until they post her in the morning about the bullets."

"You want me to take care of the autopsy for you?"

"No way." Dino's voice rose as his stomach contorted in a familiar knot. "It's my case, and I'll be there."

"Okay." There was another brief silence, broken by Paul once again, "So, what's the boyfriend's story?"

Dino gave a brief rundown of Juba's story and ended it with a shrug.

"Interesting," Paul nodded. "Interesting."

Dino closed his eyes again and asked, "Now tell me what the witnesses said."

Snowood summarized the statements in a couple of brief sentences. According to the occupants of the house, Angela and Juba were the perfect couple, although one six-year occupant of a rear apartment was sure Juba had brought another girl home one afternoon. Two people saw Juba leave alone that morning and return.

"Could anyone see the door to their apartment?" Dino asked, remembering that the way the door was situated, it would take someone in the rear yard to see the door.

"Nope."

"Did they see anyone else?"

"Nope."

"They didn't see a white man run away?"

"Nope."

"They just happened to see Juba leave and come back?" Dino asked.

"That's because the witnesses were in front, and ol' skinhead over there was running all the time."

Dino thought a moment, "He did say he was late." Catching sight of the clock, he sat up. "Damn, I gotta call Lizette."

"Bad day at the office, huh?" Lizette asked when she answered.

"Yeah. We had another Thirty."

"I know. It was on the news," her voice was soft and concerned. "It's another whodunit, isn't it?"

"Yeah," Dino was drained, "two shots in the forehead, small caliber."

"Oh no!" After a moment, she added, "Is it going to be an all nighter?"

"No. But it feels like it anyway."

After a moment of silence, she went on, "It was on the news. They said it was in Bywater."

"Yeah."

"That's not far from the St. Maurice Wharf, is it?"

"You been studying street maps lately?"

"As a matter of fact, I have," Lizette admitted as her voice perked up. "I even know where Soraparu Street is now."

Dino closed his eyes and leaned back in his chair.

"You sound beat. Have you eaten?" she asked.

"I had some coffee."

"Coffee?" her voice sharpened. "No wonder your stomach's in knots."

"It's in knots because of the pressure. You remember what it was like during the Slasher." Dino had explained the Homicide pressure cooker to her before. She had seen the pressure work on him, and he had just admitted it was working on him again.

Her voice dropped an octave. "I think the pressure's self-induced and your stomach hurts from too much coffee and not enough food."

"The pressure is self-induced. I work better this way," Dino rationalized.

She huffed and let it go for the moment, "How about supper later?"

Dino glanced at the clock again, "We shouldn't be much longer. I'll call you when I get home."

"Call me when you leave, and I'll meet you at the dungeon with everything, including dessert."

"It's a deal."

"Boy," Paul started right in on him as soon as he hung up, "that gal sure takes care of you."

Dino tried ignoring him.

"I don't know what the fuck she sees in you."

"You sound just like Mark." Dino remembered Mark's identical words back when he first started going out with Lizette.

"Me? Me?" Paul got so excited, brown spit splashed out on his chin. "You're his fuckin' little brother. You sound like him, walk like him, dress like him, smell like him. If I didn't see you two at the same time, I'd swear you *were* him."

"You're so full of shit." Arguing with Snowood was habit-forming.

"Then ask Mason. He don't lie." Paul wiped his chin with one of the Bywater statements. "Mason says you and Mark even think alike."

LaStanza was too tired to think.

*   *   *

124

It was dark by the time they dropped Juba Dishu back on Piety Street. "That dick-head looks like he's got a penis on top his shoulders," Paul concluded as he pulled the Chevy away. Dino was still watching Juba standing in the street beneath the hanging magnolia, waving his long-fingered hand at the Chevy as the detectives left.

When Paul turned the Chevy off Piety, Dino leaned back in the seat, propped his knees up against the dashboard, and closed his eyes. After a minute of silence, Dino said, "Do you know what Stan Smith plans to call his son if it's a boy?"

"I can only imagine."

"Shank."

"Why don't he just call him Prick?"

"Prick doesn't have that nice ring to it like Shank Smith."

"Huh?" Paul started laughing, "That boy's crazier than a rattlesnake on loco weed."

By the time the Chevy pulled up on North Murat Street in front of the dungeon, Paul's mind had already changed. "You know, Shank Smith does have a nice ring to it."

"Just pick me up in the morning," Dino mumbled as he climbed out of the car.

"Make sure you get some sleep tonight," Paul grinned as he pointed to Lizette's black Alfa parked in the driveway behind Dino's Volkswagen. He was still laughing when the Chevy pulled away.

She met him at the door and wrapped her arms around him, letting her fingernails run up and down his back twice before kissing him softly on the neck. She took his briefcase and pulled him into the dungeon. Her red high heels were already kicked off and lying on the carpet.

125

In her silky red jumpsuit, her face made-up and pretty, she was a sight to behold. Dino watched her walk toward the kitchen, soft and easy. "I hope you like Chinese."

"I'd rather eat you," he said, moving up behind her, pulling her back to French-kiss her. She kissed him back and then pulled away. "Dessert comes after the meal, Monsieur LaStanza."

He followed her into the kitchen, "Do I have time for a shower first?"

"Sure." She began warming up their dinner. "Have you ever had mandarin duck or moo goo gai pan?"

"Nope."

"Then you're in for a treat."

He left her with the white cartons stacked on his white kitchen table.

He did not realize how hungry he was until he started eating. He tried not to pig out too much in front of Lizette, but the food was very good.

"So," she said halfway through the meal, "tell me about today."

Dino paused between bites, "Her name was Angela Italiano. Black girl from Somalia. Woke up dead with two small calibers in the forehead. We'll know after the autopsy if it's the same gun. Her boyfriend says he saw a white man running away. I've got a composite of the man in my briefcase."

"I'd like to see that." Lizette passed more mandarin duck to him. "I wonder how this girl's going to be connected to the others."

"We'll know in the morning."

After a moment, Lizette spoke the name aloud. "Angela Italiano." She raised one eyebrow in a curious arch. "Somalia was once an Italian colony. That's probably how she got the name."

126

"Oh," Dino had no idea where Somalia was, except somewhere in Africa.

After dinner and dessert, Lizette's easy breathing soon gave way to sleep. But Dino remained awake. His eyes were closed, but his mind was racing back to Piety Street, to Juba Dishu's thin face, to skinny fingers patting a mouth that had just devoured a Po-boy. There was something in that face that bothered Dino, something about Piety Street that was not right. But he could not figure out what it was.

After an hour of futile attempts at ridding his mind of Piety Street, Dino left Lizette sleeping and went quietly into the living room. He turned on the lamp next to the sofa and dug out the statements from the occupants of the Piety House. After reading over the statements, he put on a pot of coffee, grabbed a pad and pen, and went to work. After going over the statements a second time and comparing them to Juba's self-serving statement, he sat back and smiled. "Well, I'll be damned."

Dino was putting the finishing touches to his notes when Lizette came out rubbing one eye. She stood in the bedroom doorway, a pillow in front of her. "Why are you writing notes at two in the morning . . . nude?"

"I'm Italian," Dino smirked.

She returned the smile momentarily before moving over to sit next to him. She put a hand on his shoulder and tilted her head. "Are you all right?"

His face beamed, "I think I just solved a whodunit."

*   *   *

127

Lizette was tired but would not let him leave in the morning without a good-bye kiss. "Wait," she called out as he started for the door. She sat up in bed and opened her arms. He moved over, cupped her breasts in his hands, and kissed her.

"Now go back and get some sleep," he told her.

She fell back on her pillow and added, "Go get 'em, Babe."

On the way to the autopsy, Dino told Paul his solution to the Piety Street Murder. "You remember the two witnesses from the front of the house who saw Juba run to his car and then run back?"

"Yeah."

"Well, one said he ran to his car but said nothing about him driving away. That was at six-thirty. That witness said Juba ran to his car and then ran back into the house without leaving. Mark took the statement, and the woman was sure it was six-thirty. The second witness said she saw Juba run to his car at seven o'clock and drive around the block and come right back. You took that statement."

"Yeah," Paul looked half asleep. "The woman with the cats. I remember." He yawned and then added, "So what? He went to the car twice."

"He lied." Dino ran Juba's statement by Paul again before adding, "And there was something else he said to me after the statement, when we were making the composite. Juba's a smart fella, smarter than your average reporter. He mentioned the news articles." Dino waited a moment, but Paul did not react.

"He mentioned the news articles!" he repeated louder. "The son-of-a-bitch knows someone's out there putting twenty-twos in people's foreheads!"

"So."

"So!" Dino slapped himself in the forehead, like a

128

good Italian. "He told me that, and it went right past me."

Paul shut one eye and peeked over at his partner. "I don't get it."

"Go with the facts," Dino said. "I knew there was something about this that didn't fit. There was something in the dick-head's face that hit me in the gut."

Snowood remained silent for a while. Dino watched his partner's face react, knowing how important gut feelings were to a Homicide man. Finally Paul started nodding his head. "So if the dick-head did it, how you going to prove it?"

"I'll bet the bullets won't even be close," Dino went on. "Then I'm going back to Piety and make sure these statements are accurate, and then I'm going to pick up Mister Juba Dishu and have a long long *long* talk with him."

"You think he'll confess?"

"The Slasher did."

Paul reached over and slapped Dino's knee and laughed. "Boy, you better come up with a confession. You got less going for you than Custer had at the Little Big Horn."

Dino found the gun hidden in a drainpipe at the front corner of the house on Piety Street. It was a Rohm RG 10, twenty-two caliber, blue steel six-shot revolver with a two-and-a-half-inch barrel, a typical Saturday night special. It was wrapped in the previous day's *Vivant* section of the *New Orleans Times-Picayune*. There was blood on the barrel and on the newspaper.

"Son-of-a-bitch!" Paul howled when Dino called him over to the drainpipe. Shaking his head in disbelief, he added, "Custer coulda used you. You are the *luckiest* wop I ever saw!"

"No luck to it," Dino corrected his partner. "It's all talent." There was not even a hint of a smile on LaStanza's face.

Dino called for the crime lab immediately. He gave Paul the necessary information to get a search warrant for Juba's apartment and a warrant for the arrest of Juba himself. Paul was still shaking his head as he left for the detective bureau. Dino sat on the bench beneath the magnolia tree and waited for the crime lab as he caught up on his notes from the busy morning's work.

After his partner pulled away, Dino started laughing so hard he almost fell off the bench. "God, am I lucky or what?"

Dino's morning work had begun at seven o'clock sharp, when two large, expressionless morgue assistants tossed Angela Italiano's dark-skinned body atop one of the stainless steel tables in the Orleans Parish Coroner's Office autopsy room. The room had two tables and one window and was the scene of mass production autopsies that began early each morning of every day of every year. It was called the Chamber of Horrors, for obvious reasons.

Angela was first photographed by a crime lab technician before the coroner's assistants began removing her clothes for the technician to collect in a brown paper evidence bag. After the pathologist made a cursory examination of Angela's naked body, the technician took fingernail scrapings and then fingerprinted the cadaver. Then samples of Angela's hair were collected, combed samples from her head

130

and vaginal area, then cut samples from each area were collected before swabs were taken of her vagina and anus to check for seminal fluid. Angela was then washed and examined more closely before the morgue assistant took a razor-knife to her, making long incisions from the tip of each shoulder to the center of her chest just above her breasts before slicing her down the middle, all the way to the top of her vagina, in a wide "Y" cut.

Dino took a step back when the cadaver was laid open, trying to avoid the initial stale smell of the interior of the body that oozed out in the tiny confines of the autopsy room. He had been in Homicide only a few months but had already witnessed over thirty autopsies. From the corner of the room he watched his curious partner standing over the body, leering into Angela's open chest cavity, and he wondered how many more autopsies it would take before he would be standing next to Snowood.

From the background he watched as Angela's ribs were snipped and removed, as blood was drawn from Angela's cadaver, and as each organ was removed, examined, and dissected. A slice of each organ was placed in a small vial for analysis. Fluid from the eye was then extracted by a long-needled syringe. Eye fluid retained traces of narcotics longer than any bodily fluid and was important in the toxicological examination of the cadaver.

Dino drew a step closer when they started in on Angela's head. The pathologist cut out each wound and put them aside for later analysis and to secure as much gunpowder as could be secured from the burned-out holes. Next, the pathologist inserted a steel rod in each bullet hole in order to determine the trajectory of the bullets. Dino made note that the trajectory was slightly *upward*. After the rods were removed, a razor-knife cut away the skin at the rear of the skull before the flesh was pulled down from Angela's head to expose the pink dome of her cranium. Then a round, electric bone saw was used to lay open the skull and expose the gray loaves of her brain. The pathologist reached in and removed the brain. When the pathologist started fishing through Angela's brains for the bullets, Paul called Dino over to show him a close look at the cranium, at the telltale signs of entry wounds in bone.

"Aha, got 'em both," the pathologist triumphantly announced when he found both bullets. He marked each with a diamond scriber before turning them over to the crime lab technician.

"The bullets are different," Dino said as he looked at the projectiles. These were not copper-jacketed, like the ones used on the Gargoyle and Coliseum. "Let's just hope it's a different gun."

Back at the crime lab it took Fat Frank less than three minutes to confirm the bullets were from a different gun. "All right!" Dino yelled as he hurried from the lab and headed straight for Piety Street. It took less than fifteen minutes to find the gun in the drainpipe.

"You think you can get anything off it?" Dino asked the technician when the gun had been carefully removed from the drain.

"I'll try." After photographing the gun, the technician placed it on an evidence sheet and dusted it with a virgin brush for fiber evidence before moving to another evidence sheet to dust the pistol for fingerprints. "Aha," announced the technician, "this looks like a pretty good one." He pointed out a partial latent before removing the print with clear evidence tape. "Looks good enough to make an identification," he added. Then the technician broke open the cylinder of the twenty-two revolver and found four unused cartridges and two spent casings.

When Paul returned to Piety Street with the search warrants for Juba's apartment and car and the arrest warrant for Juba, he and Dino started the search of the apartment. A half hour later, Juba Dishu strolled into his apartment to find two detectives going through his drawers.

"You have the right to remain silent," Dino announced as he stepped up to Juba with his handcuffs. "Anything you say can and will be used against you in a court of law." He quickly grabbed Juba's right hand and cuffed it, turning the Somali around to cuff the long-fingered hands behind Juba's back before making him lean forward against the wall.

Dino searched Juba and continued, "You have the right to talk to a lawyer before we ask you any questions and to have him with you during questioning." In Juba's pockets he found a wallet, car keys, two Trojan rubbers, and thirty-five dollars and change. "If you cannot afford a lawyer, one will be appointed to represent you before any questioning, if you wish." He tossed the contents of Juba's pockets into a small paper evidence bag before turning the Somali around to face him. "If you start answering questions now, you have the right to stop at any time. Do you understand each of these rights?"

Juba nodded, his large eyes darting from Dino to Paul and then back again.

"Good." Dino smiled as he sat Juba in one of the

133

folding chairs and went back to helping Paul with the search. They found a box of twenty-two caliber bullets behind the commode in the bathroom. The technician photographed the box before securing it. "Same as the cartridges in the gun," the technician announced after he examined the bullets. Dino shook his head at Juba, who looked down and refused to return the detective's gaze.

On their way out, Paul and the technician searched Juba's car as Dino placed the Somali in the backseat of the unmarked Chevy.

"Can I talk to you?" Juba asked after Dino climbed into the front.

"Sure. You know your rights. You have the right to remain silent *and* the right to talk."

Juba cleared his throat before asking, "Will this take long? My class is early tomorrow."

LaStanza looked back at Juba and laughed. "This might take all your life." Turning back forward, he added, "Then again, there's always the electric chair."

After Juba was fingerprinted, Dino placed the uncuffed Somali in the same small interview room where Juba had devoured the sandwich and left him alone for a half hour, waiting until the crime lab compared Juba's prints to the latent taken from the gun. It was Fat Frank who called to announce that not only was the gun from the drain the murder weapon, but the latent on the gun belonged to Juba Dishu.

Dino was grinning as he strolled into the interview room. "You are under arrest for the first-degree murder of Angela Italiano." He began reading Juba his rights again, this time using a tape recorder. Then he presented Juba with a waiver-of-rights form, which the African signed with a nod. "I want to talk."

"Okay." LaStanza sat back and began.

Juba's confession took three hours, two cassette tapes, and six waiver-of-rights forms to complete. Dino advised him of his rights on tape every half hour, having him initial each specific right on each waiver form and signing each form before continuing. It became a ritual that Juba seemed to relish. When the detective bowed to his rights and allowed him to make up his mind before continuing, Juba always continued.

Dino started by sitting across the table from Juba but ended sitting next to the Somali, close and confining, like old friends. He even let Juba ramble a bit and talk of Somalia before carefully guiding him back to Piety Street. By the time Juba started to cry, Dino and he were close, not only physically but also emotionally. By the time they were finished, it was apparent that Juba liked the detective very much. By that time, Detective LaStanza had an excellent confession to top off his case.

Juba looked crushed when he was left in the holding cell. Dino couldn't help but smile; the clang of metal bars slamming shut sounded too good. As he looked back at Juba's sad eyes, he had one thought, and that was of the dull, lifeless eyes of Angela Italiano as she lay on the stainless steel autopsy table.

*   *   *

"Why did he do it?" was Lizette's first question when he picked her up that night.

"The oldest crime in the book. He found another girl."

"Why didn't he just break up with her?"

"He didn't want to see her suffer."

"So he *killed* her?"

"It was quick and painless," Dino explained. "At least, that was his reasoning."

"Wow."

He opened the passenger door of his Volkswagen for her to climb in and added, "Love and murder go together like beans and rice."

Climbing in the driver's side, he continued, "That's an old New Orleans saying dating back to Hennessey's day."

"Hennessey again," Lizette teased as she leaned over and kissed Dino on the neck. "Tell me, Monsieur Detective, what made tonight so special. Was it because you broke the case?" She was referring to his earlier call about a big night out.

"No. Since we go on evenings tomorrow, I wanted to do something different."

"Evenings already?"

"You know it."

It was not until he turned off Carrollton onto Claiborne that she asked, "So, where are we going?" He did not answer. He just smiled and drove into Jefferson Parish. When they started up the Huey Long Bridge, she asked again.

"Somewhere far far away."

"No, really. Where are you taking me?"

"To eat," he winked at her, "far far away."

Lizette was not familiar with the west bank and had no idea where he was taking her, especially when

136

he turned on the dark River Road and proceeded past Avondale. She narrowed her eyes as she peered at the unlighted, winding road and in a quiet voice asked, "What are you up to?"

Dino still did not answer. He just kept smiling and driving. After several miles of traveling the River Road that hugged the levee and followed the twists and turns of the Mississippi, she asked, "Is there really a restaurant around here?" She saw no place appropriate for the skirt suit she wore or Dino's coat and tie. In fact she saw nothing but a few dark shapes that appeared to be houses on the side of the road across from the levee.

Suddenly the car slowed almost to a stop and turned into a pebble driveway half hidden between two large trees. She was about to ask another question when she saw a wooden sign dangling from one of the trees. "Tchoupitoulas Plantation," she sighed, "I didn't know it was this far out."

The restaurant occupied an old Creole plantation cottage and had hardwood floors and plenty of windows. Dino and Lizette sat at a table in the rear, next to a wall of windows that gave an open view of the back garden of magnolia trees, pecan trees, camellias, and azalea bushes illuminated by hanging lanterns.

Since it was not a weekend, the restaurant was not crowded. It was also very quiet. In fact, the entire night had been quiet after the initial talk about the case.

Lizette had never seen Dino so silent before. She had never seen him so relaxed. She smiled to herself as she watched him order their meal and then stare out at the garden. He looked almost tranquil as he sat across from her. It was as if his usual tenseness had simply vanished.

When he caught her staring, he smiled and picked up his glass of wine. After a sip, he began to stare back.

"Did you know," she said, "that this restaurant was started by a Madam?"

"No."

"And did you know this Madam once dated one of Al Capone's buddies?"

"Before or after?" he asked.

"Before, I think."

Dino narrowed his eyes and asked, "How do you know so much . . ."

". . . useless junk?" she ended the sentence. "I don't know. I think the nuns at Ursuline taught me that one."

"About the Madam?"

"Sure. The Ursuline Sisters are *very* liberal."

Both had a good laugh at that. Ursulines? Liberal? Never!

After their Creole meal, they each had a drink before leaving.

"Where to now?" Lizette asked, tucking her arm into his as they waited for the Volkswagen to be brought around. He just winked again.

He took her to a nightclub on Jefferson Highway named "Fay's." It looked like a regular neighborhood bar, with no windows, a handful of empty tables, a fat bartender with a white apron around his waist standing behind an old-fashioned bar, a jukebox tucked in a corner next to a small dance floor. Dino and Lizette were the only customers.

"Come here often?" she asked as they settled at a table.

"Not lately."

Dino moved over to the bar to order drinks. When he returned, he said, "Watch this," and went to the jukebox to punch up several songs. He was back at the table as the first song started.

"That's Buddy Holly," Dino leaned close. "You see that jukebox?"

She nodded as she took a sip of her Sazerac.

"That's a magic jukebox." He leaned even closer, as if he was telling her a state secret. "That jukebox only plays fifties rock-and-roll."

"Oh." Lizette wrapped an arm around his neck. She was not sure, but he seemed to be feeling his drinks already.

After downing his Scotch, Dino quickly called out, "Bartender. One more round." When he returned with fresh drinks, he put his arm around her neck. "Did I ever tell you my brother was a teen angel?"

Dino's lips moved next to her ear, "He used to take me to sock hops when I was a little boy and let me sit in the bleachers. I remember all these songs." He waved toward the jukebox and proved it when another song started. "Frankie Avalon," he announced and began to sing along. He also sang along with Fats Domino and Chuck Berry and Ricky Nelson. That was before his third Scotch.

"All right!" he yelled when another song started. "Jimmy Gilmer and the Fireballs!" Pulling Lizette on the empty dance floor, he danced and sang along to a song called "Sugar Shak."

"Beehive hair?" Lizette asked after one of the lines.

"That's right," he tried to twirl her and almost dropped her. She started laughing and could not stop all the way through the song. She started laughing again when he started singing the next song. "Johnny Tillotson, 'Talk Back Trembling Lips.'"

"I don't believe this," she got a word in when the song ended.

"What? That I can sing?"

"No! Because you *can't* sing!"

Dino roared, "I know. But I don't care!"

Lizette put her arm around his shoulders, "Neither do I."

"Oh, wow!" he shouted when the jukebox started up again. "'Come Softly To Me.'" He pulled Lizette back on the dance floor. "By the Fleetwoods. One of my all time *favorite* songs."

Lizette's laughter finally died away a half hour after leaving Fay's.

"Whew," she sighed, "that was fun."

"You bet."

"My jaws ache from laughing so hard," she complained.

"We'll put 'em to better use later." Dino was feeling no pain.

After regaining her composure, she asked, "What was that girl's name again?"

"Shelley Fabares. She sang 'Johnny Angel' and 'Johnny Loves Me' and 'The Things We Did Last Summer.' She was on the Donna Reed Show on TV." Dino grinned, "I used to have a big crush on her."

"How old were you back then?"

"Nine. Ten."

"You mean you actually remember rock and roll before the Beatles?"

140

"What? Of course. I remember the day Buddy Holly died! I heard about it at lunch in the cafeteria at school."

Back at the dungeon, Lizette kicked off her high heels, curled up on the sofa, and opened her arms. "Come over here, old man, and put a fire in this little girl's eyes."

Dino danced over to the sofa singing, "Talk back tremblin' lips. . . ."

Mason left a newspaper article on LaStanza's desk. The title of the article was, *Big Easy Crime Rate Down*. The article quoted the latest FBI statistics, which indicated that crime was down in New Orleans. Across the article Mason had written, "You'd never know it around here." There was a postscript at the bottom of the article, also in Mason's tiny script. It read, "Good Work on Piety Street!"

Dino tucked the article into his briefcase. Written praise from Mason was rare indeed. It made him feel even better than he already felt. He fixed himself a cup of coffee and settled at his desk. He still had paperwork to finish up on Piety before he could get back to the Gargoyle/Coliseum case, and he wanted to get back as soon as possible.

"Congratulations," Millie called out when she entered the squad room. "That was really nice work." She went up and patted Dino on the back.

"Thanks, Mil."

She quickly looked over her shoulder and added, "Maurice is green. He's so goddamn jealous!"

M.F. entered the squad room as Millie sat at her desk. He surveyed the room, and while still looking

141

in the opposite direction, addressed Dino in his usual way, by admitting Dino's presence: "La-Stanza."

Dino ignored M.F. and went back to his coffee.

Millie called out to Dino, "That son-of-a-gun boyfriend was some actor, wasn't he?" She began mimicking Juba crying, "Oh no! I don't want to live!"

Dino and Millie both started laughing. M.F. acted as if he did not notice. Millie waited for Snowood to enter before she started in on her partner. "So, Maurice, what was that you were telling me about how Dino is so lucky?" she asked, loudly enough to be heard across the squad room.

Maurice cleared his throat but did not answer. Paul pounced immediately, "Yeah M.F., what's that about luck?"

"I just said," M.F. looked over at Dino and Paul, but not directly at them, "I just said that LaStanza was a lucky fellow."

"Luck?" Paul roared. "There was no luck to it! It was all skill. It took him less than forty-eight hours to sew that one up completely. Fingerprints, confession, murder weapon, he got the works!"

M.F. was about to respond, but Paul wasn't finished. "Remember, bigshot, you're the one who took one look at it and punted it right away to Dino!"

Maurice rose and started for the nearest exit, another of M.F.'s annoying traits. Whenever faced with a frontal assault, he headed for the nearest exit. Millie started giggling as Paul shouted, "Just because the broad had a couple holes in her head, you threw up your hands and cried, 'Send for LaStanza. Send for a *real detective!*'"

As soon as M.F. was gone, Dino leaned over and

reminded his partner, "Hey, didn't you call me the luckiest wop in the world when I found that gun?"

"Yeah," Paul admitted. "But I can call you lucky. I'm your pardner. I gotta keep you humble. After all, you ain't solved the Gargoyle yet." He reached into his desk drawer, pulled out his gangster glasses, put them on, and smiled. "And don't let this Piety case go to your head, Hotshot. It wasn't even a whodunit! It was just a misdemeanor murder. Boyfriend kills girlfriend. Period."

Bogue Falaya

She may be called Big Easy, but there was nothing easy about New Orleans, especially her whores. After locating and interviewing seventeen Decatur Street prostitutes, LaStanza learned just how hard a whore could be.

At first he thought the difficult part would be locating the prostitutes, until he tried talking to them. None of them had heard of Sondra, none had ever seen her or knew anything about prostitution. Several had never even heard of Decatur Street.

In a city that once boasted a legal red-light district with fine houses where large-breasted Madams doted on their prized girls, where ragtime rolled off the nimble fingers of black piano players and jazz was weaned, prostitution in New Orleans had degenerated to its rightful place. It had been forced into dark corners, along with the cockroaches and other creepers of the night, into the sleaziest bars and rundown hotels in the dirtiest neighborhoods of the city. In a laid-back, easygoing city where the miasma of tropical days and sweltering nights slowed the blood and caused nineteenth-century men to dream of cool bedrooms and wet women, women that were paid handsomely for their charms, long nights in Storyville had been replaced by the American quickie of hit-and-run sex.

"How do you talk to a whore, a real whore?" Dino asked himself before starting through the names on the list of prostitutes. At first, he figured he would appeal to their sense of survival. Someone had killed a whore, and he wanted that someone badly.

"Say what?" asked the first whore in response, "you better wise up if you think I gives a *shit* 'bout some whore got herself killed!"

The second prostitute would not even talk to Dino and Paul when they located her sitting in a Greek bar on a Thursday afternoon when business was slow. Suddenly the whore was too drunk to talk.

The third whore had to be brought to the Detective Bureau when she flipped, "Fuck off!" after Dino flashed his badge. She left them no choice but to drag her in by her hair, which turned out to be a wig. There was no way detectives could just leave a bar after a whore flipped, "Fuck off!"

They tossed her into an interview room and made her wait an hour before taking her out, putting her in the backseat of the Chevy, and driving halfway to Baton Rouge before pulling alongside pitch-black Airline Highway.

Finally Dino spoke to the whore. "Now, what did you say to me back there?"

"Nothin'."

"You want to apologize?"

"I apologize," answered the whore, her chin resting against her chest, her narrow eyes watching the detective intently.

Dino showed the whore the picture of Sondra and

asked if she'd ever seen that face. He received the usual response. When shown a picture of Thomas Jimson, the whore said she'd never seen that face either. After several more questions, all of which received the same negative response, Dino climbed out of the car and opened the back door. "Get out," he ordered her.

"What you doin'?" asked the whore.

"Just get the fuck out of the car!"

When the prostitute stepped out, Dino slammed the back door shut before climbing back into the passenger side and telling Paul to drive off, leaving the whore to find her own way back to town.

"Fuckin' asshole," Paul said.

"They've been fucked over by so many men," Dino sighed as he leaned back and closed his eyes, trying to fight the ever increasing frustration rising in him. "They don't know when someone's straight with them or not."

"Fuckin' asshole," Paul repeated.

By the time whore number seventeen was interviewed, LaStanza's frustration was mounting. He had thought about asking Fel Jones to come along, figuring a black face might help. Only he was not ready to admit defeat. That was, until whore number seventeen.

Her name was Newella Norman. She was only twenty, but she looked like fifty miles of bad road, pot holes on her mulatto face, tire marks across her midriff. She had the nerve to wear a cut-off T-shirt that revealed long stretch marks across her stomach. She had orange hair with black roots, large breasts, large hips, and the blackest eyes Dino had ever seen. Newella was a Fifth District whore who lived in a rundown wood frame house on Alvar Street.

Newella answered her door wearing the cut-off

T-shirt and tight iridescent yellow running shorts. She took one look at LaStanza and Snowood and moaned, "Oh no!"

"Oh yes," Dino assured her as he brushed past her into the house. He stopped immediately as soon as the interior colors struck him full force, like a kaleidoscope of scarlet red and lime green, sulphur yellow and indigo blue. The room was plush, thick carpet and velvet sofa and a chrome coffee table. Paul started laughing as soon as he stepped into it.

"You got a warrant?" Newella asked in a huff.

"We don't need a damn warrant," Dino snapped back.

"Yeah? Well we'll see." Newella stepped toward her telephone but did not figure on LaStanza's temper. He took one quick step and kicked the phone off the end table, sending it crashing against the wall.

"Sit down!" he ordered. The whore took a step back, glaring at LaStanza but refusing to sit. "We don't need any *fuckin'* warrant to talk to you, you fuckin' slut! Now sit!" Dino lunged toward Newella, who fell back on the sofa.

Paul chuckled throughout the interview, which only made Dino feel worse, knowing he had blown it. He'd lost it before he was even started, which added to his frustration.

"You look like you're fit to be tied," Paul told him when they piled back into the car and left Alvar Street. "You gotta lighten up."

"I give up on these sluts!" Dino shouted. "They don't give a fuck, and neither do I! I hope he kills every one of them!"

But the next night he was back at it, this time in Parish Prison, with Fel Jones and Snowood, taking his time, returning to his polite self as he interviewed every prostitute and tramp in Parish Prison who would talk to him.

"You sure are one strange wop," Paul commented when they left the prison. "Last night I thought you were gonna kick that whore's lungs out, and tonight you're buttering up to those bitches like they got gold between their legs."

Dino yawned, "I lost it last night. But I ain't giving up."

"You sound more like Custer every day."

On the following evening Dino received a phone call from the St. Tammany Parish Sheriff's Office. "This is Detective Rex Carson, St. Tammany. Is this Detective D. LaStanza?"

If Paul Snowood was not sitting directly in front of him, Dino would have sworn ol' Country Ass was on the line. "Yes," he answered, "this is LaStanza."

The voice on the line drawled, "I got a teletype here that says if we find any bodies with twenty-two calibers in the head to contact Detective D. LaStanza, NOPD Homicide. I guess that's you."

"What?"

Detective Carson continued without missing a beat. "We got an unknown white male up here with two twenty-twos in his forehead. This teletype says you had a similar thirty."

Dino put his hand over the mouthpiece and shouted, "Anybody know anything about a teletype we sent to St. Tammany about the twenty-two killer?"

Paul shrugged and Mark peeked out of his office and shook his head "no."

"I'm sorry," Dino said when he removed his hand, "can you run that by me again?" He took some quick

149

notes as Carson explained how two days earlier a fisherman had found the body of an unidentified white male next to the Bogue Falaya River near Folsom. The victim was between forty and forty-five years old, with brown hair and eyes, six feet tall, weighing two hundred pounds, not including two copper-jacketed twenty-two magnums dug out of his forehead at the autopsy.

"No ID?" Dino asked.

"No ID."

"How long had he been dead?"

"'Bout a week. Some varmints got to him, but they didn't do nothin' like the job the pathologist did on him," Detective Carson chuckled. Dino could have sworn he heard Carson spit after the chuckle ended. Before getting off the phone, he arranged to meet the St. Tammany detective the following morning in Covington to compare bullets.

"Sure," Carson agreed. "Just one more thing—we got a pretty good suspect."

"Yeah, who?"

"I'll tell ya' when you get here." Again the detective chuckled before hanging up.

Dino put down the receiver and began to rub his stomach, as if rubbing the growing knot would in any way soothe the pain. He did not see Mark move up behind him.

"I just got off the phone with Mason," Mark announced. "He sent teletypes to all local agencies in case any other bodies pop up with twenty-twos in their heads. Son-of-a-gun's always thinking when we ain't."

Dino looked back at his sergeant and gave a quick summary of Detective Rex Carson's phone call.

"They got a suspect?" Mark asked incredibly.

"Yeah, but he wouldn't elaborate."

"Sounds fishy to me," Paul injected.

"And the son-of-a-bitch left me hanging on purpose."

"What?" Mark snarled. "Fuck that!" The grizzly sergeant bounded back to his office in three strides and was already punching out numbers on his phone when Dino and Paul entered. It took him less than a minute to locate the St. Tammany Chief of Detectives. Dino and Paul settled in two chairs across from Mark as their sergeant retold the story of Detective Carson's phone call, ending with, "If you got a suspect, Chief, I wanna know who the fuck it is right now."

Mark nodded a couple times. "Yes. Yes. I see. Well, I don't give a fuck if Rex *is* a good ol' boy who likes to joke a lot. Murder ain't funny!"

Mark nodded again and jotted some quick notes. "Well," he concluded, "we'll be over first thing in the morning, and we'd appreciate you keeping the jokes down."

He slammed down the receiver and sighed, "Their suspect's a rancher whose property was near where the body was found. They ain't got shit!"

Paul smiled, "I knew it."

But Dino did not smile. He kept thinking about the copper-jacketed magnums. If they were from the same gun, his problems had just tripled.

"Cheer up," Mark told him. "At least no country-assed yahoos stumbled on the solution."

"I almost wish they had," Dino heard himself saying. "This killer may be trying to set a record." He wondered what was worse, country police solving his cases, or the possibility of the twenty-two killer leaving more bodies lying around.

That night he had a hard time sleeping. After talking with Lizette for an hour, not mentioning the

151

St. Tammany matter, he took some medicine for his stomach before turning in. He tried thinking about Lizette and how excited she had been about her preparations for her new classes, but his mind kept returning to his case.

A cop's mind works in funny ways. Dino began to wonder, "What if the rancher *was* a good suspect?" After all, raising racehorses was a major business in the Folsom area, and racehorses meant gambling, and gambling and the Mafia went together like beans and rice. And *he* was not coming up with any suspects. Maybe, just maybe the rancher was connected. He did not sleep much that night. That's how a cop's mind worked.

It was not the first time Dino had said he would drop by after work and did not. It was not even an important night. They were just going to be together for a while. What surprised her was that it bothered her. She lay awake thinking about it.

It did not help when her father had put in another hint about her seeing too much of Dino. She was not used to the pressure. She felt as if her entire family was watching her. And she was afraid there would be many more nights when she would be left alone while he was out chasing bodies.

The St. Tammany detectives were anything but yahoos, although good ol' Rex Carson tried his best to prove he was just that. Between Rex's insufferable drawl and Fat Frank's incessant chatter, LaStanza did not think he would make it through the day.

His headache began early as he rode with Mark and Frank across the causeway bridge to the north shore of Lake Pontchartrain. Frank never stopped yakking the entire way to Covington until they dropped him off at the St. Tammany Crime Lab with the pellets from the Gargoyle/Coliseum Murders.

Detective Carson was waiting outside the crime lab. Good ol' Rex was a barrel-bellied, red-faced country ass who stood about six-five and wore suspenders and a straw hat he called a fedora. Dino did not know much about hats but was sure Rex's hat was something besides a fedora.

Rex's partner was a thin, sandy-haired man in his late thirties, Jeff Simpson, who had once been a U.S. Marshal before he'd married a north shore girl and settled in Mandeville. Rex introduced his partner. "This here is Jefferson Davis Simpson, no relation to Jefferson Davis *or* O.J. Simpson!" Rex roared after his introduction and spat a large wad of brown spit into a styrofoam cup cradled in his left hand. Immediately Dino thanked God that Snowood had not come along.

Jeff Simpson drove the foursome to the crime scene. He was a quiet man who said little until the four detectives arrived. Then he took over, leading Dino across a pasture, through a clump of piney woods, to a cool spot where the Bogue Falaya wormed its way through the suspect rancher's property. Rex dragged behind, talking to Mark, who made the sacrifice of listening, giving Dino some relief from the countrified chatter.

"The body was over there." Jeff pointed to an open area next to the river. "We found no human footprints anywhere near it. Just some coyote's and a bobcat's."

"Coyote prints?" Dino asked. "In Louisiana?"

"That's what I've been told. I've never seen one, but the Wildlife and Fisheries people tell me coyote migrated from Arizona and Texas years ago."

Dino started to draw a rough diagram of the scene

until Jeff stopped him. "I've got one to scale I can give you if this is connected to your case."

"Cases," Dino corrected Simpson.

"What?"

It was Dino's turn to advise. He explained about the Gargoyle. Apparently Mason's teletype mentioned only the Coliseum Murder. Dino spoke quickly before Rex arrived.

Rex was talking loudly as he approached, loud enough for Dino to hear, "Sorry I got the little fella all pissed off."

Dino ignored the remark as he asked Jeff, "Was he killed here?"

"No, just dumped."

"Was he in the water?"

"No."

"So somebody just walked in and dumped a dead man right here?"

"Seems that way," Simpson answered as he began to move back toward where Rex and Mark stood. Dino walked the other way, down the bank of the Bogue Falaya, glancing at the dark brown water rushing past. The river was not very wide at that particular point, although it was swift moving.

"Better watch out for snakes," Rex called out as Dino rounded a curve in the river. He clenched his fist and fought off the growing desire to tell good ol' Rex to go fuck himself. He stopped a few steps around the curve and looked around at the woods. If he hadn't known better, he'd have sworn the nearest civilization was light-years away.

On their way back to Covington, Rex told the story of the rancher on whose property the body had been found. The rancher raised thoroughbreds and housed racehorses from the New Orleans Fairgrounds during the off-season. The rancher had financial troubles and had been handled by Rex

154

before, which automatically made him a prime suspect.

"How do you work with him?" Dino asked Jeff after they arrived back in Covington and Rex left for the bathroom "to take a mean shit."

"I ignore him most of the time," Jeff answered as he led them back to the crime lab.

Fat Frank was munching a jelly doughnut when the detectives entered. He smiled broadly and said, "Bingo. It's a match!"

All the way back to New Orleans, Dino's stomach did a slow, twisting turn.

Mark waited until they were back in the Detective Bureau before stating the obvious, "We got real troubles."

"I know," Dino scowled. "I know."

"My mother asked me to invite you to dinner Sunday," Lizette said as she poured Dino a cup of coffee. Turning to face her boyfriend, who sat at her kitchen counter, she began to mix the coffee the way he liked it: cream and one sugar.

As she stirred, she brushed a strand of hair from her face. Dino watched her. He liked to watch the way she moved, the delicate twist of her shoulders when she stirred the coffee, the way she craned her neck when brushing away a strand of long hair.

He leaned over and kissed her on the cheek. Her lips found his and returned the kiss. When he leaned back, he said, "It's been a while since I've seen your parents. I was beginning to wonder if they still lived here."

She sat across from him with a cup of tea and explained, "They've been keeping busy. On purpose."

Dino nodded and rubbed his tired eyes. Nothing

more need be said about a family who was trying to forget the unforgettable.

"You sure you don't want something to eat?"

"No, I had a hamburger." He peeked from between his fingers at the raised eyebrow on her face and added, "Really."

Both took a sip from their mugs before Lizette asked another question, "So, what were you telling me about that rancher on the phone earlier?"

"He's been cleared. He was in Europe at the time of the Gargoyle and Coliseum murders. The man just got back a week before they found the Bogue Falaya body."

"So what are the detectives in St. Tammany saying now?"

Dino shrugged as he finally quit rubbing his tired eyes, "Their sheriff said the killer's probably back in New York or Chicago by now."

"Seems we've heard that before," Lizette smirked. Dino almost smiled but let it go, as if his face did not have the energy to smile. She hesitated a moment, watching him, seeing how wound up he was, wound up and tired at the same time. "What if he is from New York or Chicago?" she asked. "What if he's flying in to do it?"

Dino rested his chin in the palm of his right hand, his elbow on the counter, and answered in a weary voice, "Mason's already checked every plane in and out of New Orleans for the last three months. He's cross-checked names, flights, and dates, and he came up with nothing. He even checked the trains." He raised the cup to his mouth, hesitated before sipping, and added, "Of course our killer could be driving a Winnebago, stopping in Slidell for gas, Hattiesburg for supper." He smiled at his own remark before his voice turned sharp. "The son-of-a-bitch is right here, probably sitting with his girlfriend right now, laughing his ass off."

She changed the subject as soon as she could, trying to get his mind away from the case. But she knew that was impossible. She could see it in his eyes. Finally, after two futile attempts at changing the subject, she asked, "What are you going to do next?"

"You got me."

Paul answered the phone with his usual, "Howdy, this here's Homicide." After a second he said, "Sure. He's right here." Reaching over without getting out of his chair, he handed the receiver to his partner. "It's the Princess."

"Hey, Babe," Dino said as soon as he had the receiver against his face.

"Detective LaStanza?" asked a woman's voice.

Dino glared at Paul and cleared his throat, "Um. Yes it is."

"This is Gina Jimson."

"Oh, hello."

"I've been wondering if there were any—" Gina's voice hesitated before finishing, "—developments."

It was Dino's turn to hesitate before answering, "I'd prefer to tell you in person. Is that okay?"

"Yes. Any time."

He quickly set an appointment for the following afternoon. After he hung up he let his mind run through the case. He thought about what he would tell her, wondering what he should reveal about Coliseum and Bogue Falaya. He thought about it a while and decided maybe he should tell her. Maybe it was time to light a fire.

Dino went alone to the wedding cake house. He

half expected Rosenberg's frog face to answer the door. He did not expect the harsh face that answered, that familiar streak of white through the center of a head of wiry hair, the acne scars glaring at Dino.

"Police," Dino said as he put his credentials in front of that face. "Mrs. Jimson is expecting me."

Harold Lemoni opened the door and pointed to the living room. Without a word, he turned and walked toward the rear of the house.

Gina Badalamente Jimson was waiting in her living room. She smiled slightly and extended her right hand to shake when Dino stepped in. Immediately he saw a change in her. She looked prettier, healthier, her face made up with fresh red lipstick and eye shadow. She was dressed in a gray suit. In her burgundy designer eyeglasses, she looked like an attractive librarian.

"Thank you for coming," she said, motioning for Dino to sit before sitting in the same easy chair she'd been in the night the detectives had come to notify her.

"I took the liberty," she added, waving her hand toward a maid who was entering with a tray of coffee. After the maid left, closing the door behind her, Dino quickly asked, "Where's Rosenberg?"

Gina smiled again, "I sent him back to my father."

"Replaced him with good ol' Harry, huh?" Dino asked, letting her know that he knew exactly who the man with the harsh face was.

"Harry's my first cousin," Gina explained as she began to pour the coffee. "He's felt responsible for me ever since my brother left." Dino thought about that remark, curious that good ol' Pus-Face had felt responsible since her brother had gone to jail, not since her husband was murdered. He remembered it was about a year ago that Baddie's only son was sent to Atlanta Federal Penitentiary on a racketeering conviction.

Dino took a sip of coffee; it was made the way he liked it. As soon as Gina finished her first sip she spoke. "Sister Camille tells me you used to get into fights at Holy Rosary, over girls."

Dino was supposed to be the one springing surprises, but this woman already had him leaning back and shaking his head. Before he could even think of a response, she continued. "Sister speaks fondly of you, although she said you started too early, with girls."

"Sister's wrong," Dino said. "I never fought over any girl. I fought for them." He could hardly believe he was explaining something that had been misunderstood for so many years, and by just about everyone. "When I was little, my father taught me never to hit a girl. Well, one day this bully pushed a girl down in the playground. So I hit him."

Images of the red brick of Our Lady of the Holy Rosary School flashed in Dino's mind like snapshots illuminated by a strobe light, images of red brick walls and a concrete playground and the large church dome across Esplanade Avenue from St. Louis Cemetery Number Three.

"I'll bet you were popular with the girls."

"Not at all. I just got beat up. Little girls like winners. I lost."

Gina smiled again, "My brother and I went to Holy Rosary. Of course, that was before you. Sister Camille taught me also. Now she's the principal." Gina took another sip of coffee. "I still go to church there. Do you still go to church?"

"Not at all."

There was a pause in the conversation as Gina sat up straight and set her eyes on his, speaking in

159

almost a whisper. "The truth, please. It's not often people tell me the truth. I would like to know what you've discovered about my husband's death."

He watched her closely as he told her about Sondra. "We are certain of the link between your husband and this woman." When he explained precisely what he meant, he felt as if he was confirming a long-standing suspicion.

She nodded her head and sighed, "There have been other women before." For a moment Dino thought he saw a hint of pain in her dark eyes, but her face remained still. With his eyes riveted to her, he asked, "Prostitutes?"

Gina nodded in resignation. "Every kind of woman imaginable."

Dino tried to hide his disappointment. The Gargoyle's sex life was no secret to his wife. As a motive for his murder it was fuckin' useless.

"This woman was killed exactly like your husband," he told her.

"In the forehead?" Her eyes widened.

"Yes. And with the same gun."

She turned her head slightly as if she was focusing her right eye on him and whispered, "The same gun?"

"Absolutely."

For a moment her eyes narrowed before she sat back and sighed again. He waited before mentioning Karen Koski. Gina's face did not change, but her hands clenched into fists. "She was at the funeral," he explained, "hiding behind a crypt . . . with good ol' Harry."

Gina's face snapped in the direction of the closed door for an instant. "She was with him?"

Dino nodded, "And that isn't all. Her name was the last notation in your husband's appointment

160

book. We asked her about that. She had no idea why."

"Neither do I." Gina recrossed her legs.

"What exactly," he asked the next question slowly, "was Karen Koski's connection to your husband?"

"He was probably screwing her," Gina snapped. "Wasn't everyone?"

For a moment he thought she was going to cry, but Gina Badalamente Jimson would have none of that. Within seconds she had it under control as she reached out and picked up her coffee cup without a hint of shaking in her hand.

"So," she restarted the conversation, "do you have any suspects?"

"No."

"Any leads?"

"Oh, we've got leads," Dino told her, "but nothing substantial yet."

If there was a spark in Gina's eyes at the word "leads," it went away quickly. Her eyes softened again as she continued, "I know there are things you cannot tell me yet. But as soon as you can, I would truly appreciate it if you would. I want to know."

"I'll tell you."

"Good. Thank you."

She offered him a second cup but he declined. "I'm grateful, Detective LaStanza." Gina rose and extended her hand again.

Dino was not surprised to look up and find Harold Lemoni's angry face scrutinizing him from the foyer. Harold's eyes leered at him when he passed. Dino let his face go expressionless and stared back.

At the door, he turned back to Gina and asked, "How's your father? I didn't see him at the funeral."

Gina shot a quick look at Harry and answered, "He's been out of the country. He just came back."

161

Lemoni was still glaring hard at LaStanza. Dino paid him no attention as he added, "Tell Sister I said hello."

"I will," Gina answered with a friendly smile.

On his way to the office Dino thought about that smile. There was something about that woman he liked. For a woman trapped in the Badalamente labyrinth, Gina Jimson showed remarkable strength. Dino was certain she was far brighter than anyone suspected.

Later, while sitting in the office planning his next move, he realized he had not mentioned Bogue Falaya to her. Maybe that was better. Since St. Tammany was not anxious to broadcast the news, why should he?

Later still, on his way to Exposition Boulevard, Dino thought about how Signore Badalamente had been "out of the country." That maneuver was as old as the Mafia itself.

"What? Somebody was murdered? But I was *out of the country!*"

On the second night of the surveillance of Karen Koski, the woman called Minky put on a show for Dino and Paul. The detectives were staked out in their Chevy on King Louis XIV Ring, a semicircular drive across from Koski's apartment house on Robert E. Lee Boulevard. Just as Paul was complaining again about how bored he was, Dino watched the icy blonde stroll into her bedroom, flick on the light, throw back the curtains, open the French doors of her balcony, and strip.

He began chuckling in a low, guttural laugh that gradually increased as Koski tossed her T-shirt on the bed, followed by her bra, jogging shorts, and then bikini panties to stand naked in the open doorway, brushing her hair.

"What are you cacklin' at?" Paul complained.

Dino handed the binoculars to his partner, "Something you don't see every day."

Snowood lazily placed the glasses against his eyes. After a moment of adjustment, he lunged forward, nearly impaling himself with the binoculars when he crashed against the windshield. "Son-of-a-bitch-Jesus-Christ-oh-my-God!" Paul screamed before his mouth dropped open for almost a full minute as Dino continued laughing and shaking his head.

"You got a camera?!" Paul asked, his eyes still pressed hard against the binoculars.

"Nope."

"What kinda combat photographer are you? No camera? *Fuck!* She's out on the balcony now!"

It was another long minute before Paul pulled the glasses from his face and snapped, "Let's go!"

"Where?"

"Your house. Get your camera." He started pushing Dino's shoulder. "She just went in the shower. If we go Code Three, we just might make it!" Paul reached under the seat, pulled out the blue police light, and slapped it on the roof, hurriedly plugging the cord in the empty cigarette lighter. "Come on!" he yelled at Dino, who had not moved at all.

"Whoa, cowboy," Dino started chuckling again. "We're not getting any camera."

Paul was bouncing on the seat in exasperation. He glared at his partner, slamming the binoculars back against his eyes. "Right—she'll probably be out before we get back."

Dino waited a minute before starting up the engine.

"Whoa!" Paul yelled, "where ya' going?"

"We're leaving," Dino stated as calmly as he could, "she knows we're here."

"I know that!" Paul continued pressing the binoculars hard against his face. "Turn off that goddamn engine before I take out my buck knife and make a gelding outta you!"

Dino turned off the engine and sat back.

"Oh, wow," Paul said a minute later, "she's back." That statement was followed by a series of moans. Dino sat up and glanced around to make sure some civilian wasn't watching them watch the naked woman across Robert E. Lee Boulevard.

His partner continued moaning until finally he pulled down the glasses and slumped back against his seat. "She put on a robe," Paul announced in disgust.

Dino started the engine. As he began to pull away, Paul had one more look. "Shit," was his only remark as the Chevy pulled out on Canal Boulevard and drove away from the woman and the balcony.

"You might as well take me home," Paul said dejectedly. "I might as well go fuck my wife."

"That's real nice of you," Dino needled his partner.

"Shit. I got a hard-on of steel. She ain't had it this good since the owl came home."

Dino was not about to ask.

"Completely naked?" Lizette asked, her eyes widening.

"As a jaybird," Paul answered before Dino had a chance. "Big ol' titties. Nipples like silver dollars. Little bitty waist. Blond on blond pubic hair."

Dino shook his head as Lizette asked him, "And she stood in the doorway?"

Dino pointed to Paul, "Ask him. He was the one watching."

Lizette leaned over her kitchen counter, her face right next to Dino's, "And you didn't watch?"

"He saw first," Paul explained. "But after I got a hold of them binocs, he didn't see no more."

"And just how long did you watch?" she teased, poking a finger into her boyfriend's ribs.

"He watched her get naked," Paul explained again.

Dino shrugged in acknowledgment, "Guilty."

Lizette laughed as she reached over and playfully took a bite at Dino's lips.

He pulled back and asked, "Is our coffee ready yet?"

"Yes sir," Lizette sat up in mock attention and saluted before jumping off her stool and moving to the coffeepot.

"Mind if I use the phone?" Paul asked.

"Sure," Lizette answered as Dino moved behind her and put an arm around her waist.

"Can I help?" he whispered in her ear.

"Don't come here looking for anything, mister," she continued to tease, "until after you've taken a cold shower. I don't want anything from you that some naked blonde started."

He had a good laugh at that.

"Damn woman!" Paul complained as he hung up. "I wonder where my goddamn wife is."

"Joe the grinder?" Dino asked, getting full pleasure at his turn to needle his partner.

Paul's face contorted into a mock grimace, "I couldn't be so lucky."

Dino started laughing again, reminded of how mad Paul had been when he found his wife was not home, punching the dashboard and then insisting on accompanying Dino to Lizette's to make sure Dino was not going to get any if he didn't.

"This has been one useless night," Dino said after they all settled over coffee.

"Did you really expect to discover anything following her?" Lizette asked.

"Not really," he admitted. "We're just spreading ants. Getting 'em mad so maybe they'll do something."

"Why Karen Koski? Aren't there some Mafia men who you can follow?"

Dino nodded toward his partner, "He chose her."

"Don't blame me," Paul snorted, "you're the case officer."

"And you haven't been haranguing me for days about her!"

"Yeah," Paul admitted, "and all I got is a . . ." he stopped in midsentence adjusting himself as if he was in agony. "Damn woman! This has been one frustratin' evening."

"In more ways than one," Dino agreed.

Later, on the telephone, she told Dino, "Sometimes I need an interpreter when ya'll are talking."

"Why?"

"I think I know what 'spreading ants' means, something to do with stirring things up. But who's Joe the grinder?"

"That's the Joe who's grinding the wife while the husband is out working."

"Oh. And public hair? He did say 'public.'"

"Mook talk," Dino explained. "In the projects pubic hair is as public as you can get."

"And a mook?" Lizette left her question open ended.

"A project black."

She sighed, "I've been right about you all along, Detective LaStanza."

"About what?"

"You have the makings of a fine liberal Democrat."

On the following evening, the Narcotics Division blew up Canal Street. Eleven narcs dressed in various guises, from a filthy version of Fagin to an iridescent Tinkerbell, opened fire on two "dealers" who just happened to have their own arsenal.

The front windows of D.H. Holmes were taken out with the first salvo, two mannequins killed, four interior display counters destroyed, ten decanters of the strongest perfume obliterated, the facade of Holmes given a swiss cheese facial by automatic fire which even destroyed the clock. The clock above the front doors of D.H. Holmes, known simply as the clock, was the rendezvous point for generations of New Orleanians . . . "Meet me under the clock."

Sixteen cars and two vans parked on the downtown side of Canal Street suffered bullet wounds. A huge neon sign high above the street was similarly executed. The Maison Blanche Building suffered the same fate as Holmes, only moreso because "hot" magnum rounds used by two of the narcs set off the sprinkler system. Nine other stores between Bourbon and Dauphine Streets suffered penetrating gunshot wounds. Three streetlights were murdered, as well as the signal lights at Canal and Dauphine.

Two automobile wrecks were caused by the running gun battle among thirteen heavily armed human beings. Yet throughout the holocaust no one was hit, although every narc, to a man, insisted he'd hit at least one of the "dealers." The "dealers" were never found.

The blowout on Canal Street occured at ten p.m. By the time Homicide was notified, one casualty had resulted when a First District patrol car rammed a car driven by a "hippie" and a "terrorist," which turned out to be an unmarked narc unit. The "terrorist" narc crashed against the windshield, vastly improving his face by the dislodging of four front teeth.

When Detectives LaStanza and Snowood arrived, they found Detective Sergeant Mark Land in front of D.H. Holmes, screaming at a Mexican bandito who turned out to be the narc sergeant in charge of the operation. "I want every fuckin' gun given to the crime lab *right fuckin' now!*" Mark moved his face right up against the bandito's. "And I don't give a fuck what your mother-fuckin' captain says."

The narc's fists were clenched as if he was about to punch Mark until Paul moved up behind and patted him on the shoulder. "I wouldn't do that," he told the narc. "Mark'll fuck you up real good."

Suddenly outnumbered, the narcotics sergeant took a step back and began barking orders for his men to turn over their weapons to the crime lab. Mark continued to glare at the narc sergeant as he began to bark his own stream of orders to Dino, Paul, Maurice Ferdinand, Millie Suzanne, and the other two teams of detectives which made up the entire Homicide evening watch.

Mark remained on Canal Street with the bulk of the watch, processing a crime scene that ran four blocks. LaStanza and Snowood were assigned to take statements from the narcs and soon found themselves back in the Homicide office with tape recorders and a mob of the unruly, unshaven, and undisciplined of New Orleans' finest.

While Mark loathed narcs, Dino had no particular dislike for them. Then again, Dino had not been in Homicide long. As he and Paul secured the statements, he tried ignoring the narcs storming around the office, cursing and yelling. Paul was less forgiving.

Interrupting the statement he was taking, Snowood stepped out of the interview room and shouted, "Shut the fuck up! This is a police station, not a goddamn kindergarten."

When some of the narcs began to yell back, Paul raised his voice even louder. "Hey, we can do this easy or hard! We're willing to take down your little fantasy verbatim. But if you wanna be hard-asses, we can start asking some embarrassing questions. You got me?" In no uncertain terms, he reminded everyone that when it came to police shootings, Homicide was in charge. Dino had to smile. During Paul's tirade, his accent was noticeably gone.

It took until three in the morning for the statements to be completed. In the end, Dino concluded those were the most vanilla statements he had ever taken. "No wonder Mark hates 'em," Paul said as they drove back to Canal Street. "I'd like to make the lot of them take a urine test and watch the test tubes explode!"

"Dope fiends with badges," Dino added, quoting Mark's favorite description of the narcs.

Dino parked just beyond the police barricades at Canal and Burgundy. They found Mark leaning against the front of Maison Blanche, dripping in his own sweat from the night's heat.

"Assholes," Mark grumbled aloud. He looked at Dino and asked, "Have you seen the kinda artillery these assholes were packing?" He pointed in the direction of the narc bandito who was standing with

169

the narc captain. "Forty-four magnums, forty-five automatics, nine millimeters, thirty-twos, twenty-fives, even a fuckin' German Luger with a swastika on it!" Mark groaned.

It took until five in the morning to recover forty-seven pellets and take the necessary measurements at the scene. At ten after five, Mark, Dino, and Paul were seated at the rear of the Café DuMonde with steaming coffee in front of them. "Bring me some beignets," Mark ordered the waiter.

"I tell you," Paul said, "those fuckin' narcs are the worst, the absolute worst."

Mark agreed and began to exchange horror stories with Snowood about the Narcotics Squad, the pariahs of the department, the unclean cops with their dope fiend "snitches" and easy money.

Seated at the rear of the table, his back to the seawall behind the café, Dino listened in silence, his eyes staring blankly at the empty café and Decatur Street beyond. As Mark continued with his stories, Dino remembered a recent incident when he'd called the duty judge at night to get a search warrant signed on a misdemeanor murder. The judge asked, "Are you from Narcotics?"

"No sir," Dino had said, "Homicide."

"Okay, you can come." Upon Dino's arrival, the judge declared, "I don't sign narcotics warrants anymore. Those sons-of-bitches lie more than a TV evangelist."

Between stories, Mark wolfed down two orders of hot beignets, solid, square donuts generously sprinkled with powdered sugar. Paul chomped down his own beignets as Dino began his third cup. The donuts had a visible effect on both Mark and Paul.

After downing his sixth hot beignet, Mark licked the powdered sugar from his fingers and actually smiled at Dino.

"You look beat," Mark said.

"You don't look so hot yourself."

"So how're your whodunits coming along?"

"They're still whodunits."

"I got a message for you," Mark continued, "from one of the best detectives you know."

Dino moaned and refused to look at Mark.

"According to world famous Detective Maurice Ferdinand," Mark announced, "you've been going about it all wrong."

Snowood began to howl.

"Maurice says that just because it's the same gun doesn't mean it's the same killer."

"That boy'd fuck up a wet dream," Paul snorted.

Mark laughed so hard the powdered sugar in the two saucers in front of him mushroomed up in a cloud of white fog. Dino had to swish it away with his hands.

He wondered why his partners and expartners relished heckling him. A half hour ago Mark was a surly bear, his oversized eyebrows drooping, his mouth turned down in a scowl. Now he was a jolly Santa. For the hundredth time Dino reminded himself that as long as he lived, he would never understand the psyche of Napolitano Italians.

It was nearing six in the morning when Paul told Dino, "I'm gonna let Mark drop me off. You keep the car."

LaStanza nodded as he waved for the waiter. "One more cup," he told himself, "and maybe the caffeine will hit the bloodstream."

Mark stretched his huge arms and declared, "I've got one thing more to say about tonight." He slowly

171

reached into his coat pocket, removed a pair of gangster glasses, and put them on. "Let's beat it," he told Paul, who was laughing so hard he almost collapsed.

Dino was the last customer left in the all-night café. The waiters had gone inside the closed area. He could see them through the windows, joking over coffee and cigarettes, waiting for the morning rush.

He was so tired he wished he could just inject the caffeine straight into a vein. When he lifted the cup, his elbows ached; his knees ached when he crossed his legs; he ached everywhere.

Outside the café, it was the blackest part of the night, the dead of the night just before the sun begins to crawl into the sky. Decatur Street was quiet, still. Not even a car passed on the street.

Dino took another sip and then suddenly turned around and looked behind him at the walkway between the rear of the café next to the seawall. Then he looked around at the empty tables, noting the stillness. The incandescent bulbs of the café lights cast a soft amber glow under the canopied roof.

Reaching to take another sip, Dino felt something . . . needle pricks on the back of his neck. It was a familiar feeling. The same feeling that used to grab him when he was a little boy playing hide-and-seek in the cemetery and he felt as if someone, something was behind him.

Slowly Dino turned again, and saw an Ernest Hemingway face staring back at him with shark-black eyes.

"I understand you've been asking about me," said Alphonso Badalamente as he took a step toward Dino. Baddie's black eyes, like a mannequin's, stared blankly at the detective as the man moved up to the table. "Mind if I join you?"

Dino nodded as Badalamente sat. A waiter materialized, moving quickly toward the table. Without looking over his shoulder, Baddie announced, "Two coffees." The waiter retreated. Dino had to fight the urge to look around, certain that Signore Badalamente was not alone, but he dared not show his concern.

Detective LaStanza and Signore Badalamente continued to stare at one another with unblinking eyes until after the waiter had left fresh café-au-lait for both. Dino tried to match Badalamente's leering eyes with his own. But the eyes of the elder Sicilian seemed to stare right into the detective's eyes. Dino could feel them.

Baddie drank his coffee straight. Dino followed suit, foregoing his usual sugar. He watched Badalamente's hand as it wrapped around the steaming cup. The man's fingers looked like the gnarled branches of a magnolia tree. The man's face was craggy, the well-tanned face of a weathered fisherman that stood out in contrast to his full mane of white hair and moustache. Since the elder Sicilian had picked the meeting, Dino waited for him to speak first.

"So," Badalamente said with a deadpan expression on his face, "you're the detective who caught that Slasher fella."

"Yes sir." He answered, unsure by the monotone of Baddie's voice if the man was mocking him or not.

"That was good work." Badalamente's face continued to give no hint of expression. He reached for his coffee and added, "He was German, wasn't he?"

"I guess so," Dino's voice sounded scratchy. "His name was Hemmel. Jerome Hemmel."

"German," Badalamente nodded, his black eyes

173

narrowing. "I hear they make the best killers."

Dino refused to blink as long as the shark eyes remained fixed and open. "I thought Sicilians made the best killers," he said. His jaw felt tight from the tension.

Badalamente grinned like a mortician. "I let you in on a little secret," he said as he leaned forward, "Sicilians do make the best killers. We just have better press agents than the Germans." He leaned back and smiled a wicked smile.

"Al Capone didn't have such a good press agent," Dino came right back, trying to loosen his jaw with a quick response.

"Capone wasn't Sicilian," Badalamente was still smiling, "He was Napolitano. Just like your sergeant and your chief of police."

"Well," LaStanza responded quickly, "you know the old saying . . . Sicilians make the best gangsters or the best cops." The sparring made him feel combative, less rigid, less afraid.

The smile was gone. The mannequin eyes once again reached out at Dino. They were unfeeling eyes, alert and yet dull at the same time, the eyes of a dogcatcher.

"My daughter tells me you have made progress in the murder of my son-in-law."

"Yes sir."

"She tells me she is convinced that you are handling the case satisfactorily."

Dino nodded again, not daring to look away, trying to keep from blinking first. Badalamente's stare continued until he had to blink first. Then the man said, "If there is anything I can do to help, feel free to call upon me."

"Yes sir," Dino responded automatically, his jaw tightening again.

174

"If I happen to hear anything," Badalamente continued, "I'll let you know."

"Fine."

Signore Badalamente finished his coffee, returned the cup to its saucer, and added, "You're a polite boy. Your father teach you that?"

"Yes sir."

"He teach you to say 'Yes sir' and 'No sir'?"

"Yes sir."

"Good," Signore Badalamente nodded as he rose to leave. Dino noticed how large the man seemed, far larger than his six feet. If the man weighed two hundred pounds, it was lean weight.

After a couple of steps, Baddie turned back and asked, "Is there anything you wanted to ask me specifically? You did ask my daughter about me."

"I just noticed you weren't at the funeral."

"Yes. I was out of the country."

"Yes sir."

When Badalamente turned to leave, Dino asked, "Is that why you dropped by, to see what I wanted?"

"No." The lifeless eyes turned on Dino again, "I wanted to see the Siciliano who caught the Slasher."

"Oh."

Turning once again, Badalamente strolled through the café to Decatur Street. It was not until the man was halfway through the empty café that Dino noticed Badalamente was wearing a dark gray silk suit, shiny as the skin of a hammerhead.

When Dino left the café, the dawn light was creeping through the narrow streets of the French Quarter. All the way to his car, he felt the needle pricks on his neck, as if someone was . . . but he refused to look. His hands were shaking when he put the keys in the door of the Chevy.

"Fuck him!" he said aloud as he moved in behind

the steering wheel. "Fuck 'em all!" The words came out harsh and mean, the way Dino wanted to feel.

It has been said that New Orleans never tried to impress anyone and never cared if it did. The Louvier family seemed that way to Dino. Maybe it was their French Creole blood, the old blood of the original French who came to Louisiana first and refused to assimilate into the American culture after the Yankees bought the land.

The Louviers had lived on Esplanade Avenue for generations. Their bank catered to the Creole money, the old money of the French and Spanish until the Civil War came and eradicated most of the remnants of old New Orleans. The Louviers eventually abandoned the old town and moved to the American section, but they never forgot the old ways.

Although the Louviers always treated Dino politely, he felt uneasy around Lizette's parents. At first he thought it was because of Lynette's murder, that he was a constant reminder of it. But he realized he did not make them as uncomfortable as they made him. When he was alone with Lizette he felt comfortable, but once the Louviers were there, it was as if he was visiting a rich neighbor's house.

Unlike the LaStanzas, who'd come to America in the hold of a filthy ship with the refuse of Europe, the Louviers migrated to Louisiana long before the French Revolution. In the Louvier library there was a letter in a gold-leaf frame, hanging over a Louis XIV desk. The letter was from Robespierre himself, addressed to Lizette's great-great-great-great grandfather, Henri Louvier, thanking Henri for his financial support for the Revolution. At least that was what Lizette told him. It was in French.

Sunday dinner at the Louvier's was served in the dining room by two maids. Mr. Louvier sat at the head of the table. He was in his mid-forties, a lean man with thick, curly black hair, graying at the temples, and deep-set eyes. He looked the part of the bank executive at leisure in his dress white shirt and neatly pressed dress pants. Mrs. Louvier sat next to her husband. She was a pretty woman of indeterminate age, with short dark hair and an athletic, slim build. She looked like she could be Lizette's older sister. Alex, Lizette's eight-year-old brother, sat across from Mrs. Louvier. He was a thin child, quiet and intelligent looking, the kind of boy who was well read for his age. Lizette sat next to her brother in a white LaCoste shirt and designer jeans. Dino sat at the end of the table, in his own dress white shirt and jeans, facing Mr. Louvier.

After grace, as the salad was served, Mr. Louvier started the conversation. "I had lunch with your boss the other day."

"Yes sir."

"Please don't call me sir. It's Alexandre."

Dino nodded and glanced at Lizette, who winked at him.

"Your chief tells me he and your father used to be partners," Mr. Louvier continued. "He also told me about your brother."

Dino nodded again.

"We didn't know about him," Mrs. Louvier added.

"What happened to your brother?" Alex asked, which seemed to surprise even Lizette.

"He was a policeman," Dino told Lizette's brother.

"He was killed."

"How?"

Mrs. Louvier was about to correct her son, but Dino answered too quickly. "He was shot by two burglars."

"Did you catch them?"

"Yes," Dino answered and could not help but smile at the boy's anxious eyes.

"What happened to them?"

"One was shot by the police, and the other was killed in a drug deal."

"Oh, wow," said the boy as he dug into his salad. "You still carrying your Magnum on your ankle?"

"Yep."

Alex was wound up. "He showed me his Magnum once," he told his mother. "He carries it in an ankle holster."

There was a pause in the conversation until Mrs. Louvier spoke, "If you wouldn't mind, I'd prefer that Alex stay away from guns." She was looking at Dino with stern eyes.

"I understand," he told her.

After another tense pause, Mr. Louvier asked Dino, "What do you see yourself doing five years from now?"

Dino watched Lizette cringe. He hesitated a moment, fighting back the automatic urge to snap off a barbed retort such as, "Sending fuck-heads to the electric chair." Instead Dino answered, "I'll still be where I am, probably, unless I get transferred."

"Ah," was Mr. Louvier's only response.

But Mrs. Louvier was not finished, "Has everyone in your family been a policeman?"

Lizette covered her eyes with a hand and shook her head. Dino set his eyes on her mother and answered,

178

"No, my grandfather was a fruit peddler." He tried his best to control his sarcasm, but it still came out. "I'm sure Grandmother Louvier sent her maid out to buy fruit from my grandfather when he used to peddle along Exposition Boulevard."

When he looked back at Lizette, he could see she was livid.

"I thought you were mad at me," he told her when they stepped into the library after dinner.

"No. *Them.*" She closed the door and pulled Dino to the large easy chair.

He thought he would be helpful, "It doesn't bother me . . ."

"It bothers me," she snapped. "And it goes way back."

"Oh."

She snuggled next to him, and he could feel the tension in her. He could feel the tightness in her jaw when she placed it against his neck. But he could think of nothing to say or do.

Finally Lizette sighed. "My father asks everyone what they plan to be in five years. He always has five-year plans for investments. . . ."

"I guess I don't fit their idea of what your boyfriend should be."

"It only matters if you fit my idea."

"But if they don't like me?"

"It's not you, and it doesn't matter anyway," she told him. "It's me."

Then she told him how Lynette, her sister, had always been everyone's favorite. "That's why I went away to college. I had to get away."

It was more than that, but Lizette did not want to

179

go into the other reasons she and Lynette had grown apart. This was not the time to talk about the other boys.

He wanted her to go on, wanted to know more but when she fell silent, he knew better than to ask. She would tell him when she was ready. He was even going to tell her how Joe had been his parent's favorite son, which was natural for the firstborn, but he said nothing. Something in the way her jaw was set told him that he should just listen.

"You know," she added a little later, "that was the most my brother has said in weeks."

"Until your mother cut him off."

"I know," Lizette admitted, "she has that way about her."

Dino nodded.

"She's probably mad because he's really taken to you."

"I know."

"And so has his sister."

"I know," Dino smiled.

Lizette looked up at him, her gold eyes staring into his. She craned her neck and kissed him. When she pulled back, she continued to look into his eyes.

"You know," she said, "sometimes when you stare back at me, it's as if you're staring right into me. I can feel your eyes."

"It's a Sicilian trait."

According to Detective Jeff Simpson, St. Tammany was having no luck with the third body. 'I'm trying every way I can to identify him," He told LaStanza over the phone.

"I know," Dino said.

"As soon as I come up with anything, I'll call you

right away," Jeff added.

"I'll do the same," Dino said before hanging up. What he did not say was what he feared most: with a third of the puzzle blank, the chances of solving the case were greatly diminished.

The next afternoon, Dino dropped by Burke Playground and found Rawanda Jones walking along Annunciation Street with her little brother. "How about a snowball?" he asked the two.

"Yeah!"

Dino drove the pair to a snowball stand on Magazine Street where Rawanda ordered a strawberry, her brother got spearmint, and Dino ordered chocolate, his favorite flavor. The trio sat on a wooden bench alongside the stand and dug into the flavored ice.

He waited until Rawanda had eaten a few bites before telling her, "I've got a couple questions for you."

"Okay," Rawanda nodded.

Dino asked if she had heard anything new about Sondra.

"Nope," she answered, not looking up as she dug into her snowball with a plastic spoon. The huge eyes of Rawanda's silent brother, who must have been about four years old, stared intently at the detective.

"What about friends?" he asked. "Sondra have any friends?"

"You axed me dat," she reminded him. "I don't know nothin' about Sondra, 'cept she be a whore."

"Oh," Dino shrugged.

"And she be dead," Rawanda added.

"Yeah."

It was Rawanda who broke the ensuing silence with, "You talk to dat other man yet?"

"What other man?"

"The one askin' 'bout Sondra."

It took a few minutes for Dino to get the whole story of the other man. He was a large, white man, driving a long black car. He wore shiny sunglasses. "Like these?" Dino asked as he donned his gangster glasses.

"Yep."

Dino retrieved the file from his car and went through several sets of pictures with Rawanda until she casually pointed to one photo. "Dat's him."

"Are you sure?"

"Uh-huh," Rawanda answered and poked her little brother. "Ain't dat de man askin' me 'bout dat whore?"

The little brother nodded.

"What did the man ask?"

"Same things you been askin', and I told him I don't know nothin'. He be askin' all kindsa people 'bout Sondra."

Dino looked down at the photo, at the large face of Frank Porta.

West End

Frank Porta lived on a long white yacht moored at a private dock on the east end of West End Park. The yacht bore the name *Lil Gina* and was registered to the Pomodoro Corporation. According to Felicity Jones, the Pomodoro Corporation was a Badalamente family holding company.

From their surveillance point in the parking lot of the Southern Yacht Club, Detectives LaStanza and Snowood watched Porta's comings and goings for five humid and steamy days and nights. Even the occasional Lake Pontchartrain breeze did nothing to relieve the stifling heat. Their only respite was the occasional suicide, misdemeanor, murder or killin' they were pulled away to handle.

The detectives could set their watches by Porta's routine. At seven o'clock sharp, the large man rose and climbed on deck in his gym shorts to retrieve his milk and newspaper. At seven-thirty he returned to the deck dressed in a white shirt, a tie, and dress pants to read his paper and drink one cup of coffee. At eight o'clock he donned his suit coat and gangster glasses, climbed into the black limousine parked next to the private dock, and left West End for the short ride down Lakeshore Drive to the Badalamente house. At eight-fifteen the limousine left the house and proceeded directly to the New Orleans central business district, to the Sentinel Building on Common Street, where Signore Badalamente's penthouse office was located on the thirty-sixth floor.

After parking the limo in a private lot behind the Sentinel Building, Porta positioned himself in the lobby of the high-rise. Like an uncomfortable gorilla, trying to get his large frame comfortable, he remained in the lobby, awaiting Signore Badalamente's whim.

At precisely twelve noon, Porta was sent out for lunch. At exactly five o'clock, the limo, driven by Porta and carrying Badalamente, departed the central business district to worm its way through the evening traffic back to Lakeshore Drive. By seven o'clock, Porta was back at the yacht, where he removed his tie to await the arrival of whatever woman whose night it was to drop by.

On Tuesday and Thursday nights a flashy red-headed woman arrived in a Lincoln shortly after eight o'clock and stayed until three in the morning. Around midnight, music and uproarious feminine laughter could be heard echoing through the yacht harbor from the *Lil Gina.*

On Wednesday night at nine o'clock, a large blonde woman arrived in a Cadillac and left at two in the morning. Not fifteen minutes after her arrival, all the lights were extinguished on the yacht and never came back on. Although Snowood tried his best, he could hear nothing from the yacht that night.

"Does the boat look like it's rockin' to you?" Paul asked his tired partner.

"I'll bet he's pile drivin' her right now, and we sit

184

here sweating our asses off," Paul added. "Tell me again exactly why we're out here." Dino said nothing.

On Friday, when the blonde came back, Dino was alone as Snowood went to assist Mark with a barroom killing on Chef Menteur Highway. He had to use a motor pool car that was so noisy it ran off the sea gulls every time he cranked it up.

Although he was certain Porta did not see him that day, the big man probably heard him. Again the yacht was silent that night. Dino had plenty of time to think about how futile surveillances could be.

On Saturday, the surveillance was terminated early when the detectives were called to assist the day watch with a tedious canvass of Brechtel Park in Algiers after the body of a strangled woman was found there. Later LaStanza and Snowood were sent across town to Milneburg to handle the suicide of a fifteen-year-old born-again Christian daughter of a charismatic minister who was in New York raising money for his church . . . with his private secretary. The victim's mother found the girl and called police.

The girl was lying naked on her bed. After bathing, she had put on fresh makeup and dusted her entire body with baby powder and perfume before taking enough sleeping pills to kill a rhinoceros. The girl's long black hair had been carefully brushed to lay neatly around her shoulders, almost reaching to her small breasts. Her hands were folded across her flat stomach. Her legs were straight. The hair between her legs stood fluffy, as if it had also been freshly brushed. Dino found a hairbrush on the floor next to the bed.

The girl left a suicide note on the nightstand next to the empty pill bottle which read, "Father. Forgive me. For I have sinned." There was a postscript at the bottom of the note which read: "Daddy, I'm still a virgin."

"What a fuckin' waste," Paul declared when the detectives left the suicide house.

Dino was already thinking ahead, of the inevitable autopsy. "I'll take care of the post in the morning," he told his partner when Paul was finished complaining.

"No you won't," Paul argued. "I'm taking you straight to Exposition Boulevard and I don't wanna see you until Monday."

"What's got into you?" Dino asked his suddenly rowdy partner.

"That girl didn't look like the Princess to you?" Paul asked incredulously.

"Not really."

"The fuck she didn't!"

The unit suddenly accelerated. Dino watched his partner's face, at the anger masked on Snowood's profile. After a while Paul snapped again, his mouth resembling a safety valve going off sporadically to let out steam. "You're not going anywhere near that fuckin' autopsy!"

"Hey, it's all yours," Dino agreed.

When the unit came to a grinding halt at the dead end of Calhoun Street at Exposition Boulevard, Paul exhaled loudly and nodded to the door. "I don't wanna see you until Monday."

Dino hesitated a moment before asking, "Are you all right?"

"Yeah!" Paul was still agitated. He turned to Dino and asked again, "That girl didn't remind you of the Princess?"

Looking into his partner's distressed face, La-Stanza finally realized what Snowood meant.

On Monday afternoon, Mason called Dino into his office. Seated, feet up on the desk, the lieutenant set his lean jaw as Dino entered. He lit a fresh cigarette with the butt of the cigarette already in his mouth.

"So," Mason said after Dino sat down. "Any luck on your intelligence work?"

"Nope."

"Has Porta gone near Soraparu Street or Burke Playground or anywhere near your witness?"

"Nope."

"Has he done anything interesting?"

"Nope."

Mason took a deep drag before continuing. "I think it was a good idea to follow him around for a while." The lieutenant was doing what he did best. Dino realized he was being let down easily.

"You got to see what he was up to," Mason rationalized, "get some intelligence, spread some ants. It's good to put pressure on people who are not supposed to feel pressure."

Dino nodded in agreement.

"Anyway," Mason added, "I think you should hit him sporadically. Every so often pick him up out of the blue. That'll put more pressure on him. Keep him off balance."

"I see your point."

"Then maybe we'll pick him up one night. Bring him up here and see how cool he really is."

Dino stretched his legs and added, "Yeah, these sixteen hour days ain't cuttin' it."

It was Mason's turn to nod in agreement. "You know, I've been thinking about this Twenty-Two

187

Killer of ours. He's no pro." Mason let that statement linger in the smoke-filled air for a moment.

Dino responded, "because we keep finding the bodies."

"Right," Mason's voice rose as he spoke, "and moreso because he keeps using the same gun. He has to keep it somewhere safe."

Dino instinctively thought of the yacht.

"Whoever he is," Mason said, "He's doing this on purpose. He's leaving the bodies so they can be found." Kicking his feet off the desk, Mason leaned forward and continued, "He's bragging. He's using the same gun, the same M.O., bragging that we can't catch him."

"He's bragging all right," Dino said, "and I'm listening."

"And we're gonna catch this fool," Mason declared confidently. "He'll slip up. We just have to give him time." He leaned back and put his hands behind his head. "Sometimes it takes a while for a case to fall into place."

Dino was nodding again at Mason's confident face, but he felt anything but confident. The Twenty-Two Killer was taunting him, and that bothered the hell out of LaStanza.

When he received the photos of the Bogue Falaya victim sent to him by Jeff Simpson, he took them to Intelligence immediately and showed them to Fel.

"This man's dead," quipped the black man.

"I know, but who is he?"

The Intelligence detective examined the close-up of the dead man's face and shook his head. "I don't know him. But I'll ask around."

"Thanks." Dino left immediately.

At the Missing Persons Bureau, he checked on every white male reported missing in the last five years, with negative results.

The arduous task of contacting a missing persons bureau in each surrounding parish was divided between LaStanza and Simpson, with Dino taking the southern and Cajun parishes, while Jeff took the north shore up to Baton Rouge.

"I'm gonna contact Mississippi and Arkansas," Jeff explained later.

"I wouldn't stop there."

"I know," Simpson replied. "I gotta contact the entire fuckin' world on this one."

"So where are you?" Dino asked when Lizette called.

"I'm at the dungeon," she answered. "I figured I might catch you here."

"Don't move," he said. "I'll be right there."

"You can get away?" She realized how anxious she was.

"It's only eight o'clock on a Friday night," he said, "but if they want LaStanza, they'll have to come get him. I'll be right over."

When he pulled up, Lizette met him at the door with a Scotch on the rocks. "Hello stranger," she purred, "don't I know you?"

"Yeah, I'm the fella with the wide tongue." Dino stepped up and planted a big wet kiss on her mouth. He was bone tired but his kiss was anything but tired.

After the two settled on the sofa, Lizette handed him his Scotch and told him, "Your mother called a little while ago."

"Yeah?"

"She says she doesn't care how many murders

you're working on. You will be at dinner next Sunday. She said she's giving you enough notice to make it. She's fixing tortellini."

"Tortellini," Dino smiled, "my favorite." He took a gulp of Scotch and paused before adding, "I guess it's about time you met my parents."

"Actually, I was beginning to wonder if you were ashamed of me, being a princess and all."

"Could be," Dino shrugged as he leaned back on the sofa and kicked his feet up on the coffee table.

Lizette kicked her feet up next to his and took a sip of her Sazerac before asking, "Any luck on identifying your Long River victim?"

"Long river?"

"That's what Bogue Falaya means in Choctaw. It's a Choctaw word."

Dino narrowed his green eyes at her, "Sometimes I wonder if you just make this stuff up."

"Actually I looked it up. A good historian doesn't know everything, just where to look things up."

"Well then, come here," Dino told her. "I wanna look you up."

Lizette put her drink on the coffee table and leaned toward Dino, but held back from kissing him. She ran a finger along his ear and asked, "By the way, who's Jessica?"

He pulled back and closed one eye. "Don't tell me my mother thought you were Jessica."

Lizette nodded as she ran a menacing finger across her boyfriend's throat, repeating her question. "So, who's Jessica?"

"My mother thought she was Jessica," Dino told Mark the following Monday afternoon when he explained how he had to have the next Sunday off.

190

"So, who's Jessica?" Paul injected.

Mark answered, pointing a thumb at LaStanza. "He was fuckin' Jessica before he was fuckin' the Princess."

"Ah," Paul nodded.

Mark looked back at Dino. "You're off Sundays already."

"That don't mean shit around here," he reminded his sergeant. "I just wanna be sure."

"You got it."

"Yeah," Paul cut in again, "you gotta get your mama straight on who you're fuckin' now."

Sometimes it was hard to ignore Snowood, but Dino did his best. He had enough on his mind without having to spar with his partner. He had two unsolved murders on his hands, an unknown body lying unburied in St. Tammany Parish, paperwork still to be completed on the Bywater Murder and the Brechtel Murder canvass, as well as the Born-Again-Christian Suicide. And to top it off, his mother forgot he'd told her he'd broken up with Jessica months ago. Or did she forget?

"Better hurry up with that Bywater paperwork," Mark advised a few minutes later when he handed Dino a subpoena. "You got a preliminary hearing Thursday."

"Fuck me," Dino scowled before tossing his other paperwork aside and picking up his incomplete report on Juba Dishu. After rereading what he had already written of the report, he went to work. He was able to finish composing exactly one new paragraph when the sergeant stormed back into the squad room.

"We gotta roll!" Mark bellowed. "Some douche bag just jumped off the Mississippi Bridge and the Seventh District's screaming for us at some fuckin' hospital called St. Larry's! Fuck!"

191

"Double fuck!" Paul roared even louder.

Dino was speechless. The Homicide pressure cooker had just been turned up a notch, and his stomach knotted for the hundredth time since his ascent to the big leagues from the relative calmness of the Bloody Sixth District.

Mark took the jumper and sent LaStanza and Snowood into the bowels of the Seventh District. Paul drove as Dino sat mute, his stomach knotting, his blood pressure rising, wondering if you could actually feel blood pressure rise. The Homicide pressure cooker was relentless, especially when you let it have its way. He wondered, as the Chevy drove across the high bridge over the Industrial Canal, why he allowed the pressure to worm its way into his stomach.

It was not until they were past the Bullard exit that Paul realized he had no idea where he was going. "Where the fuck is that hospital?" he yelled before picking up his radio and asking headquarters. The Chevy had to turn around at the Paris Road exit when they found out the hospital was back on Morrison. Paul let out a litany of curses Dino had not heard since his days at the Sixth.

Somewhere between Read Boulevard and Crowder, while the Chevy was roaring down the dark interstate, something crept into Dino's mind, something wicked, something funny. It has been said that the mind has a defense mechanism that clicks on when the pressure is too much. The click can bring on dark mania or complete lunacy or cause everything to become unbearably funny.

For the first time since they'd left the office, Dino spoke.

"Who the fuck is St. Larry?" he shouted, causing Paul to jump in his seat. "I've heard of some strange saints," he continued. "St. Roch, St. Aloysius, St. Stanislaus, but who the *fuck* is St. Larry?"

Dino glared at his partner, who just shrugged. He threw back his head and screamed at the roof of the car, *"Who the fuck is St. Larry?"*

St. Larry's Hospital was a one-story brown brick building that looked more like a methadone clinic than a hospital. Inside its small emergency room a lone Seventh District officer was waiting for the detectives. Upon entering the room, Dino noticed an obese man clad only in bloody boxer shorts lying on a trauma table. The man's skin looked as white as the small portion of his shorts that was not bloodied.

The patrolman greeted the detectives and began relating the story of the fat man. Dino left Paul with the patrolman and moved to the trauma table. There was a hole in the obese man's leg that was still oozing blood. When he stepped up Dino saw the man was smoking a cigarette.

The fat man noticed LaStanza and nodded. Dino nodded back and turned to his partner. "I hate to tell you this, but this fella's not dead."

Paul interrupted the patrolman by putting a hand in the patrolman's face, "What was that?"

"I said this guy ain't dead. He ain't even close."

Paul's head snapped back to the patrolman as he roared, "Is that our victim?"

"Uh, yes." The patrolman rocked back on his heels.

Snowood lunged forward and put his face against the patrolman's, like a Marine Corps drill instructor. "Are you fuckin' me?"

"No," the stunned patrolman hesitated, "my sergeant told me . . ."

"I don't give a rat's ass what your fuckin' sergeant told you." Paul's face was nearing a purple hue, and his eyes bulged as he fumbled in his coat pocket for one of his business cards. Dino moved behind his partner. He had seen this routine before and liked it a lot.

"You see this card?" Paul yelled into the patrolman's face.

"Yeah." The patrolman was getting angry.

"See what it says?" He put the card right in front of the patrolman's eyes. "It says *homicide*. It don't say *almost homicide!*"

The patrolman retreated angrily while Paul was still yelling, "Unless they're fuckin' dead, we don't give a fuck!"

As this last remark echoed through the narrow corridors of St. Larry's, Snowood stormed out of the emergency room, followed by his partner. But Dino did not follow him out to the Chevy; he took a right in the corridor and strolled up to the information desk in the front of the tiny hospital.

Behind the front desk sat a matronly woman with an extremely bored look on a face of granite. When she did not even acknowledge Dino's presence, he tapped the desk top with his portable police radio. The woman looked up at him with a snide "Yeah?"

"I have a question."

"So?" the woman muttered as she rose and walked away from the desk. Dino raised a hand to object, but the woman cried out, "Just hold on a minute, wise guy. I got something to do right now." The woman vanished from sight into a doorway marked "Employees Only." After a minute she came out of the room with a magazine. She returned to her chair, plopped the magazine on the information desk, and began thumbing through it before asking, "So, what do you want?"

"I wanna know who the fuck is St. Larry?"

"See, I told you," Paul chided his partner as they drove away from St. Larry's, "you're just like Mark. He'd done that. Curse out an old woman. Abso-fuckin'-lutely nuts!"

Dino was about to remind Paul of the ring episode with his son, but he saw something that caused him to shout out, "Wait!" He pointed out his window at a cemetery next to St. Larry's. "See that? See that?"

"See what?" Paul yelled back.

"That cemetery," Dino shouted. "See it? The people are buried in the ground!" It was the only cemetery in New Orleans Dino had ever seen where the corpses were actually buried.

"So what?" Paul argued as he hit the accelerator.

"Goddamn! Not only is St. Larry's affiliated with some un-fuckin'-known Protestant sect, but they bury people in the ground!"

"It used to be landfill," Paul told his partner, the aggravation still in his voice.

"What?"

"That cemetery used to be landfill. My aunt lives near here, and when I was a kid, that cemetery was landfill. That's why they can bury underground."

"Jesus fuckin' Christ!" Dino screamed. "You mean they just toss the coffins in with the toxic waste and the soap powder boxes?"

"Not to mention the used sanitary napkins."

"Aw, fuck!"

Mark was standing in the right lane of the Mississippi River Bridge when Paul pulled the unit up behind him. With a notepad in hand, their sergeant examined the late-model Buick four-door that was parked on the bridge.

"So what's happening?" Paul asked as he stepped out of the Chevy.

Dino took his time getting out. He hated standing on the bridge. He had done it before as a patrolman when a Mardi Gras float had broken down crossing from its den in Algiers. It was extremely disquieting to stand on a bridge hundreds of feet above a churning river, a steel-and-concrete bridge that swayed and bounced like a catwalk in a windstorm.

When Dino finally stepped out of the car, he made sure to keep clear of the side of the bridge. When the bridge swayed suddenly, he felt his knees buckle slightly. He felt as if he was on a bamboo bridge held up by rope.

"The douche bag left his car running," Mark explained when Dino joined the two.

"Anybody see him jump?" Paul asked as he walked over to the railing to lean over and spit a wad of brown saliva into the river. Dino nervously took a step back.

"No witnesses," Mark answered as he reached in and turned off the ignition key, then moved to the trunk to finish logging the contents of the car so it could be towed. When he popped the trunk, he took a step back and there was a shout. Dino watched his sergeant fall back on his ass. A man stood up in the trunk shouting, "Boo!"

Dino's radio fell where he dropped it as he quickly knelt and drew his .357 Magnum from its ankle holster. Before anyone could move, LaStanza was on the man climbing out of the trunk, grabbing the man's long stringy hair, pulling the head down, and

196

shoving the barrel of the Magnum against the man's throat.

With a handful of greasy hair, Dino yanked the man from the trunk and pushed him all the way to the side railing of the bridge, pinning him there.

Dino had been shouting all the while, letting out his own litany of curses, but did not realize he was yelling until he had the man against the railing and heard himself screaming, "Let me see your fuckin' hands! Let me see your fuckin' hands!"

The man was smiling at LaStanza. Dino yanked hard on the man's hair again, causing the man's head to bend far back as the barrel of the gun dug into the guy's throat . . . finally he obliged and raised his filthy, but empty hands.

Dino then planted his right foot solidly and shoved the man forward, knocking him to the pavement, then jumped on the man, the gun against the base of the man's skull. With several quick movements LaStanza let go of the hair, retrieved the handcuffs tucked in the rear of his pants, and quickly cuffed the man's hands behind the back.

"You motherfuckin' idiot!" Dino screamed when he jumped off the man. "I oughta throw you off the fuckin' bridge!"

Mark arrived in time to stop Dino from drop-kicking the man. The large sergeant passed Dino to Paul, who wrapped his arms around his short, angry partner. "Whoa!" Paul shouted as his partner struggled.

The handcuffed man began to yodel.

"Fuckin' lunatic!" screamed LaStanza.

Paul did not release his partner until after a patrol

unit had removed the yodeling man from the bridge. When Dino was released from his partner's grip, he pulled away and kicked the air.

"You okay?" Paul asked as Dino continued to pace in front of their car.

"Fuckin' lunatic scared the hell outa me," Dino admitted.

"You sure are a fast little fella."

Dino stopped pacing and bent over to put his gun in its ankle holster. "Just get me the fuck outa here," was his final remark.

"Let me get your radio first."

As the detectives were driving off the bridge, they received a call from headquarters to return to St. Larry's.

"We've already been there, headquarters," Paul responded angrily.

The communication's supervisor repeated her request and added, "They say the man's not gonna make it."

"Ten-four," Paul answered before releasing the transmit button and screaming, "I'm gonna kill somebody tonight!"

"You fuckin' me?" Paul asked the patrol sergeant waiting for the detectives at St. Larry's.

"Nope," the sergeant responded, "He's dead."

"I don't fuckin' believe it!"

"Go look for yourself."

Dino led the way into the trauma room, where a skinny black janitor was mopping up a large pool of blood beneath the table where the now-dead obese man lay.

"What the fuck happened?" Paul asked aloud. The janitor just shook his head. The sergeant, who had followed the detectives back into the trauma room, responded, "Looks like he bled to death."

Dino looked at his stunned partner and could not stop himself from laughing, which caused the janitor to laugh along. Paul looked at his partner with glassy eyes as LaStanza moved to a chair.

The humorless sergeant put the finishing touches to his report before pirouetting and waving good-bye on his way out, "It's all yours now."

"I don't fuckin' believe it," Paul said again as Dino laughed even harder.

"Where's the doctor?" Snowood asked the janitor, who shook his head and shrugged.

From the hallway a chubby nurse in white appeared. She entered and stammered, "I uh, have uh, details you uh, might need."

Paul wheeled and shouted, "I want the doctor who killed this man!"

The nurse took a step back and said the doctor was unavailable.

"You mean he's hiding!" Paul yelled.

The nurse just blinked and looked as if she was about to cry. Paul reached over and snatched the clipboard from her hand. "Give me that."

As he scanned the medical report and began taking notes, he heard the nurse add in a quivering voice, "We just couldn't save him."

Dino was laughing so hard his sides began to ache, and he could hardly catch his breath. Somehow he managed to laugh even harder when Paul had to call Central Lockup and instruct the desk sergeant to rebook the man already charged with aggravated battery of the obese man with a new charge of first-degree murder.

Drained and disgusted, Paul departed St. Larry's Hospital with his partner, who was still laughing.

Pulling away, Dino suddenly added, "I just realized who St. Larry is."

When Snowood would not respond, he told him, "He's the patron saint of malpractice!"

When Lizette asked Dino how his night had gone, he told her, "What would you like to hear about first? The man hiding in the trunk on top of the bridge or, the man who bled to death in the emergency room? Or how about the patron saint of malpractice? Or what about bodies buried with used sanitary napkins?"

It had been a pressure-cooker night, of that she was certain. She let Dino talk, let him tell his stories, let him vent his frustrations. She lay back on her bed and listened to the excited, weary voice of her boyfriend as he told her stories that would be hard to believe if they were not true.

Lizette had never been inside the criminal courts building at Tulane and Broad until Dino's preliminary hearing on the Bywater Murder. She had difficulty parking and arrived late. He was already on the witness stand when she walked into the nearly vacant courtroom. But he saw her right away, stopping in midsentence to give her an inquiring look before stating, "I'm sorry, counselor. Could you repeat the question?"

Dino's voice echoed through the large room, amplified by a microphone on the witness stand where he sat. A man in a mauve suit standing next to Dino threw up his arms in exasperation and said, "I asked if you read Mr. Dishu his rights when you took his statement the first time you spoke to him."

Lizette continued up the center aisle of the courtroom as Dino looked at the man in the mauve suit and answered, "No."

"And why *not?*" asked the man, who was overacting.

Lizette was about to sit in the third row when she noticed two grungy-looking white boys in coveralls, each giving her a wicked, semi-toothless smile.

"Because he wasn't a suspect at the time," Dino answered as Lizette sat down in the front row. He was looking at her as she settled in her seat. In his black suit, with his thick black hair and light green eyes, he was a handsome sight. He was wearing the red tie she had given him recently. He looked sharp sitting there next to the judge, who Lizette noticed was also looking at her, as were the uniformed officers standing behind the judge.

"And when exactly did Mr. Dishu become a suspect, therefore entitled to his constitutional rights against self-incrimination?"

"The following day," Dino responded. It was apparent by the expression on his face how much he loathed the man questioning him.

The man in the mauve suit crossed in front of Dino and pointed to a thin black man with no hair seated at a table facing the judge. "And in your conversations with Mr. Dishu, what language did you use?"

Dino rolled his eyes and answered, "English."

"Are you aware, Detective," the mauve-suited lawyer lectured, "that Mr. Dishu barely speaks English? That his native tongue is Somali? That he came to this country . . ."

"Objection!" A trim woman with a pageboy haircut and wearing a neat tan skirt suit stood up from another table and repeated, "Objection. If counsel for the defense would refrain from asking multiple questions, I'm sure Detective LaStanza would be better able to answer."

"I'll rephrase the question," said the man. He asked Dino again if he was aware that the defendant did not speak English well. As Dino responded, Lizette watched the thin-lipped lawyer and was reminded of Bela Lugosi. If the man in mauve had had a Hungarian accent he could have been Bela.

"Where did you find the gun in question?" Bela asked.

"In a drainpipe on the south side of the house."

"Why didn't you find this gun on your first search of the crime scene?"

Dino responded flatly, "I didn't look in the drainpipe until the following day."

"And why not?"

There was another objection from the woman lawyer and a big discussion with the judge. Lizette watched Dino closely as he leaned back in the witness chair and again rolled his eyes at her. She smiled back at him.

When the discussion ended, the defense lawyer went back on the attack. "Isn't it true you terrorized this man," again pointing to the defendant, "into giving you a confession?"

"No." Dino's face remained passive, yet Lizette could tell there was anger within.

Bela's face was anything but passive. "Isn't it true you slapped this man?"

"No."

"You never hit him?" Bela's face was reddening.

"No." Dino was beginning to lean forward, his voice rising slightly.

"Didn't you prey upon this man's misunderstanding of our language to coerce a confession from him?"

202

"No."

"Detective LaStanza, how many times have you been accused of police brutality?"

"Objection," voiced the woman lawyer who stood up and was about to continue when the judge raised his hand.

"Sustained," said the judge as he leaned back in his chair and closed his eyes in obvious boredom.

"Detective LaStanza," Bela went right back on the attack, "How many men have you shot in your career?"

"Objection."

"Sustained." The judge spoke without opening his eyes, "Counselor, you know these questions are not pertinent."

Bela nodded but moved closer to Dino, "Detective LaStanza, are you telling the court you never beat Juba Dishu?"

"That's right." Dino was getting annoyed. Lizette could see how he was trying to control his temper as Bela moved even closer.

"Detective LaStanza, what if I told you we have doctor's reports—medical evidence—that the defendant was beaten severely shortly after his arrest? What explanation would you have for that?"

"Jail's a tough place," Dino answered, suddenly calm as he leaned back and winked at Lizette. Bela shot a look at Lizette and stepped away from Dino, "If you would pay attention to your testimony instead of watching the occupants of the courtroom . . ."

"Objection," said the woman attorney, "Detective LaStanza is required to answer the defense's questions, not pay attention."

"If you two do not stop cat-fighting," the judge said, his eyes still closed, "I'm going to lock you in my chambers together and you'll miss lunch."

The lady lawyer appreciated the judge's humor. Bela did not as he huffed and walked back to the defendant's table to look at some notes. After an inordinately long pause, Bela asked, "Detective La-Stanza, didn't you trick the defendant into signing a confession?"

"He never signed a confession."

"You don't have a signed confession?" Bela exclaimed as he dropped his notes on the table.

"No."

"Your Honor, we have been misled," Bela pleaded, raising his arms in emphasis. "We were advised there was an inculpatory statement."

The woman lawyer rose and explained in a starched voice, "Your Honor, the statements are recorded statements."

The judge nodded. "I see." At that point he finally opened his eyes and called both lawyers to the bench. Dino leaned back again and shot a wink at Lizette, who pursed her lips and blew her boyfriend a kiss.

When Lizette looked back at the judge and the lawyers, it was obvious from their body language that Bela was not having his way in the hushed conversation.

From the corner of Lizette's eye, she noticed the two grungy white boys had moved up to her row and sat on the other end of the long bench. They both were hungrily appraising her legs. She fought the automatic urge to pull at her tight skirt, but decided ignoring the grungies was best. From their angle, all that could be seen was a little thigh. If they hadn't seen a thigh before, then let them gape.

Whatever occurred at the bench resulted in a quick ending to the hearing, which went against Bela and his client. Lizette watched Dino descend from the witness chair and move directly to her. He waved at the woman lawyer and the woman nodded in response.

Dino was angrier than he acted. He grabbed Lizette's hand as he began to lead her out quickly. When she resisted the rush, he paused, looked back into her face, and sighed.

Then he smiled. "You look terrific," he told her.

She tucked her arm in his and gave him a conceited smirk. "I know."

He got a kick out of that and laughed. "I didn't think you were coming until you strolled in that way." He pulled her aside and put a hesitant hand on her waist as he looked around the courtroom. "You know how to make an entrance."

She leaned over and pecked him gently on the lips. "How about lunch?"

The woman lawyer passed with a "See ya' later." Bela followed a second later without a word.

"Yeah. Lunch," Dino nodded.

"Can we stop by the dungeon first?"

"Sure."

She leaned close and whispered, "For a nooner?"

Propped up on an elbow, Lizette ran a finger over Dino's naked chest and said, "My brother announced today that he wants to be a detective when he grows up."

"I'll bet your father had a cardiac."

"No, last year he wanted to be a garbageman. Ride on the back of garbage trucks."

"From a garbageman to a policeman. He's going down the social ladder."

Lizette poked a fingernail into the soft flesh of Dino's side.

"It could be worse," Dino continued in a voice that was more sarcastic than he intended it to be, "he could plan to be a retired cop. A civil servant for life!"

Lizette climbed out of bed and scooped up her clothes on her way to the bathroom. "That's not fair," she said, closing the door behind her.

When she came out she was dressed. Dino watched her tuck her pantyhose into her purse and asked her, "What do you see yourself doing five years from now?"

Lizette narrowed her eyes at him and said, "Don't. Don't say anymore." After a long hard stare, she started to leave.

"Where are you going?"

She hesitated in the bedroom doorway and declared in a voice husky with emotion, "I don't give a damn what my father thinks! Or what you think! I'll do whatever I want to do!" Then she walked out, slamming the front door of the dungeon.

Dino lay there for a minute before shouting, "You are one dumb fuckin' Wop!"

Stepping back into the bedroom doorway, Lizette cocked her head and said, "That's the most intelligent thing you've said all day."

Dino was hoping for a quiet ending to the week, but what chance had he on a sweltering Friday night? Mix high temperatures with humidity and a little human anger and you get murder, mayhem, and manslaughter. He never even made it to the office. Fifteen minutes into the shift, three simultaneous calls came in for Homicide. With only LaStanza, Mark, and Millie manning the evening watch, the hot night began to seem interminable. On his way to the first call, Dino wondered how Snowood always knew the right night to take off.

While Mark handled an unclassified death in Gentilly Terrace and told headquarters to hold the suicide in Gentilly Woods, Dino assisted Millie with a killing in the Magnolia Projects. In the wonderful and picturesque Sixth District, someone found the body of a black man who had been sliced to death between two buildings of the Magnolia.

The usual crowd had gathered by the time Homicide arrived. Sergeant Stan Smith was there, keeping the curious clear, especially the curious cops who had never seen a man sliced to death before, not to mention the old ladies and the equally curious children of the housing project.

"Looks like he got caught in a meat grinder," Stan told Dino.

"Looks like they autopsied him before he was dead," Dino added as Millie and the crime lab began to process the scene.

"At least this one's gonna be easy," Stan explained, pulling Dino away from the cadaver to a crowd of the curious, where he pointed to three eyewitnesses. "They saw the whole thing."

Detective LaStanza took separate taped statements from each of the three witnesses. It was the third witness, a half-brother of the victim, who provided the all-important moniker for that particular killing when he described the perpetrator. "She bad. She a mean, straight-razor–totin' bitch! She totes a straight razor around wif her. Slice your ass off *right now!*"

Less than an hour after the Straight-Razor–Totin' Bitch Killing, Dino caught a killing at a honky-tonk bar on Elmira Street, Algiers Point. He handled it alone, as Millie tried to put her anxious hands on the Straight-Razor–Totin' Bitch and Mark went to the suicide in Gentilly Woods.

He was thinking of naming the murder after the bar on Elmira Street. The Suspicion Bar sounded like an excellent name for a killing until Dino questioned the perpetrator, a bovine white boy wearing a tank top three sizes too small and a pair of blue jeans that were brown with sweat and the dirt of New Orleans' west bank.

The perpetrator, Bubba Jeffries, formerly of the great state of Texas, shot his buddy, Dave "The Snake" McNally, three times in the chest. Bubba's reason: "He was gettin' up in ma face." After a quick process of the scene, Dino booked Bubba for the Gettin'-Up-In-Ma-Face Killing of his good buddy The Snake.

Friday night turned into Saturday morning when Dino and Mark assisted Millie with the apprehension of the Straight-Razor–Totin' Bitch, who wound up turning herself in at Central Lockup just before dawn.

"What a night!" Millie exclaimed after she had secured the confession of her perpetrator. The Straight-Razor–Totin' Bitch had claimed the killing was accidental. "I was trying to cut off his thing, but the bastard kept protecting it, so I cut anything I could."

"Sounds logical to me," Mark admitted.

Dino, who had been particularly quiet most of the evening, had one thing to say on his way to the autopsy of The Snake. "Fuck this shit!"

Lizette decided that she would put her hair in a ponytail and wear a white LaCoste shirt, pink shorts, and white jogging shoes to the LaStanzas' for dinner on Sunday. She put on light makeup with only a hint of lipstick and waited for Dino to pick her up. She realized as she waited that she was nervous. She realized just how little she knew of Dino's parents. She knew much more about his dead brother.

On the way from Exposition Boulevard to Dino's parents' house on North Bernadotte Street, she asked Dino what his mother was like.

"She's very old fashioned, about four feet tall, with a hunchback. But she's not a bit self-conscious about the hunch, just don't mention the warts on her nose."

"I don't even know her name," Lizette said slowly, hoping Dino's humor would give way once he realized how nervous she was.

"Hortense," Dino answered. "Hortense Immaculata. And my father's name is Pasquale Appassionato."

Lizette bit her lower lip and stammered, "Would you *mind* being serious. I *am* a little nervous here." Sometimes, she was learning, she had to tell him things outright.

"I'm sorry," Dino apologized. "My mother's name is Virginia but everyone calls her Jennie, only she prefers Mrs. LaStanza. My Pop's name is Anthony but just call him Captain . . . okay?"

Lizette nodded and unclenched her fists.

Captain LaStanza was sitting in his front room with a beer in his hand, watching a baseball game on television. He greeted Dino and Lizette warmly but was anxious to get back to his game. "Yankees and Red Sox," Mr. LaStanza explained as he sat back in his recliner. "If you're a Sox fan, young lady, you can leave now," he added, pointing to the front door. "Those Beantowners still don't understand the damn Yankees are the best."

Dino just shook his head and led her by the hand

through the next two bedrooms, following the rich scent of tomato gravy to the rear kitchen, where Mrs. LaStanza was working on the meal. As soon as she saw Dino's mother, Lizette knew where Dino got his bright green eyes and smile. He looked so much like his mother. But it should not have surprised Lizette that he looked nothing like his father. Mr. LaStanza looked like anyone's idea of the typical Sicilian, dark skinned, burly, hairy, with a wide face and deep brown eyes. Mrs. LaStanza, like her son, had a delicate look about her, a lighter complexion and those green eyes.

"Smells great," Dino said, releasing Lizette's hand and moving over to the stove.

"Don't you dare," Mrs. LaStanza scolded her son when he reached for a spoon. "You go out with your father. Dinner will be ready shortly."

Lizette was about to ask to stay in the kitchen, but Dino grabbed her hand again and laughed. "Okay, Boss Lady. We'll go out with Grumpy. I just hope the Yankees are winning."

Mr. LaStanza just popped open a fresh beer and was smiling, "Mattingly just emptied the bases with a triple. Three-zip, Yankees. Want a beer?"

Dino shook his head no. When Lizette sat, she noticed the small refrigerator behind the recliner. "So that's where he got the fresh beer," she told herself as the captain continued to praise the Yankees, never taking his eyes from the TV until Mrs. LaStanza came in to announce dinner was served. Actually Dino's mother said nothing. She just walked in, gave Dino a wink, and flipped off the TV before returning the way she'd come. It was Dino who announced dinner was ready. Captain LaStanza said nothing. By that time the Yankees had ten runs.

Mrs. LaStanza said grace before serving everyone

personally at the small kitchen table. As she served the Italian bread, spaghetti sauce, and tortellini, the captain spoke. "I hear you've been busy, Son."

"A little," Dino answered as his mother served up a heaping plate for her son. "That's enough," he told her as she put two more scoops on anyway.

"I hear you're working on some LCN murders?" his father added, which caused Dino's mother to pause momentarily.

"That's right, Pop."

"Are you getting anywhere with them?"

"No. Too many other cases and not enough leads," Dino responded as Mrs. LaStanza handed Lizette a plateful of strong-smelling tortellini covered in a deep red sauce. The tortellini looked like small ravioli, but it had a cheese taste that was better than any ravioli Lizette had ever tasted. The strong scents of tomato, garlic, and cheese were rich and sweet in the air.

She had waited until Mrs. LaStanza seated herself before sampling the meal. "This is delicious," Lizette said.

"Thank you," replied Dino's mother warmly.

"I hear you got a body across the lake too, huh?" Mr. LaStanza asked.

"I think that's enough shoptalk," Mrs. LaStanza injected.

The captain shrugged but never lost a beat. "My Poppa wouldn't allow anyone to even mention the mafia in his presence." The captain was now addressing Lizette. "He would either bop you on the head or just walk out of the room as soon as the word *Mafia* was heard."

"Dino," Mrs. LaStanza said, "reach over and bop your father for me." Which caused Dino to laugh and the captain to smile.

"So, young lady," the captain asked, "what does your father do for a living?"

"He's a banker."

The captain's eyebrows rose. "What is your last name?"

"Louvier," Dino said as he turned to Lizette and explained. "He's just wondering if it was Rosenberg or Rothschild."

"Dino!" Mrs. LaStanza corrected her son.

"Louvier," the captain repeated, "Alexandre Louvier?"

Lizette nodded.

"I know your father," the captain said. "He's an old friend of Chief Rosata, isn't he?"

"Yes he is."

"We met your parents at a Rosata family reunion." Dino's father continued, explaining to his wife, "Remember the one in Abita Springs?"

Mrs. LaStanza shook her head, "That was a large reunion, Tony." She looked apologetically at Lizette and added, "But New Orleans sure is a small town sometimes."

Lizette insisted on helping with the dishes, even though Mrs. LaStanza maintained that guests did not work in her house.

"Then may I dry?"

Mrs. LaStanza gave in. The dishwashing and drying finally put Lizette's nervousness to rest. By the time the women moved back into the living room, she felt much better.

Until she heard the captain speaking. ". . . and this has been a gangster town for over two hundred years."

She could see in Dino's face that he was keyed up

again as he spoke. "Of course I'm taking it personally. The LCN is very personal. Just like the old country."

Lizette sat next to Dino, so close their legs touched.

"Baddie's a powerful man, son. He's as ruthless as they come."

"I know," Dino responded. "You can see it in his eyes. He's got eyes like a goddamn shark."

Mrs. LaStanza hesitated as she entered the room. "When did you ever see his eyes?"

"The other night." Dino sat back and told them about the Café DuMonde. As he described the meeting, Lizette felt her breath seeping away from her as the air became heavy with tension. She was as surprised as Dino's parents about the meeting.

Captain LaStanza's voice was solemn when he spoke. "You do realize what this means, don't you, Son?"

"I know what he's telling me," Dino's voice rose, "but I'm as Sicilian as any of them, and I'm gonna get 'em."

The captain nodded as he leaned back in the recliner. "There's an old Sicilian saying that revenge is a dish best served cold."

Dino narrowed his green eyes, nodding as he added coolly, "Ice in the veins when it counts, Pop. Ice in the veins."

"So, Lizette," Mrs. LaStanza tried to change the subject. "How did you two meet?"

"Mom," Dino answered quietly, "her sister was one of the Slasher victims."

On their way to the dungeon later, Lizette asked, "Why didn't you mention that meeting before?"

"I . . . uh. . . ."

"If you're going to start keeping things from me, then we're going to have problems." Her voice was low and serious.

Dino turned to face her and said, "I don't want to keep anything from you. I just didn't want to smother you with all this."

"You can't smother me. I love you."

She remained quiet for a while before asking another question. "What does LCN mean?"

"La Cosa Nostra. It's another name for the Mafia," he explained. "Literally it means 'our thing' or 'this thing of ours.'"

Lizette ran the phrase through her mind, this thing of ours, and she felt frightened.

Paul finally got to meet Karen Koski the following evening when Dino went to show her the picture of the Bogue Falaya victim. She answered her door in a crimson Danskin, columbian blue stockings, white leg warmers, and jogging shoes, a gym bag tossed over her shoulder. Automatically she shot him an annoyed look.

"I'm on my way out," she announced, remaining in the doorway, posing again with one arm up on the door frame, her hip pointed toward the detectives. "What do you want this time?"

"He's got something to show you," Paul answered as he gave her a long look up and down. "But I came to see the pictures of you with no clothes on."

Koski quickly recovered from the surprise comment as she twisted her head and stepped out of the way. "Help yourself," she said, smiling broadly at Paul. "They're to your right."

She regarded Dino with an annoyed look.

"I have a picture I'd like you to look at," he told

her, "see if you recognize someone."

"Okay, just make it fast. I'm late for exercise class."

"There's one more thing," LaStanza added. "This guy's dead."

"What?"

"The man in the picture is dead."

Koski crinkled up her nose again, as she had when he'd mentioned the word *gargoyle* at their last meeting. "You want me to look at a picture of a dead guy?"

"Exactly."

"You're kinda kinky, aren't you?" Koski ran a hand through her white-blonde hair.

"No. I just work with a lotta dead people."

"I like kinky," she smiled, using the same flirty smile she'd used on Snowood. "It rhymes with my nickname, Minky."

Paul returned in the middle of that last remark and injected, "And what kind of name is Minky, anyway?"

Koski's flirty smile turned to Snowood as she purred, "It refers to a part of my anatomy. The part you were just ogling in the other room."

"You know," Paul moved closer to Koski, "you probably don't remember, but we met once, a long time ago."

"Really?" Koski's flirting was at full power.

Dino was about to cut in, but Paul was too quick. "Yeah. We met in a wet dream I had, back in the seventh grade."

Surprise once again visited Karen Koski's face, but only for an instant as she started laughing a deep, nasty laugh. "And was it a very wet dream?" she asked wickedly, blinking her blue eyes.

"Very very wet."

"Good. I wouldn't want to be accused of leaving a

215

man unsatisfied."

Paul was smiling so wide, Dino thought his teeth would pop out. Stepping between the two, he shoved the picture in front of Koski's face.

"Oh," she said with a start as she examined the photo. After a moment she added, "You're right. He's dead. And I have no idea who he was." She handed the photo back to Dino.

"Never saw him before?" he asked as she stepped out and locked her door.

"Nope."

"Can we go to class with you?" Paul asked.

"It's for women only."

"All the more reason," Paul flirted back. "Maybe there'll be a short one for him."

"Don't get discouraged," Mason told LaStanza. "There's no such thing as a perfect investigation. Just keep working at it; it'll all fall into place."

Dino nodded in agreement.

"Come on in my office," Mason offered, "and we'll plan a little strategy."

Paul joined them with his styrofoam cup and brown spit. At least he kept quiet as Dino reviewed his case in brief for Mason.

"So," the lieutenant concluded when Dino had finished, "except for your Bogue Falaya mystery, everybody you mentioned so far is connected to Badalamente." He leaned back and continued thinking aloud. "That means they're all mobbed up. Therefore they're all pros. Therefore they ain't gonna tell us shit."

"All except one," Dino stated.

"Who?"

"Karen Koski."

216

"She's a pro," Paul argued. "Any broad who brags that she fucks like a mink is a pro."

"But she ain't Sicilian!"

Mason caught on, "Weak link?"

"Could be," Dino rose and tapped Snowood's shoulder. "Come on, padna. We got a weak link to work on."

Paul Snowood's teeth nearly did pop out.

Robert E. Lee Boulevard

"This broad's fruit for shoes," Dino said after the fourth day in a row in which Karen Koski visited a shoe store.

"Now that's a downright sexist statement," Snowood told his partner. Without any prodding, he elaborated, "I'm learning such things as what's sexist and what ain't from my lovely wife, who's gonna drive me stone-fuckin'-crazy if she keeps reading those women's magazines."

Sitting in their Chevy outside the Uptown Square Shopping Center, Dino was feeling pretty good for the first time in a long while. The mood change had not gone unnoticed by his partner who, upon readjusting himself for comfort behind the wheel, asked, "Is the Princess taking extra good care of you lately?"

"As a matter of fact she is."

"I thought so, because you've been a lot calmer. Especially after that bridge scene."

LaStanza's arrest of the man on the bridge had been the talk of the Detective Bureau for days. Millie asked to hear the story three times, she liked it so much. Some members of the evening watch refused to believe Snowood's account but had to accept the story once Mark verified it. Only Maurice Ferdinand did not believe a word of the story.

When Felicity Jones heard the story, he nonchalantly said, "That's just his Sixth District training." Which caused Dino to smile for the first time about the incident. After all, veterans of the Bloody Sixth were a cut above.

Dino was smiling as he sat outside Uptown Square, but he was not thinking about Lizette or even about the man from the bridge. He was thinking about how quiet it had been the past few days. In Homicide, that was a true blessing. But woe to the detective who mentioned it out loud. Superstition proved that if anyone so much as hinted that it was slow a triple murder would immediately occur, followed by renewed carnage. Open your mouth and somebody died right away. It had happened so many times in the past that it was legend.

The most recent violator, Cal Boudreaux, had opened his mouth just prior to the current holocaust, which was devastating the evening watch when he declared, "It's sure been quiet around here. What we need is another Slasher!"

Boudreaux was transferred to the Fourth District the following morning by a livid Lieutenant Mason after two killings, two misdemeanor murders, and a quadruple murder occurred the evening of Boudreaux's remark. "I'd rather be shorthanded than keep that fuck up!" Mason screamed. "I hope they put that Fuck Head in the middle of the Fisher Projects by himself!"

Dino continued to smile, thinking how nice it was working nine-to-five with no autopsies the following morning. He could concentrate on his Twenty-Two Killer every day and on Lizette every night.

Lizette and Dino were spending the majority of

their evenings together, always dining together, usually at the dungeon. Some nights she would stay over, but some nights he would take her home, especially when her parents were in town or if she had something to do the following day with her brother, who was beginning to talk to his sister more frequently.

Although Lizette had seemed upset after the tortellini dinner, he had made it up to her by telling her everything, as he promised. This was helpful not only in calming her, but in letting her bright mind wander through his case, making comments and giving him fresh insights into the mystery from a civilian's point of view. Lizette was especially curious about Karen Koski and her habits.

"Okay," Paul started to complain again. "We been following her around four days. She ain't led us to nothin' but shoe stores."

"Don't forget the exercise classes," Dino sparred.

"Yeah."

"And the French Quarter strolls."

"Yeah, and you ain't any closer to solvin' this damn . . ."

"You don't get it," Dino told his partner. "We're just putting pressure on the weak link, pushing her until something pops."

Snowood readjusted himself again in a vain attempt at comfort and groaned as the armrest dug into his hip.

"You don't have to be here, you know," Dino reminded him.

"I know, but I can't help myself. I can't keep my eyes off the bitch."

"Why don't you go in," Dino nodded toward the shoe store, "and look up her dress again? That'll cheer you up."

"I just might."

Back on the first day, when it was obvious that Koski had spotted them, Paul had given up hiding and just went and tried looking up her dress as she tried on shoe after shoe, sitting in a miniskirt in the D.H. Holmes Department Store. As soon as Karen had seen Paul spying, she winked at him and raised her knee higher.

"Couldn't see a damn thing," Paul griped after the Holmes spying. "I don't see how a woman can try on shoes in a miniskirt and I can't see no drawers!"

"It's an art."

He had a gut feeling about Karen Koski, but not the usual cop's gut feeling about a criminal; it was an old-country feeling, an innate Sicilian instinct of preying on weakness wherever weakness presented itself. It came naturally to someone named LaStanza. If she was the weak link, he would prey on that.

It took Paul four days of surveillance to realize that important facet of LaStanza's Sicilian mind. "You know," he said as he stared at the door of the Uptown Square shoe store, "we're putting this girl on the front line. Even if she don't know nothin', they might think she does and get worried that we're . . ."

Dino smiled slyly, "Exactly."

Paul frowned as he looked back at his partner. "Now I know why you people wear gangster glasses."

Dino adjusted his glasses and nodded toward Koski as she strolled out of the shoe store carrying a fresh bag in one hand. She walked languidly across the parking lot in her ice-blue minidress, passing her BMW and moving up to Snowood's window. Bending at the waist, she rested her elbows in the open window and smiled at the big Country Ass.

"I thought you were coming in for a peek." She batted her eyes at him.

"I was about to." He leaned out the window and looked down at her legs.

She turned her eyes across Paul to Dino. "Why are you still following me? I'm not going to lead you anywhere, except in circles."

"We're following you so he can look up your dress," Dino pointed to his partner.

"And you don't want to?"

"Not particularly."

"What's the matter? You don't like girls?"

"No, I just don't like you," Dino stated matter-of-factly.

So she asked Paul, "Does he even have a girl-friend?"

Paul, whose eyes were riveted to Koski's legs, answered slowly, "He sure does. His girlfriend's a princess."

"Is she pretty?"

"Yep."

"Is she a good lay?"

Dino's face remained still as his eyes stared at Koski without any emotion.

"Well," she continued to flirt, "I'm going to Lake-side now. There are plenty shoe stores there."

As she moved away in her easy, smooth walk, both detectives watched until she climbed into her candy-apple-red BMW and drove off. When she climbed in, her skirt rose high up her thighs, which caused Snowood to moan a long, low moan.

That evening, after finishing the red beans and rice and breaded pork chops Lizette had fixed, Dino settled on the sofa with his princess to watch a Woody Allen film on cable. When the phone rang a half hour into the movie, he answered and was surprised to hear Karen Koski's voice on the other end.

"I missed you at Lakeside," she purred.

He recovered quickly from the shock of having Koski call his unlisted number. "Is that why you called?"

"No. I just want to save you some time tomorrow."

"Yeah. How?" His voice was sharp and stiff.

"You won't have to follow me in the morning. I'll be in City Park, by the concession stand, posing for some fashion pictures. Why don't you and that good-looking partner of yours join me?"

"We might."

"Good," she flirted. "'Bye now."

"Good-bye," Dino was about to hang up when he realized she was still on the line.

"Is your princess with you?"

"As a matter of fact, yes."

"That's nice." Koski hung up.

Lizette gave Dino an inquiring look. When he did not volunteer an explanation, she asked, "Who was that?"

"That was Karen Koski."

"Are you kidding?" Lizette sat up suddenly.

"Nope."

"How did she get your number?"

He shrugged his shoulders. "I guess Baddie's got connections with the phone company."

When he offered nothing more, Lizette pressed on. "What did she want?"

"She called to tell me about a fashion show she'll be at tomorrow so we don't have to follow her in the morning, but that's not why she called." He paused a second before explaining, "She called to let me know she had my number."

"Is that supposed to be a threat?"

"Maybe," Dino smiled.

"Come on." A hint of concern crept into her voice. "What does it mean?"

Dino's smile broadened. "It means my actions are getting reactions. And that's good."

She watched him resettle next to her, still smiling. After a while it was obvious that Dino was not in the least bit concerned. He was displaying a confidence that made her feel apprehensive.

After two hours of watching Karen Koski posing in various outfits, Dino realized he was watching an efficient model. With a wave of her hand she moved the cameramen, who were supposed to be in charge, around like puppets. She would move and pose herself as the three photographers buzzed around her, clicking like insects with fifty-millimeter eyes.

With her face made up to perfection, Koski looked stunning as she moved between the dripping, low branches of the great oaks of City Park. She wore a long white gown with a high collar and a plunging back and posed using a minimum of expression and yet reeking of sensuality.

Paul began his low moaning early, especially after Koski changed into a red evening gown and then a tight-fitting navy blue dress with a daring slit up the front. "That is one beautiful fuckin' woman," he whispered to his partner.

At first Dino would not admit it, not even to himself, but he was becoming excited watching Koski's sensual movements, especially when she would focus her icy blue eyes on him. Her face remained expressionless as she stared at him, yet her eyes refused to pull away.

Koski was an efficient model, with no wasted movements. She was an equally efficient seductress, of that Dino was certain.

They had to leave City Park early so Dino could file charges with the DA against Bubba Jeffries for the Gettin'-Up-In-Ma-Face Killing. Koski waved good-bye, winking at LaStanza.

"She keeps winking at me like that," Paul said as they pulled away, "and I'm gonna give her all she can handle."

All the way to Tulane and Broad, Paul acted as if he had itching powder in his pants. Finally settling down when they parked, he added, "You know. My wife's not a bad lookin' woman."

"I know that." Dino stared curiously at his partner, who seemed to be thinking real hard. Paul indicated he was thinking real hard by the way his eyebrows moved closer together.

"She ain't got a body like Minky's, but at least after I fuck my wife I don't have to worry about no twenty-twos in the skull."

"You could say that," Dino agreed as he narrowed his own eyebrows at his partner.

"Yeah," Paul concluded as he climbed out of the car, "I think I'll bring my old lady a present when I go home later."

"Really?"

"Yeah. I gonna give her this hard-on ol' Minky done give me."

"You're all heart."

"Thanks. Mighty nice of you to notice."

*　　　*　　　*

226

"But I don't know anything," Koski insisted the following morning when Dino knocked on her door. She neither let the detectives in nor slammed the door in their faces.

Dino met her reply with a cold stare, which made Paul fidget. He stared hard at her as she leaned in her open doorway in another of her Danskin outfits. After putting a defiant hand on her hip, she started to speak again but was cut off.

"Look," Dino said in a louder voice, "we can keep playing little games as long as you want. But I just want you to know that you're not fooling me one bit. You know what I'm looking for. I just want to give you the opportunity to make it easy on us all." He ended his remark with an unfriendly smile.

"You are a little bastard," she replied indignantly.

"You know my number. At work and at home," he told her. "Call me." And with that he turned and walked away.

She was still laughing when the detectives climbed into their Chevy and drove off.

When the Louviers went to Florida for the weekend, Lizette invited Dino to stay with her on Exposition Boulevard. He forwarded his phone to Lizette's just in case Koski called, which he knew was highly unlikely, but you never knew.

They never left the house the entire weekend, cooking together, sleeping late in the morning, reading, watching movies on the video recorder each night. When Dino found that the Louviers had the uncut ten-hour version of *The Godfather*, they watched it all day Saturday while it rained outside from dawn to dark.

"Best gangster movie ever made," he told her when

it finally ended. Although Lizette had seen it before, it had never seemed real to her. It had been as foreign as a science-fiction movie until now.

She asked a few questions, mostly during the parts when DeNiro spoke in Italian and Dino could interpret what was said. He seemed to understand every nuance of the plot, even the subtle mannerisms of the actors. He especially liked DeNiro. Lizette always liked Pacino best, but it was not until seeing the movie again that she realized how much Dino looked like Pacino and reminded her of the young Michael at the beginning of the film, before he was gobbled up into the gangster life-style. Put a moustache on Pacino and he could pass for Dino's twin.

After a Sunday evening feast of cracked crab, boiled shrimp, and Zeller Schwatz Katz wine, Lizette led Dino out to the tiny backyard of the mansion. Attached to the rear of the kitchen was a wooden deck with a Jacuzzi. She moved to the controls, turned on the water and the low lights around the hot tub, and then began to strip.

Dino glanced around the small yard, near the tall banana trees with their elephant-ear leaves and over to the high wooden fence and realized that no one could see into the yard unless they were in the empty Louvier Mansion. When he looked back at his girlfriend, she was climbing out of her shorts. Calmly, without looking back at him, she tossed her bra aside and then her panties before descending into the bubbling water. When she did turn back to him, she grinned, "Come on, Short-Dark-and-Italian. Strip."

Lizette watched him remove his clothes, her breasts resting at the water level, her nipples pointing and waiting. When he finished, he moved into the Jacuzzi and eased over to her. She kissed him quickly, but then pulled away and asked, "What did she look like naked?"

228

His hands groped under the water for her body. "Who?" he asked.

"You know who," she leveled her gold eyes at him. "Minky."

"Oh," Dino snickered as he leaned back against his side of the tub. "Not bad. Not bad at all."

He quickly moved against her and added, "But you've got it all over her."

"You're just saying that because you've got your hands on my ass."

"No," he argued, removing his hands as he settled next to her. "Just take her face," he continued. "It's perfect, but there's an edge to it, not a hint of softness."

"Go on."

"And you've got much prettier boobs."

"What's wrong with hers?"

"Nipples are too big."

"You are such a sexist."

"I know," he apologized.

"Don't apologize, so long as you're *my* little sexist."

She kissed him, wrapping her arms around his neck, and pulled him around the tub, sinking into the water and kissing him again underwater.

When they emerged, Dino asked, "Is it hot in here or is it just me?"

After spitting a mouthful of warmed water into his face, Lizette climbed out and turned the heat completely off before going in to get more wine. Dino watched her walking naked back into the kitchen and then coming out with a fresh bottle and two glasses.

"Now this is the life," he acknowledged after she resettled next to him in the gurgling water.

She pursed her full lips and said, "Now tell me again how much finer I am than Karen Koski."

"I don't wanna talk about her anymore."

"Not your type, huh?"

"Why would I want a tramp when I've got a princess?"

"You don't know the half of it, mister." Her face turned away smugly as she took a sip of wine.

"And what does that mean?"

"Have you ever heard of the House of Valois?" Lizette continued in a saucy voice.

"The what?"

"The House of Valois. It preceded the House of Bourbon as kings of France." She pronounced Bourbon as "Borbon," not "bourbon."

"You mean like Bourbon Street?" he asked.

"Exactly. Before the Bourbon Kings, the House of Valois ruled France. Anyway, the Louviers are directly related to the Valois," Lizette added. "King Henri III of France was my Great-Great-something-or-another-Uncle." She took another sip of wine. "Of course, that was long before the Louviers came to Louisiana and sent money to the French Revolution."

Dino's mouth was open. She noticed and started giggling, "So . . . ?"

"I'll be damned," Dino exclaimed. "You really are a princess."

When Dino returned to the office Monday morning, there was a large envelope waiting for him. In the upper left corner of the envelope, postmarked "New Orleans" the preceding Saturday, the name "Minky" was printed.

"Do you know anything about letter bombs?" he asked Snowood as he reached for his letter opener.

"Why do you ask?" Paul answered as he turned the

230

page of the sports section he was reading.

"Because this," he held up the envelope, "is from Minky."

"No shit?" Paul looked over the top of his paper at Dino.

"No shit."

Dino held the brown envelope up to the light and shrugged, "What do you think?"

"If you don't slit that thing open right now, you ain't got no balls."

"I was thinking about maybe bringing it by the crime lab first." Dino's even voice was void of genuine concern.

"A real policeman would just open it," Paul egged his partner as he went back to his paper. "If it blows, it blows."

Dino laughed as he began to open the envelope. "And what the fuck do you know about real policemen? When did you ever work the Sixth?"

The envelope contained one eight-by-ten-inch nude photograph of Karen Koski inscribed, "To a real little bastard!" Dino examined the full-length nude of Minky leaning seductively against a column of Pop's Fountain in City Park. It was a copy of one of the photos that hung in her apartment. There was nothing else in the envelope, except two thin pieces of cardboard between which the photo had been sandwiched.

"Is that a picture?" Paul asked from the other side of the photo.

"It's a nude of Karen Koski."

"Yeah. I am sure," he went back to his paper.

At that moment, Millie Suzanne entered the squad room behind LaStanza and as she approached exclaimed, "Oh my God!"

Dino turned and nodded, "Not bad, huh?"

231

"Who is that?" she asked as she stepped up.

Dino noticed Maurice Ferdinand entering behind Millie and held up the picture for him. "Hey M.F., ever see anything like this before?"

Maurice took a step in LaStanza's direction and took in the picture for a full second before turning away in a huff.

Dino looked back at Millie. "It took him a couple seconds to recognize it."

Millie could not take her eyes from the picture. "Where did you get that?"

"From a fan." He pointed out the inscription.

By that time Snowood's curiosity had forced him to put down his paper and mosey on over. When he saw the front of the picture he opened his mouth to speak, but nothing came out.

"There's a first time for everything," Millie patted Paul on the back. "I've never seen anything shut *you* up before."

It did not take long for word to pass throughout the Bureau, causing every detective to congregate around LaStanza's desk. Some came by themselves, some came in packs, but they all came. From Robbery they came, from Burglary, from Juvenile, from every corner of the Bureau. Fel Jones even came down from Intelligence to examine the picture.

Since Dino would not allow anyone to touch it, Fel had to stand over the picture as he rubbed his chin and nodded. "Not bad for a white girl." Pointing to the inscription he added, "Knows you pretty well, don't she?"

"What can I say?"

Before leaving, Fel had one more comment. "I don't know how I'd feel fuckin' a broad with blonde publics. I like my publics black and rough, like Brillo." At that point he noticed Snowood brooding

232

across the desk. "What the fuck's his problem?"

Dino nodded to the picture.

"Why don't you just let him take it into the bathroom for a minute?"

When Mark came to see the picture, he had one question for LaStanza, "You sure you ain't fuckin' her?"

"I oughta know."

"He knows better," Mason said when he walked up to take a look. "Once you crawl into the gutter, there's no getting out." He put a hand on LaStanza's shoulder and reminded him, "I told you she liked you." But he quickly added, "You're getting reactions, and that's good." After a few more seconds of staring at the picture, the lieutenant asked, "You know what to do next, don't you?"

"Ignore her for a while."

"Absolutely," Mason agreed as he headed back to his office. "Abso-fuckin'-lutely."

"You see," Dino told Lizette later when he showed her the picture, "your boobs are much prettier." Although his comment was in a sarcastic voice, his face looked almost innocent, like a little boy who'd found something he should not have found.

Lizette's surprise gave way to a deep curiosity the longer she looked at the picture. "Why?" was the only question that came to mind.

"Reactions," he answered cryptically. "We act and she reacts."

"But she's sending you naked photographs of herself."

"Yeah, to the office, so everyone will see." His answer made sense, only Lizette was too busy fighting a new feeling inside. She felt jealous. And if

233

there was one thing she did not want to face again, it was the specter of jealousy.

"She's trying to get her own reactions," Dino explained. "And it looks like she's getting her way. She's got Paul brooding and you curious as hell."

Lizette remembered what jealousy had done to her and Lynette, how it had driven a wedge between them. She handed the picture back to Dino and watched him put it back in its envelope.

"I liked it better when you were in the pressure cooker," she said and immediately regretted it.

"What does that mean?" Dino readjusted his weight from one leg to the other as he stood there looking uncomfortable in Lizette's foyer.

"Never mind," she mumbled, "I didn't mean it." She felt vulnerable, while he was feeling anything but. Ever since the dinner at his father's house, Dino seemed more self-assured, more cool, as if he had discovered an inner strength, as if he had discovered something within himself that made him more confident in working this LCN case of his.

She took his hand and led him back to the kitchen for the iced tea she had just made. When she looked back at him, sitting across the counter, she wondered if he could see the worry in her eyes. But as soon as he started up again about his case, she knew he had not seen it. Or maybe he just wasn't looking.

"Babe, I've got to make them think I'm on top of this, one step ahead of them, that they can't get to me." He looked like a little boy at confession, "I'm just following an instinct. It's the only way to fool with these people. They prey on weakness and confusion," he was pointing his finger at the counter now, "and I can't afford to show them either."

She heard herself repeating Dino's own statement to his father, "Ice in the veins, huh?"

"That's right," he agreed. "Ice in the veins."

Dino waited four days before reinstating the surveillance of Karen Koski and then decided to watch her at night. Since Snowood was "too disgusted" to watch her, he went alone, parking the Chevy on King Louis XIV Ring.

He did not expect Koski to stay home on a Friday night, but she did, exercising in her living room, eating alone before showering and settling in front of the television. Near midnight, just when he was about to pull up, he noticed he was not alone. To the left of the Chevy, in the grassy area between King Louis XIV Ring and Robert E. Lee Boulevard, there was a man in dark clothing standing behind a tree not fifty yards away. Instinctively Dino sank lower in the seat and reached down to withdraw his Magnum. In the dark he could not tell if the man was looking at him until the man lit a cigarette. The match flashed, illuminating the profile of a face and a streak of white hair.

"Lemoni," the name rang in LaStanza's mind as the man tossed the match down and moved to Dino's side of the tree. After the movement, the distant street lights of Robert E. Lee provided enough light to see that Lemoni was looking at Koski's apartment.

When Dino glanced back at the apartment he saw Koski standing in her balcony door, doing her striptease. She moved slowly and sensually as she removed everything and then stood there dancing naked.

He caught the movement of Lemoni's cigarette as it was tossed to the ground and looked back in time to see Harry start across the grass directly for the apartment. When he arrived, he let himself in with a key. Not sixty seconds after he entered, all lights went out

235

in the apartment and never came back on.

After an hour, Dino began to wonder how Lemoni had arrived. Maybe he'd taken a bus; Dino had never heard a car. There was a bus stop at Robert E. Lee and Canal Boulevard. Or maybe Lemoni's car was parked nearby. After another half hour, Dino climbed out of the Chevy with his portable radio, his Magnum tucked in his belt, and searched the area in vain for the Cadillac Seville registered to Lemoni.

By four o'clock, Dino had set his mind. "I'm gonna wait him out and see how he leaves." But by four-thirty he was so tired he almost gave in. Instead he climbed out, stretched, did a couple of jumping jacks, and then began to think about Lizette in order to keep awake.

He remembered what she had said to him after the tortellini dinner, when she'd told him she loved him. He had heard it but said nothing. He wondered why. It registered, deep inside, but he had not even acknowledged it. Maybe that was why she was acting nervous lately. . . .

When the sun crept up, hot and sticky, Dino began to yawn so much he almost missed Lemoni walking out of the apartment. Harry went straight to a taxi that had just pulled up.

Dino tried to follow the cab, but the driver made a quick turn on Canal Boulevard and he caught the light and by the time Dino was through the inter-section the taxi was nowhere in sight.

At least he got a couple hours' sleep before the phone woke him at ten o'clock. It was Mason. "I got a message for you."

"Uh-huh," Dino answered groggily.

"From Gina Jimson."

"Really?" He started to wake up.

"She says Karen Koski got beat up last night. She's at Ochsner."

"Wow! Wait . . . wait," Dino sat up in bed and asked Mason to repeat the message. After hearing it a second time, he told his lieutenant that he had been there all night. "And she wasn't alone. Harry Lemoni was with her, he left at six."

"Who?"

"One of Baddie's men."

There was a pause on the other end of the line before, "You need any help?"

"Sure."

"As you can see I got nothing better to do on a Saturday. The wife and kids are raiding the shopping centers."

"Sure. Sure," Dino started to climb out of bed.

"Good. Pick you up in forty-five."

On their way to Ochsner Foundation Hospital, LaStanza asked his lieutenant, "What exactly did Gina say?"

"Just what I told you, except she asked that you not call her back."

"She didn't say how she knew about it?"

"No."

On their way to Jefferson Parish, Dino had him pull over at a large drugstore on Claiborne. He went in and bought a cassette tape. Mason bought a couple extra packs of cigarettes, "Just in case."

Karen Koski was in a private room in the large hospital. When the detectives entered, she was applying makeup to a face that was swollen on one side. As soon as she saw them she gasped and almost dropped her compact mirror. "What are you doing here?"

"My job," Dino told her as he stepped up to her

237

bed. "Somebody got hurt and I'm a cop."

"I'm not telling you a damn thing," she declared, going back to her makeup.

Dino walked around the end of the bed to get a better look and shook his head. "Any broken bones?"

She tried ignoring him, but when Mason sat in the chair near the door, she said, "You can't stay here."

"What are you gonna do about it?" Dino asked as he sat on the foot of her bed, "call the police?"

"I'll call the sheriff's office. You're in Jefferson Parish."

Dino pointed to the phone, "Go ahead, we got lots of J.P.S.O. friends."

"And we haven't seen them in a long time," Mason added as he lit up.

Koski's icy eyes looked at each detective in turn with her hardest *fuck-you* look. Dino reached in his coat pocket and tossed the cassette tape to her.

"What's this?"

"I owe you one cassette, remember?" He nodded to Mason. "The snoring routine?"

She did not change the frigid look in her eyes. She just went back to applying mascara, only now her hand was shaking.

Dino reached over and touched her arm, and she almost jumped. He left his hand where it was as he asked quietly, "Are you all right?"

Koski's cold blue eyes were wide and oval. She looked down at his hand until he removed it. In a chilly voice she said, "It's the painkillers. They cause the shakes."

"You know," Dino added in a voice little more than a whisper, "you're gonna have to talk to me sooner or later."

"No I don't."

He continued in a voice so low that she'd have to

238

concentrate to hear. "I already know. I just want you to confirm it."

She would not look back at him, so he added in a slightly louder voice, "I know it was Harry."

She tried to hide the effect of his statement, but she looked stunned. Her hand shook so much she had to stop, but she would not look at him. He had hit on something. He held his breath and waited for her, but she only looked away.

So he told her, "We know Pus Face was at your place last night before midnight and left by taxi at six this morning."

When a hint of relief crept across Koski's face, it was Dino's turn to feel surprised. He could not understand why she felt relieved.

"I wouldn't call Harry that to his face." She went back to her makeup, her shakes gone. "You might as well get lost. I'm not pressing charges." She was cocky again, but he no longer felt like sparring.

When the silence grew into minutes, he took out his card and put it on the table next to her bed and then left. He felt this girl had something to tell him, and maybe wanted to tell him, only she was afraid. If there was one thing a good investigator had to learn, it was patience, and the ability to let someone take his time to decide. He knew one thing for sure: there was more to Koski's fear of Lemoni than what had happened the previous evening.

"That was a nice touch," Mason said as they drove away, "leaving like that."

"Yeah?"

"Especially the way you touched her arm."

LaStanza was going on instinct, like a man in suspended animation trying to fight his way out of a plastic bag.

"You had her for a second there."

"I know."

Dino ran it back through his mind, what he said, what she said, what he said again, and then that stunned look on her face when he said, "I know it's Harry. . . ."

Slapping himself on the forehead he blurted out, "Maybe she told me something after all."

Mason, never one to miss a detail, added, "I think that you just may have a suspect now."

"It ain't much," Dino admitted.

"Right. It *is* slim."

"But it's more than I had before."

When a red light stopped their car, Mason turned his steely eyes to LaStanza and said, "You better watch yourself."

"Yeah, I'd better."

He tried to rest later but could not. He took off his clothes, climbed into bed with the air conditioner on high, and closed his eyes, but it was no good. He tried thinking of Lizette, daydreaming about their date later that night, when it would be his turn to take her to Commander's Palace.

He closed his eyes and tried thinking of Lizette, but another drowsy vision came to mind, a vision of a shotgun. Dino's vision included himself, at night, standing in the doorway of the dungeon, and there was a shotgun, the inevitable shotgun that haunted his Sicilian dreams. Deep within his mind lurked a fear of the inevitable shotgun blast, a vision of a key turning in his hand as he opened his front door and then a blast from behind.

He must have fallen asleep because when Paul called, it woke him and he felt terrible.

"Say, pardner, what ya' doin'? Taking a siesta?"

Dino grunted in response.

"Look, can you get yer butt up and give me a hand?"

"What?"

"Remember that old murder I was telling you about, the one by U.N.O.?"

"No."

Paul explained about a coed murder a couple years ago that LaStanza had never heard of.

"Come on, ride with me tonight." Paul urged, "I know it's an old murder, but I got a lead." He waited for a response.

"I don't give a fuck! Period. Listen," Dino shouted, *"I don't give a fuck!* I'm not working tonight!"

It took a while, but they compromised. Dino agreed to work Sunday with Paul, who responded, "Thanks, pardner. I'll pick you up at eight in the morning."

By the time he picked up Lizette later, he felt the tiredness creeping back into his legs and arms. Even as he returned her smile, he felt weariness pulling at his face. Her bouncy walk did little to rejuvenate him. She was up, feeling good, and looking good in a white dress whose top was loose and whose skirt was tight.

The luscious meal at Commander's perked Dino initially, soothing his hunger, but left him full and content, which allowed the weariness to return in full force.

Lizette dominated the conversation, telling him all sorts of things about her upcoming classes and how her brother was beginning to smile more and had even laughed earlier that day when a squirrel had

241

fallen into their Jacuzzi.

"Thank God it was off," she added, slicing into a piece of blackberry pie.

When he did not respond, she continued the one-sided conversation. "My parents went to the condo in Florida." She winked at Dino, "We've got the house to ourselves again."

Before leaving Commander's, she asked, "How about some more coffee?" His weariness was obvious.

The extra coffee did no good, but he tried perking himself up on their way to a new nightclub Lizette had heard about at West End Park. The club was nautical in design, with fish nets on the ceiling and oars and plenty of stuffed game fish nailed to the walls. The place was on pilings over the black lake water and was relatively new. The combination of loud music and dancing fast with an energetic Lizette caused Dino to become actually light-headed.

He was too tired to even make a pass by the *Lil Gina*.

"Whew," she said as she led Dino into the Louvier library when they finally made it home, "that was *fun*." She kicked off her heels and climbed into the big easy chair to nestle next to him. It was obvious by the slump of Dino's body and the droop of his eyes just how tired he was.

After snuggling for a few minutes, she moved her lips over to kiss him and woke him with a start.

"I'm sorry, Babe," she said as she resettled next to him.

"I'm the one that's sorry. I'm just so tired."

"It's no wonder, after the last forty-eight hours," Lizette added sympathetically. He had told her, on their way from the nightclub, about his all-nighter

242

and about the hospital.

"And then I take you dancing."

When he tried to get up a few minutes later, she held him back. "Just stay here tonight, Babe."

"No," Dino rose slowly. "Paul's picking me up in the morning. He needs help on an old murder."

"You're working tomorrow?"

"He's working. I'm gonna sleep in the car. That is, if I can even get up in the morning."

She followed him to the door, gave him a big good-bye kiss and hung onto his neck with her arms wrapped around him. "You're too tired to drive. Let me drive you."

"No. I'll be okay."

She watched him walk like a punch drunk to the gate and then stand there stretching as he stared out at the darkness of Audubon Park.

The park was extra black that night and extra quiet. Without any wind to rustle the leaves, even the trees were silent. Dino yawned before turning to glance back at her house. Lizette was still in the doorway, leaning against the door frame. Her lively face smiled as she gave him a big wink before going back inside.

Turning down Exposition Boulevard to the side of the Louvier Mansion, he stopped again and stretched before heading to his car. He had parked on the dead end of Garfield across from the Louviers. Crossing the street he glanced up at Lizette's bedroom windows. The lights were already on.

The sound of her balcony doors opening caused him to look back when he reached his car. She stepped out on the balcony in her long white robe and spoke. "Hark, who goes there?"

"Me," he answered before he caught on to her mock English accent.

She put her hands on her hips and sighed, "You're supposed to say, 'But soft! What light through yonder window breaks? It is the east and Juliet is the sun!'"

"What?" Dino yawned again.

"The balcony scene," she sighed again. *Romeo and Juliet?*"

"Oh, yeah," he shrugged. "That was a good movie."

Lizette huffed as she took a step back and added, "Only this balcony scene is 'R'-rated." With that she untied her robe, letting it fall, and stood totally naked above him.

Standing across the narrow street, he could see her clearly in the bright light from her room and the streetlights on Garfield.

"Am I supposed to climb up there?"

"No. This is supposed to keep you awake until you get home."

"Oh."

"Tell me, Detective LaStanza, did Blondie look this good?" Lizette placed her hand behind her head and took a slow, sexy turn.

His exhausted face was smiling as she scooped up her robe and went back into her room. With the balcony door still cracked, she added in a mock southern-belle accent, "Ya'll come back real soon." Then she closed the French doors and did not come out again.

Dino stood there for a moment and debated which way to go, back into the house or to the car. If he wasn't so damn tired . . . then he heard something behind him and wheeled quickly to see a young boy standing outside the gate of the house across Garfield. The boy's wide eyes stared from behind thick eyeglasses, up at Lizette's balcony. The boy was about ten years old and stood there like a statue. Turning to Dino, the boy asked, "Did you see that?"

The phone was ringing when he got home.

"Good," she said, "you're home safe."

"Does a little boy about ten years old with blond hair and glasses live across from you on Garfield?"

Lizette's voice dropped to almost a whisper. "Yes. Why?"

He fell on his sofa and laughed, "Well, after you finished on the balcony, I ran into him."

"Oh no!"

"Oh, yes. He was standing by his gate staring up at you."

"Oh no! That's my little brother's best friend. Oh my God!"

"Exactly."

He couldn't sleep. He lay awake in bed trying to fall asleep but realized after a while that he was too excited to sleep. He had his eyes shut tight but continued to see Lizette's naked body on the balcony and then the little boy's wide eyes staring up at her.

Only the eyes were not the eyes of the little boy with glasses who lived across the street. They were Dino's eyes, and it wasn't Lizette at all, it was Jennifer, and Dino was eight years old again.

Like videotape, Dino's memory had rewound itself back to a night when he was eight and he saw a naked girl for the first time in his life. He had been hiding in his brother's room when the girl next door entered her room and stripped. Her name was Jennifer, and she had long brown hair and took all her clothes off that evening in her room across the narrow alley between their houses on North Bernadotte.

She was sixteen and had a crush on Dino's big brother, but it was Dino who saw her naked. She was his first sexual fantasy. She moved away from North Bernadotte soon after, and he never saw her again, except at night in his dreams. Even in Vietnam, Dino dreamed of her. The memory was that vivid.

It occurred to Dino that Lizette was now another little boy's fantasy, and that excited him as he lay awake. He was sure his eyes were just as wide as the boy's when he was looking at Jennifer. He lay awake, getting more excited by the minute. He could opt for a hot towel in the bathroom. In the jungle he would have given anything for a clean towel or a clean woman.

Lizette was asleep when he called. "I'll come over," she said, but he insisted on returning and did, arriving in record time. When she let him in, he grabbed her in the foyer and sank his mouth against hers, his hand reaching under her robe for her naked ass.

She responded instantly and kissed him back, hard and hot, and then he had her robe off and his hands racing over her from her pointy breasts to the softness between her legs. She tore at his clothes and found that he was wearing only a loose T-shirt and nothing beneath his tennis shorts.

Dino continued his attack on Lizette, pushing her against the railing of the stairs and then pulling her down on him as he turned and sat on the third step, spreading her legs around him. She sat on top and he was inside her and they were moving in unison, still kissing, until Lizette suddenly leaned back and started pumping vigorously until Dino came with ferocity deep within her.

After they made it up to Lizette's bed, they lay

246

exhausted in each other's arms. When she caught her breath she asked, "What brought this on?"

"Balcony scene."

"You better be talking about *my* balcony scene."

"Of course. Yours and a girl named Jennifer."

Lizette's head rose from the comfort of Dino's shoulder, "Who?"

So he told her about the time he was eight and about Jennifer and about how a sexual fantasy will remain vivid through years and years.

"So what are you telling me? I'm gonna be a fantasy?"

"Yep. And don't worry about him telling your brother. He won't tell anyone. Until he's grown."

"You sure?"

"I know what I'm talking about," Dino assured her. "This is more than a secret. It's a sexual fantasy."

Lizette leaned up and kissed him gently. He smiled back at her when she pulled away and asked, "Ready again, little girl?"

"I don't know why the fuck I brought you along," Snowood complained as they pulled away from a house where Dino had never gone inside because he was sleeping in the car. "First I had to pick you up at Audubon Fuckin' Park and then drive you home and wait for you to dress and what do you do all day? Sleep!"

Dino did not answer. He was sleeping. He vaguely remembered Snowood bringing him straight to the dungeon later.

The next morning, as Dino sleepwalked into the office behind his partner, Paul was conducting a one-sided conversation, complaining how autumn was long overdue. "It's so fuckin' hot!" he moaned as he picked up his paper and sat at his desk.

When Mason entered, he took one look at Dino and asked Paul, "What's wrong with him?"

"Fuckathon," Paul muttered in a disgusted voice.

"Oh." Mason nodded and went into his office.

Mark did a double take on his way in and went up to Dino to ask, "What the fuck happened to you?"

"Fuckathon," Paul explained from the other side of his paper.

"Oh." Mark left it alone and went into his office.

When Millie saw Dino, she rushed over. "Are you all right?"

"Fuckathon," Paul snapped.

"What?"

Snowood threw down his paper and reached over for the dictionary and started fumbling through it. "See," he pointed at the open dictionary. "Fuckathon." Paul looked where his finger pointed and pretended to read aloud, "A term commonly used by policemen meaning 'to stay between a woman's legs all night' . . . cunnilingus . . . suckalingus . . . lickalingus . . . fuckalingus!"

When Paul finished shouting, Mark yelled from the confines of his office, "I just wanna know one thing. Who was the fuckee, Blondie or the Princess?"

Dino's response to the entire tirade was directed to Millie when he pointed to Snowood and asked her, "Did you ever notice when he gets mad, he loses his accent?"

LaStanza knew that murders were never solved while detectives sat in the office, but he also knew that knowledge was power and decided he would take time to learn everything he could about Harold Eugene Lemoni, alias Harry Lemon, alias Harry

248

Lee, alias Pus Face. From every conceivable source of information he traced Lemoni from his birth certificate through grade school, all the way to his present ownership of Club Morocco in the wonderful four-hundred block of Bourbon Street.

After exhausting all available police records from the Record Section and Intelligence, he secured whatever information the state had on Lemoni's driving record, record of automobile registrations, and liquor licenses. Then he secured Lemoni's records from the Louisiana Department of Employment Security, from the local electric company, from the gas company, from the telephone company, from the retail credit bureau. Then he started in on securing any information on anyone who had ever been arrested at the club, who had ever worked at the club, who ever had any contact with Club Morocco and the man known as Pus Face.

After, he sat back and made a plan.

"Why not a quiet evening?" Lizette proposed.

"Slow Dancin'?" Dino asked as they climbed into the Alfa.

"That would be nice."

So they went to Slow Dancin' on the last night before he started the evening watch once again and listened to soft music while dancing in subdued light. Embracing her on the dance floor, Dino ran his fingers slowly up and down her back. She was wearing a strapless, low-cut black dress. Dino was in his shirt sleeves, his coat tossed on a nearby chair. It was a mellow night, a warm night, a quiet night in which they drank enough to feel a glow inside but not enough to bring on a buzz.

On their way out, it was Dino who first noticed. He

stopped suddenly and pulled Lizette behind him as he stepped in front of a couple who were just entering Slow Dancin'.

Lizette recognized Karen Koski from her picture. She was tall and stunning with her light blue eyes and perfect face and long blonde hair. She wore an icy silver slinky dress and spiked silver high heels. Around her neck she wore a diamond necklace and earrings to match.

Koski's face was made up to perfection, so much he could not see where it had been injured. Placing a hand on her cheek, she looked down at Lizette for an instant before stating, "Dino, your little girl is lovely."

Lizette searched for an appropriate response but lost her voice completely when the man who was with Koski stepped around the tall blonde and stood close to Dino's face. The man had the harshest face Lizette had ever seen, a pockmarked face with a scowl on it and deep-set, piercing eyes.

Dino stared back into Harry Lemoni's eyes for a long time, making sure he was not the first to blink. He also made sure his face remained placid. Let the Mafioso scowl, LaStanza would show no emotion.

As the leering continued, Dino realized he was looking into eyes of pure evil. He searched those evil eyes and found what he was looking for. Lemoni was not even trying to hide it, did not seem even to care that Dino had discovered it. It was as though he was challenging the detective. Lemoni's eyes said, "Yeah. I did it. What are *you* going to do about it?"

Finally, Pus Face broke the stalemate with a snarling remark. "Yeah, your little girl is real pretty."

"Come on," Koski pulled at Lemoni, leading him into the club. Dino waited for the way to clear before he continued straight ahead, Lizette's arm tucked tightly around his arm, until they were outside.

She watched Dino look around as they walked, watched him keenly take in the surroundings like a bloodhound sniffing for whatever was there. What struck her was the smooth, easy way he moved, opening her door and locking her in before walking around to the driver's side.

He took a roundabout way back to Exposition Boulevard and only after checking several times in the rear view mirror did he make a swift turn onto Garfield to pull into the Louvier garage.

He seemed to ease up once he was inside. She led him to the kitchen and put on a pot of coffee, her stomach suddenly queasy. As she poured the water into the pot she told Dino, "That girl likes you."

"What?" Dino immediately recalled Mason's similar remark after leaving Koski's apartment the first time.

"A woman can tell," Lizette continued, her back still to Dino, "by the way another woman looks at a man."

Dino was not thinking about any blonde. He was not even thinking about Lizette. His mind was on the man with the acne scars. But when Lizette made her statement, he refocused his attention to her. When she turned to put the coffeepot on the stove, he asked, "By now, don't you realize nothing can come between us?"

Lizette nodded as she set her golden eyes on Dino, eyes that looked especially huge. "I know," she whispered. "I just wanted you to know that she likes you."

She watched his face become placid again as he stared out the kitchen window. His eyes finally moved from the window when she poured his coffee and placed it in front of him. He looked down at the cup momentarily, took a sip, then looked back at the window.

"Is there something out there?"

"No," he looked back at her and smiled.

Lizette felt a twinge inside when he smiled because he was confusing her with his changes. He smiled at her, but it was obvious that she was not the reason he smiled.

"So what is it?" she asked.

"My murders. I'm getting close. I can feel it."

Bourbon Street

Her name was Sharon Dufrene, and she was a Bourbon Street whore before she gave up the neon lights for the swamp. She lived in a house high above a sluggish bayou, elevated on pilings of cypress logs. The house, less than two hours from New Orleans, had never been painted. Its exterior was bleached to a dull gray by the persistent Louisiana sun. If Dino had not driven to the house himself, he would find it hard to believe there was any city within a thousand miles of the place.

Sharon was a small woman, a little on the heavy side, with reddish hair cut very short and a wide, hardened black face. As soon as she found out the man standing on her front porch was a policeman, she slammed her screen door in LaStanza's face and stormed back into her house. Dino waited at the door for a minute before removing his coat and sitting on a front porch bench. He found it peaceful on the bayou, a warm breeze easing its way across the flat land, an occasional snowy egret glided overhead, a black hawk circled in the distance.

A half hour after the woman slammed the door on Dino, her son came up the steps of the porch and did a double take upon seeing a man in a suit sitting on the bench before running inside. A few minutes later the boy came out with a slice of cantaloupe and sat next to the detective. The boy was six years old and said his name was Christopher. He asked Dino several questions about his notepad and pen and why the detective was wearing a suit before Sharon Dufrene came out and ran the boy back inside the house.

"What you want?" Sharon snapped at Dino.

During the interview Dino noticed Sharon's coarse hands and worn dress, much like Christopher's tattered jeans. You don't make much on the swamp.

When the interview was finished, Sharon had one question for LaStanza. "How did you find me?"

He almost told her the truth, that he got lucky in finding her, but caught himself. He rose, picked up his coat, and looked down at Sharon before answering in a cocky voice, "I'm a detective."

And that was how he left her, as a cocky detective. After all, if he found her, they could find her. And if they did, he left them something to wonder about.

On his way back to New Orleans, Dino thought about Christopher and his torn jeans and about Sondra's boy sleeping on Soraparu Street. Lizette said he had the makings of a fine liberal. He wondered about that but soon drove thoughts of the boys from his mind. He had more important things to think about.

"The Coliseum victim used to work at Club Morocco," he told Mark when he returned to the office that afternoon.

"So?" Snowood responded, even though he was not included in the conversation up to that point.

"So, now I've connected Lemoni to the Coliseum victim as well as the Gargoyle."

"So what?" Paul countered.

Mark cut in, "Don't you know better than to argue with him?"

Dino knew better but could not help himself. He shrugged and continued explaining to his sergeant, "I found an ex-Bourbon Street whore today who remembered Sondra Joseph used to work out of the Club Morocco. Sondra and Harry Lemoni were pretty tight a couple years ago, before Harry ran her off."

"Ex-prostitute?" Paul snorted, "no such animal!"

Dino paid no attention to his partner. "Her name is Sharon Dufrene, and she used to work at Morocco's." He began to fix himself a cup of coffee. "She wouldn't even talk to me until I told her about Coliseum Square. Then she opened up."

"Honor among whores, what's the world coming to?" Paul declared.

"That's good," Mark said. "You're getting closer."

"So did Custer," Paul added.

Club Morocco was a typical sack-a-roaches dive in the four-hundred block of Bourbon Street. It was a narrow strip joint sandwiched between a t-shirt shop and a fast food stand that sold corn dogs, egg rolls, and burritos from an open window. Morocco's facade was adorned with a huge neon sign that read, *Topless and Bottomless Girls*. A smaller sign above the front doorway identified the place as Club Morocco. There was no door because the club never closed.

Morocco's was a tired place, beat up and worn out, kept perpetually in the dark by walls painted black. It had a long bar on one side with a dance floor slightly higher than the bar. There was a curtained doorway at the rear of the dance floor where the dancers emerged to gyrate and expose the pasties over their nipples and the g-strings over their crotches. On Bourbon Street, topless and bottomless meant pasties and g-strings. Expose a nipple or one pubic hair and it was Central Lockup time.

Club Morocco, keeping faithful to its North African motif, dressed its strippers as belly dancers and put a fez on its bartender's head. Above the rear bathroom was a crude drawing of a camel. When Dino first entered the place and took a walk around, not daring to sit or touch anything, he thought the camel was a dog. Snowood, during his subsequent walk through, corrected his partner. "It's a camel. It's got two fuckin' humps."

For the remainder of the evening's surveillance, Dino and Paul positioned themselves across the street from the club, nursing one beer apiece, waiting for Pus Face.

Dino passed the time watching the obnoxious barker who stood outside Morocco's front doorway, screaming at passersby, hooting and howling, attempting to entice any unfortunate creature to venture inside. The barker had long curly hair of indescribable color somewhere between brown and green, and a reddish-pink complexion. He weighed about three hundred pounds and wore a blue paisley shirt and striped orange pants. What amazed Dino was how many people actually went in Morocco's.

When Pus Face had not shown up by midnight, Paul had enough. "Let's go see if he's at Minky's."

Dino agreed, and by twelve-thirty they were

knocking on Karen Koski's door. She opened it dressed in a pair of man's pajamas, frowning at Dino until she saw Paul. Then she smiled weakly. She opened the door wider and said listlessly, with a look of resignation on her face, "Come on in, why don't you?"

Dino stepped into the living room and looked around. "So, where's Pus Face?" he asked when Koski stepped up behind him.

"How would I know?"

He turned and examined her face. "Looks much better," he said as he carefully reached up to touch it. There was only a hint of discoloration left, easily covered by makeup. It was then he noticed she was wearing no makeup. She didn't need much.

She withdrew a step before he could touch her and moved to the sofa to flop down between the two standing detectives.

"What's the matter?" Dino asked. "You haven't recovered sufficiently from your fuck-me, slap-me-around routine with Harry?"

"You don't know what the fuck you're talking about," she argued. "Harry doesn't fuck!" She moved her eyes from Dino to Paul and asked, "Want a beer?"

"Sure."

"Can you get it?" she pointed to her kitchen. "I'm a little tired."

"Sure," Paul obliged. "Can I get you anything?"

Koski nodded. "A Dr. Pepper."

When Paul returned, Dino said, "That's all right. I didn't want anything anyway."

"Figured the little lady's hospitality didn't extend to you," Paul smiled, "just like the coffee at Jimson's house, remember?"

Dino waited for Koski to look back at him and then

asked, "Why doesn't Harry fuck?"

She stared back at him for a long time as her frosty blue eyes searched his. "Harry," she said softly, "doesn't like women. And he likes men even less." Her face became expressionless as she seemed to look beyond the detectives, beyond her living room. "Sex is degrading to Harry. He sees it all the time, with the whores at Morocco's and the weak, sniveling men." She took a sip of Dr. Pepper, put the bottle down on her coffee table, and moved to the wet bar at the far end of the living room. "I need something stronger." She took out a bottle of bourbon, looked back at Dino, and asked, "You thirsty?"

"Got any Scotch?"

She fixed him a Scotch and herself a bourbon and told Paul to help himself as she sat back on the couch. After a swig of her drink she pulled back her hair and continued. "So, you wanna know about Harry? Okay, I'll tell you. He's mean, real mean." Koski did not seem like the kind of girl who scared easily, but there was fear in her voice when she spoke. "You know, he's never even tried to screw me."

"Because of Baddie," Dino injected.

Her eyes hardened, "You really are a Sicilian bastard, aren't you?"

Dino did not answer and kept every expression from his face.

When she did not get a reply, she went on, "As far as I know, Harry's never screwed anyone."

"Is he fruit?" Paul asked from somewhere to Dino's right.

Koski shook her head no. "He's just different."

There was more to it. Dino waited for her to continue, hoping she would elaborate, but when she did not he didn't push it. He made a mental note and planned to come back to it when he could.

When Koski finished her drink, she fixed herself another and began to perk up. She went back to her sofa, licked the rim of her cocktail glass, and looked over at Paul. "Ole Harry's not anything like me. I love to fuck. I love to feel a man inside me because right before he comes, he tenses up and grabs hard and then explodes."

Paul was beginning to breathe heavily. Dino could hear him and had to fight to keep from smiling. Karen was already smiling. She got up again and fixed herself another drink.

"I'll take one of them bourbons, little lady," Snowood huffed.

Koski reached the bar and flipped on her stereo, and when Boz Scaggs came on, she started dancing slowly. "You know what Harry says about organized crime?"

"No." It was Dino who answered.

"He can't understand the fuss," Koski giggled. "Law enforcement's organized, isn't it? Religion's organized? Why not crime?" She danced past Dino with a drink in each hand and added, "Organized crime keeps the riffraff out."

The opportunity never came back that night for Dino to find out what Karen held back earlier, about Harry and sex. She continued to drink and talk about everything from football to music to movies, but no more about Harry, until the detectives were leaving.

As Dino stepped out of her apartment, Koski added, "You know, you've got one glaring weakness in Harry's book."

"And what's that?"

"Your girl."

There was something familiar about Harry Lemoni. Maybe it was just a memory deep within the folds of LaStanza's mind, but there was something familiar. Maybe it was a memory of the sandy hills of Sicily, where the Lemonis and Badalamentes of the world preyed upon the LaStanzas and the other black dago peasants. Or maybe what Dino saw in Lemoni was something familiar because the LaStanzas came from the same clay. There was something familiar about Lemoni.

"I'll be starting classes soon," Lizette told him. He did not seem to hear her. He had been preoccupied all evening, through dinner and especially through the movie. Several times when she looked at him in the dark theater, he was not paying attention to the screen at all.

In a louder voice, she repeated, "I'll be starting classes soon," and watched his eyes move from her kitchen window to her.

"Yeah?" he asked as he took a sip of coffee. "And we'll be starting the evening watch soon, too."

"How can you tell the difference? You're working days and nights now."

At least he seemed to recognize pain in her voice as his eyes lost their hypnotic look and focused on her with that little-boy look of his. "I know," he whispered in apology.

As he looked at her, he acted as if he was seeing her for the first time that night. "Are you all right?"

"No," Lizette answered. "Besides the fact that you have not been here all evening, I'm afraid."

"Of what?"

"What do you think?" she answered quickly, her voice rising with emotion. "This LCN thing. It's been with us all night, sitting on the other side of you in the show. Don't tell me that you weren't thinking of it."

Dino looked down guiltily.

It was Lizette's turn to look out the kitchen window. "I'm not a scaredy-cat," she explained, "but I have an ominous feeling about this LCN." Her lips began to quiver as she added, "It's the exact same feeling I had when they told me about Lynette."

Dino waited a moment before telling her, "I know this may not help. But I have a feeling too, inside, a gut feeling. I'm gonna win."

"I've got a message for you from my wife," Paul told his partner the following morning on their way to the office.

"Yeah?"

"Yeah. She says she wants me to get a divorce if we continue like this." He paused a moment to spit out the window. "The divorce will be between you and me, pardner. She says you're seeing too much of me lately."

"Yeah?"

"Yeah," Paul spat again and looked at Dino. "So what are we gonna do today?"

"I'm thinking of how we could pick up ol' Pus Face and fuck with him a little bit."

"Sounds reasonable to me."

A few blocks later, Paul had an idea, "Why don't we just pull him over on some bullshit traffic offense and bring him to the bureau?"

It wasn't until Dino had half finished his first cup, sitting at his desk, that he had the brainstorm of the day. "Listen up," he told his partner, who responded by peeking over his sports section.

"Since Lemoni lives above Club Morocco, how

much you wanna bet he's got a shitload of parking tickets on that nice pretty Seville of his?" Dino need not elaborate. The French Quarter had more "No Parking" signs than the rest of the city combined.

"Okay, so his car's got parking tickets," Paul agreed after Dino checked with the Parking Bureau at City Hall and discovered the Seville had fifty-seven outstanding tickets.

"What're you gonna do?"

Dino picked up a blank arrest warrant and began to fill it out. "I'm cutting a warrant for him."

"For parking tickets?"

"Why the fuck not?"

When the duty judge started reading the warrant, he stopped immediately and asked, "I thought you were from Homicide."

"I am," LaStanza assured him.

The judge went back to reading and had no further comment until after he signed it. He handed it back and said, "This man looks like a multiple offender."

Dino nodded in agreement.

"We can't have people ignoring our parking regulations, now, can we?" the judge added as the detectives departed.

"At least he signed it," Dino said.

Paul was rubbing his hands together in anticipation. "Boy, is this gonna piss off ol' Pus Face!"

Dino was itching to search the Seville. They looked for it, but when they could not find it, he realized it was for the better. With his luck the twenty-two would be inside and any good lawyer, especially Rosenberg, would get it thrown out. The same went for breaking into Lemoni's apartment above Club Morocco. Dino itched but knew better.

262

They finally found Lemoni strolling down Bourbon Street at three in the afternoon. Paul moved across the street as he approached. Dino turned his back and waited for him to pass. As soon as he did, LaStanza grabbed him from behind and shoved him hard against the wall of a Chinese restaurant. "Police!" Dino yelled as he quickly helped Lemoni assume the arrest/search position by kicking Harry's legs apart. He yanked Harry's hands back and cuffed them before searching ol' Pus Face. Harry had no weapon.

Turning the ugly face around, Dino smiled. "Greetings, Pus Face. Needless to say, you're under arrest!"

Snowood came rushing over with, "Goddam, you're too fast." When a crowd started to gather, Country Ass turned on them. "All right. All right! The show's over!"

They took Lemoni straight in and went through their usual routine of letting him sit alone in an interview room for a half hour, still cuffed, in an uncomfortable hardwood folding chair.

When LaStanza stepped into the room with a fresh cup of coffee, Lemoni glared at him. "Tut, tut," Dino said, "now don't be like that Harry. I don't know what I'll do if you don't like me anymore."

"Just take these cuffs off," Lemoni growled.

Dino put his coffee on the table, "Just what I was going to do." He moved behind him as Harry stood up defiantly. "Now Harry, you better be good, because," he suddenly lowered his voice into Harry's ear, "you may think you're tough, but believe me, you'll lose." And with that he removed the handcuffs and returned to the front of the table to sit across from the seething man with the pus face.

"Sit down, Harry. I already know how tough you are."

When Lemoni finally sat, he continued, "Beat up any women lately? Beside Karen Koski?"

Harry would not answer. He continued to use his eyes as the only means of defiance available. Dino smiled again. The one-sided conversation continued for over an hour. The detective jabbed, and Lemoni would not move except to blink his mean eyes occasionally.

"This is not getting us anywhere," LaStanza finally sighed as he took out an arrest report and began filling it out. He asked Harry the standard questions, such as name and date of birth, but Harry refused to answer, so the detective answered aloud for him.

"Scars, marks, or tattoos?"

"Pus Face," Dino answered himself with a broad smile. Lemoni remained stoic, so Dino continued. When he got to the part where the charges were listed, he asked, "Aren't you even interested in the charges against you?" Lemoni said nothing.

"Suit yourself."

He knew there was no way Lemoni was going to crack, but he could not help relishing the way he was messing with Harry. He knew, deep down, that Lemoni was livid at the ease in which LaStanza could mess with him. The more old Pus Face hid his anger, the better Dino liked it. And Lemoni kept it up all the way to Central Lockup, even while being printed and mugged.

He watched Lemoni go through the booking process as Paul horsed around with the booking officers. And finally, after all his trouble, he saw something that made it doubly worthwhile. Dino caught Lemoni peeking at the arrest register, at his charge, and watched Harry's cheeks begin to quiver in rage.

"That's right, Harry. *Parking*. You've just been arrested for *parking!*" Dino announced as every booking officer and even some of the men in the holding cell began to laugh. Harry Lemoni's cheeks continued to tremble.

On their way out of Central Lockup, the detectives almost ran into Rosenberg himself. As soon as the counselor recognized them, he began to berate LaStanza, accusing Dino of holding his client incommunicado. "I've been trying to locate my client for two hours."

Dino continued to walk, which forced Rosenberg to follow outside. "Now you listen to me, detective!" the lawyer shouted. "I'm an officer of the court. . . ."

Dino continued to walk away, back around the corner toward the Detective Bureau. Rosenberg screamed after him, "You hold on one minute. You can't ignore me! I'm going to report you to Internal Affairs this time!"

He could just picture it, Rosenberg complaining to IAD that Detective LaStanza ignored him.

"What a fuckin' toad," was Snowood's only remark as they rounded the corner.

"She'll never be the same again," explained the doctor to the three detectives who had been waiting for two hours outside the operating room at Charity. Mark and Paul were standing, facing the doctor, while Dino was seated in a chair, staring down at his feet.

"Whoever did this to her knew what he was doing," the doctor continued as he pulled off his long plastic gloves, his eyes meeting LaStanza's for the first time when Dino looked over. "He messed up her face badly." The doctor turned to leave, hesitated and asked, "Does she have any family?"

"We don't know," Mark answered as he took the seat next to Dino.

"You don't look so hot," he told Dino.

"He shouldn't," Paul shouted, "it's his fault!"

Dino looked up at his partner's angry eyes and had to nod in agreement, which only caused Paul to kick at the floor and snort, "Are you satisfied?"

"Hold it!" Mark yelled back as he rose.

"Don't get in my face," Paul warned him. "You're as stupid as that other wop." He pointed at LaStanza.

Dino stood up and grabbed Mark's arm as the sergeant's hands clenched. Paul stood his ground in front of both men, seething in fury. "You don't get it, do you?" Pointing to the closed door of the operating room, he screamed, "That could be the Princess in there! You dumb fuckin' wop!"

Dino was too tired to argue. Besides, Paul was right. He said nothing, but just sat back down and waited until they rolled Karen Koski into a ward and waited even longer until the sheriff's office sent a deputy to guard this witness who was now, belatedly, under protective custody.

"Nobody," Detective LaStanza told the guard, "*nobody* comes near her except one of us three."

The guard was almost a foot taller than Dino, with a face blacker than his sheriff's uniform. "I know my job," the irritated guard said. "And so do the guys who relieve me."

It was four o'clock in the morning. The three detectives went straight to the office. Dino cut a warrant for Harold Eugene Lemoni for the attempted

266

murder of Karen Koski. All three knew that Koski would not follow up on the charges, but they had to do something. The motherfucker could beat the rap but he wouldn't beat the ride.

"The judge was not amused. One minute he's a parking violator, and the next he's an attempt murderer," Dino explained to Lizette later that morning. "So now we have an A.P.B. out for him, and he could be anywhere."

She had never seen him look worse. His shoulders drooped, his moustache looked haggard and tired. His reddish eyes avoided her stare as he explained what happened to Karen Koski.

"Well, isn't that what you were looking for?" she heard herself asking in a voice with an edge to it.

"Huh?"

"Your actions are getting reactions, aren't they?"

Dino admitted it with a nod, a hint of sadness creeping into his expression. "I guess so." His voice rasped from fatigue so he cleared his throat and took a long gulp of coffee. But he did not look back at her. Instead he just stared into his cup.

"I always thought you were different. But you're as callous as your partners."

Her statement seemed to have an immediate effect on him. The redness in his eyes deepened for a moment. Those wide greens looked at her, but slowly the redness went away completely, replaced in a blink with a sharpness, a look that went right through her.

He went back to his coffee and his voice was still husky. "Is there anything else?"

She shook her head no.

Then his voice became faint again, "You know what Paul said? He said it could have been you."

Lizette promised to stay inside and let no one in if Dino would catch some sleep at her house. It took him awhile to fall asleep. He was worried about Lizette, but that did not keep him from sleeping. It was another thought, a cold thought, a ruthless, crystalline Sicilian thought that crept from the depths of his subconscious and told him that she was right. He had forced Lemoni to react. He had hit the right nerve, found the weak link and preyed upon it.

What bothered Dino was, instead of thinking of ways to protect Lizette, his mind was thinking of ways to get Lemoni. "After all," he reasoned, "wasn't that the same thing?"

If Lemoni was out of control, then he was more likely to make a mistake and LaStanza would be waiting. But would it be in time?

After a short nap, Dino showered and ate, feeling a little better. He waited until Mr. Louvier came home before leaving and told Lizette he would call her later.

"I'll be here," she said.

But before he could leave, Mason came on the radio and asked Dino to call him in the office.

"I got a message for you," Mason told him on the phone, "from Harry Lemoni."

"Go ahead." Dino tried to keep his face calm as Lizette watched.

"He says he's got Rawanda. Does that mean anything to you?"

There was no hiding it on his face, no matter how

268

hard he tried. He had underestimated Lemoni again.

"That's my witness from Burke Playground."

"I see," Mason said. "I'll meet you at Burke."

"What is it?" Lizette asked when Dino hung up.

"Remember the little girl from Burke Play-ground?"

Lizette nodded cautiously.

"He's got her."

According to eyewitnesses, Harry Lemoni snatched Rawanda Jones from Burke Playground right in front of ten screaming children, threw her in the trunk of his Seville, and drove away. When Mason arrived with filler photographs, Dino composed a photographic lineup and showed the witnesses one at a time. Nine of the ten witnesses picked out the pockmarked face of Harry Lemoni as the man who'd kidnapped Rawanda Jones.

Upon signing the warrant for aggravated kidnapping, the duty judge asked, "What's next, murder one?"

Dino led the search, racing across town, sending patrol cars to check addresses and hunches through the afternoon and evening, and well into the night. But Lemoni was nowhere to be found, and the longer it took, the more discouraged Dino became.

Since Snowood was still not talking to his partner, Mark sent him to Exposition Boulevard, to watch over the Louvier house. Mark himself rode with LaStanza, bouncing across the city in the overheated Chevy.

Just before dawn, Mason called everyone together and explained the situation, "Okay. I just got off the phone with the chief. There will be two uniformed men from the second district at the Louvier's from now on, and they're increasing the watch over the broad at Charity." Dino and Mark were leaning against the fender of his tired Chevrolet. "Still nothing on Lemoni yet," Mason continued between puffs of smoke. "We've got the whole city looking for him."

He turned to LaStanza. "What we all need now is rest, so go home, get some sleep, and check in later."

Before going home, Dino went by Exposition Boulevard and spoke a few minutes with the two half-bored uniformed men sitting on Garfield next to the Louvier's before knocking on Lizette's door.

Dino was surprised when Carolyn Snowood answered the door and let him in. "She came over to talk," Lizette explained as she reached over and brushed a strand of Dino's hair from in front of his eyes. "You look terrible," she told him.

"I feel terrible." He looked over at Paul's wife as she sat on a kitchen stool. When Carolyn noticed, she stuck her tongue out at him and wrinkled her nose.

"What are you girls talking about?"

"What do you think?" Lizette answered with a question. "She's explaining what it's like to be a police widow, even though her husband's still alive."

Dino got a few hours' sleep before the phone rang. "Karen Koski wants to talk to you." It was Mason. "I'll come if you want."

"No, I'll get Snowood."

When Paul answered his phone, sounding as groggy as LaStanza, all he had to say was, "Hey, Minky wants to talk to us."

Karen Koski's face was completely bandaged except for a long slit where her mouth should have been and an opening for her right eye. The skin around her right eye was blue. She was also in traction, with both arms bandaged and her left leg in a cast.

She blinked at Dino in recognition when he leaned over her. "I've brought your number-one fan," he told her, nodding back at Paul. "He's come to peek up your gown."

She blinked twice before trying to speak in a shaky voice. "I . . . I got . . . the gun." She shivered from obvious pain and repeated, "I . . . got . . . gun. The one . . . Harry . . . used . . . on Jimson."

Dino had already started the tape recorder. "Where is it?"

"Safety deposit box . . . bank." She was in considerable pain and paused to catch her breath before continuing. "He . . . told me . . . he killed . . . Jimson . . . whore."

"Why?" Dino asked, "Why did he kill them?"

She paused as if to regain her strength. Dino hesitated a moment before asking again, "Why? What is it about Harry and sex?"

Koski whispered in response, "Harry . . . and Gina. Harry . . . Gina."

"Harry and Gina?" Dino repeated.

Karen nodded.

"Harry was fucking Mrs. Gargoyle?" Paul asked from over Dino's shoulder.

Karen shook her head no. "Gina . . . no . . . Harry wants . . . but Gina . . . no." Karen gulped and continued, "Jimson . . . weak . . . fuck around . . . Harry crazy . . . for Gina."

"He did it for Gina? Because Jimson screwed around?"

Koski nodded, "Harry . . . psycho."

271

"I know," Dino agreed. "Does Gina know?"

"No . . . Gina . . . Harry always crazy . . . for Gina . . . psycho!"

"What about Baddie?"

"Harry . . . out of . . . control. Baddie . . . looking for him."

"So are we," Dino told her as he gently touched her shoulder. "Do you know where he is?"

Karen shook her head no.

Dino leaned closer as Karen told him which bank and where the key to her safety deposit box was hidden. Paul was already on the phone with Mason, getting a warrant prepared for the safety deposit box. "All we need is the box to be in his name and we'll lose the gun," Paul explained to LaStanza when he asked why the warrant.

"We're gonna need the crime lab," Dino reminded his partner, who nodded in agreement.

Dino leaned close to Karen's ear and whispered, "I'm gonna get him. I'm gonna get that motherfucker!"

Karen nodded. *"Kill him."*

Mason finished the search warrant for Karen Koski's safety deposit box while Dino cut search warrants for Lemoni's apartment and car and arrest warrants for Lemoni for the first-degree murders of Thomas Jimson and Lutisha Joseph.

When LaStanza showed the new warrants to the duty judge, the judge said, "Didn't I call it? Murder one!"

The gun was waiting for the detectives, just as Koski had said. Dino watched the crime lab technician photograph the box before opening it and photograph the gun before dusting it for prints, securing two partial latents before taking the gun directly to the lab.

While Fat Frank Hammond was checking the test-fired pellets against the projectiles from the Gargoyle and Coliseum, Dino looked at the gun. It was a blue steel Colt Buntline, twenty-two magnum revolver with a six-inch barrel.

It took Frank less than ten minutes to match up the projectiles from the Buntline and the murders. "It's the gun, all right." He was so proud of himself, he broke open a fresh moon pie.

Only one of the partial prints taken from the Buntline could be read, but there wasn't enough of it to identify anyone positively. "It's probably Lemoni's," explained the fingerprint expert, "only there aren't enough lines and grooves for this to stand up in court."

"What are the chances it isn't Lemoni?" Dino asked.

"A million to one it's him. I think he's your man. I just can't be absolutely certain about it."

On their way back to the homicide office, Paul told his partner, "I gotta hand it to you, boy, you solved it."

Dino nodded in acknowledgment.

"I don't think it was pretty," he continued, "but you solved it."

"Don't sugar-coat it," LaStanza sparred, "just tell it like it is."

"Well," Snowood reached for a fresh dip, "just remember, Custer took lots of casualties too."

The search of Lemoni's apartment produced no results, yet Dino took his time looking through Harry's things, as if he could glean something from

273

the odds and ends of Harry Lemoni's life. Mason accompanied him on the search of the apartment above Club Morocco. During the search he asked Dino, "You know what a sociopath is?"

"I think so," Dino answered as he started in on Harry's dresser drawers.

"It's an incurable mental disorder," Mason explained as he put out his cigarette on Lemoni's nightstand. "The afflicted consider themselves blessed with a superior gift, rather than afflicted with a diseased mind." He lit up another cigarette before continuing. "A sociopath cannot change, cannot be reformed, because he's got no conscience. He's gotta be stopped, he'll never stop himself."

"And I'm just the one to do it!"

"I guess congratulations are in order," Millie told Dino when she walked into the office first thing in the morning and found him still at his desk. She took a second look and asked, "What are you doing, trying to work yourself to death?"

"No."

"Look at you—you look terrible."

"I know. Something came up," he explained.

"Where's your partner?" she asked as she sat down in Snowood's chair.

"I hope he's asleep. He needs it."

"Well, can I help you with anything?"

"No . . . but thanks for asking." He was going over his notes again, trying to get a lead, a hint, anything that would tell him where Lemoni could be.

"You know you don't have to do all this alone," Millie added as she rose, "even if you are a hotshot." When he looked up at her she turned quickly and started to walk away.

"Who says I'm a hotshot?"

She stopped and her shoulders slumped, but she did not turn around. "Some of the fellas have been wondering about you lately, that you're a hotshot sometimes."

"Since when am I a topic of conversation around here?"

She turned back to face him, "Since the Slasher."

"I was lucky with the Slasher."

"Mason says you make your own luck. But even he's worried you're gonna burn out."

Dino could not imagine Mason being worried about anything.

"Some of them were waiting for you to fall on your ass on this one," she told him, "but I guess you're just too good."

"You're only as good as your last case, huh?" he asked.

"You know it," Millie agreed. "First the Slasher, and now the Twenty-Two Killer. At least you got a good case in your past."

When she turned to leave, he stopped her. "Actually, there is something you can help me with."

"What?"

"I need somebody to go back to Burke Playground to talk to the little black girl's family."

"I'd be happy to."

Dino waited until he had gotten a little sleep before returning to the wedding-cake house. The door was answered by a tall, thin man in a black suit. He had an unfamiliar face and was wearing gangster glasses. The man said nothing as he stared at LaStanza from behind his shades.

Dino dug out his credentials and held them in front of the man's eyes. "I want to speak to Mrs. Jimson."

The tall man nodded and stepped back to allow Frank Porta to move into the doorway, like an iceberg in a black suit. Porta asked, "What do you want?"

"Hello Frank," Dino sighed, "just tell Mrs. Jimson I'm here."

They made him wait outside for five minutes before letting him in. He used the time to go over the questions once more in his mind.

Frank led him into the living room, where Gina was waiting in her easy chair. Her face was pale, her hair drawn straight back in a loose ponytail that made her look older. She wore no makeup.

"What is it?" she asked before he even sat down. There'd been a remarkable change in her since their last meeting. Gone was the smiling face, the youthful face that had gone to Holy Rosary School just a few years before Dino. Gone was the easiness that had played out between the two.

Dino hesitated, waiting for Porta to leave, but when Frank pulled up a chair, he turned back to Gina and asked, "Do you know where Harry Lemoni is?"

"No," she answered quickly, "why should I?"

"He was here last time I came by. He isn't taking care of you anymore?"

"No. Why do you ask?"

"When was the last time you saw him?"

"The day you were here." Gina's eyes searched LaStanza's, as if she could learn something from staring into them. But he knew his eyes were giving nothing away.

"Have you ever seen this man before?" he asked as

276

he handed her the picture of the Bogue Falaya victim, paying close attention to her reaction. She had to know who he was. After all, Harry did it for her.

She examined the photo and shook her head. "No, I . . ." she looked up suddenly, "is this man *dead?*" dropping the picture as if it was on fire.

"Oh yes, I should have warned you," Dino said coolly.

She was staring at him with a look she must have inherited from her father, because her eyes were suddenly lifeless, unmoving, unyielding in their cast.

"Have you heard from Harry lately?"

"No," Gina's lips began to shake. "What is going on? Everybody's asking me about Harry." She shot a quick look at Porta's stone face before pleading with Dino, "What is it?"

"Then you don't know?" Dino stared back at her coldly. He had to know if she was telling the truth.

"No," Gina was now crying. She could be acting, but there was no way he could be sure.

"Well, I might as well tell you. It'll be all over TV this evening." He watched as her crying subsided somewhat.

"Harry's wanted," Dino paused to emphasize the rest, "for murder."

"*No.*" Gina began to cry again.

"For the murder of a prostitute, for the kidnapping of a little girl, and for the murder of your husband."

Gina stopped crying immediately and shrieked, "No. No! That's impossible!"

Dino nodded. "Harry killed him."

Her tears came down in a stream. Dino waited quietly. He was still holding some of it back and wondered what her reaction would be when he told her why Harry did it. He wondered if she already knew.

277

He never got the chance to ask. As soon as she regained some limited control of herself, she sobbed at him, "Out! Get out!"

Porta rose and moved over to escort the detective out. Dino picked up the picture and left quietly. When Porta sneered at him on his way out, Dino could not resist asking, "Tell me Franco, which one's better, the blonde or the redhead?"

Dino made a quick stop on North Bernadotte Street to drop off a picture of Harry Lemoni with his father. He waited until they were outside to explain.

"Just let him show his ugly face around here," the captain grumbled, "I'll save you a lotta trouble."

"Okay, just don't let Mom go anywhere alone until this is over."

"You just take care of yourself. I'll take care of your Mom and me."

"Good."

Unless Gina Jimson was the best actress he had ever seen, Dino owed her one hell of an apology. But he was still not sure. She was in shock, all right, but he could not tell if it was from the pain of discovery or from the complicity of guilt or guilt by omission.

The layers were too thick to see through. Nevertheless she denied knowing the Bogue Falaya victim, and without her, that part of the case remained hidden in a deep fog. But Dino had something else to think about at the moment: there was a little girl in the grasp of a psychopath.

"Can I use the phone?" he asked Lizette as soon as

278

he entered.

"Of course."

He did not even kiss her as he went directly to the kitchen and dialed a number. "Let me talk to Jones," he said a moment later.

"Fel? Dino. You busy? Well, you might wanna drop by the Jimson house. The place is filthy with Mafiosi." He paused a second and ended the conversation with, "You're welcome."

Lizette was watching him. He still looked tired, but a different tired, a wilted tired. His face looked drawn. When she tried asking him about it, he answered in an exhausted voice, "How can I rest? I've tried . . . I can't."

"How about the easy chair?" she asked. When he hesitated, she persisted, "Come on, let's snuggle."

In ten minutes he was asleep, and it felt good to lie there with him in the coolness of the dark library. She too fell asleep after a while, but when she woke and he remained asleep, she did not move, content to stay there with him, as if by holding him she could make him rest.

Paul's wife was right, she thought. If you concentrated on the positive, then the negative things had a way of receding into the background. That was the way Lizette was thinking. But it was not easy.

Dino continued to sleep even after Lizette got up. It was already getting dark outside. She looked out a side window at the patrol car parked on Garfield. One of the policemen was reading a paperback while the other was standing on Exposition Boulevard, stretching and yawning.

With her brother away at camp and her mother busy with one of her garden clubs and her father working late again, she had the house to herself. Lizette liked it that way. She especially enjoyed the kitchen when the maid was not around. She fixed fresh coffee for the policemen outside and cut each a large piece of pecan pie and took it out to them. The officer in the car had red hair and looked younger than Lizette. "So you're the lady we're guarding, huh?"

"I guess I am."

"Isn't that LaStanza's unit?" asked the other officer, who stepped back for his coffee and pie.

"It sure is. He's inside, trying to sleep."

They thanked her politely, but seemed aloof. The redheaded one looked especially nervous as his eyes darted around them between bites. As Lizette turned to leave, she noticed a photo of the harsh face from Slow Dancin' pinned to the visor inside the police car.

She busied herself inside the kitchen, preparing supper and trying to get her mind off the fact that armed men were outside to protect her from a man who looked like a Frankenstein nightmare. She was putting bread in the oven when Dino came in.

"I can't believe I slept that long."

"You needed it."

They had a quiet supper, but Lizette ate little. The ominous feeling returned in the middle of their meal. It was a feeling of foreboding. Dino did not seem to notice as he talked about the case. He was telling her everything, as he had promised. He was telling her his theory of how to end the case.

"Even an immovable object has to yield to persistent pressure," he explained, "eventually."

"I see."

"We've caused a ripple effect here," Dino said. "I just hope it works."

"It may not?"

"If I were really smart, I'd know. But all I got going

280

for me is persistence, and that's just another name for pigheadedness."

Lizette thought about the men outside, wondering if they would be following her to class when she started.

Dino waited until Mr. Louvier came home before leaving. He kissed her good-bye and started to leave without another word. Only he hesitated, turned, and grabbed her. He hugged her for a long time before whispering in her ear, "You didn't eat much." He did notice. "Are you all right?"

"As soon as all this is over, I'll be fine."

Dino did not respond, but continued to hold her.

"I start classes day after tomorrow," she whispered.

"I know."

"Will I have a police escort?"

"I don't know. Maybe I'll go with you."

"I'd like that."

"I love you," he told her. "I really do." And then he kissed her.

Later that evening, while Dino was at his desk, Harry Lemoni called. There was no mistaking the voice that growled, "Hello, cocksucker."

"Hello," Dino answered.

"Recognize your name, huh?" Lemoni's infantile remark had no effect on LaStanza, but the tone of Harry's voice made his breath hard in coming.

"So, cocksucker," Lemoni continued, "If you want the black girl, she's at the Bonnabel boat launch. She's in a phone company van. You can't miss her!" Lemoni began to laugh a guttural, satanic laugh and hung up.

*   *   *

Rawanda Jones would never be ten years old because she'd once met and spoke to a detective named LaStanza. That was how Dino saw it. That was what he was thinking about as Paul Snowood, blue light and siren blaring, swerved into Jefferson Parish, taking the Bonnabel exit off Interstate 10 and then heading north toward the lake. He already knew what they would find.

The Bonnabel boat launch was a public launch that was closed at night. There were no lights at the launch; it caused the lake to seem blacker than usual. Even the city disappeared once the police car crossed over the high levee to crawl along the gravel parking lot.

When the detectives arrived, two marked sheriff's units were already there, along with a Jefferson Parish homicide team and their crime lab technicians. They were standing at the rear of a telephone company van. Its back panel doors were open.

"Which one of you is LaStanza?" asked a husky black detective whose shield dangled from his suit coat pocket.

"I'm LaStanza."

"I'm Allen Renard."

He shook Dino's hand firmly, then stepped out of the way for LaStanza to proceed to the van. Snowood remained behind with Detective Renard. Immediately Paul began to give Renard the details.

As soon as he saw the crumpled body, he sagged. Lemoni had been sloppy. There were two large-caliber wounds in Rawanda's forehead and plenty of blood. The lab technician started talking about entry and exit wounds, but LaStanza tuned him out.

Rawanda's hair was still braided, as it had been the day he met her. Her thin yellow dress had raggedy areas where the hem had worn down. Her panties had holes in them. One of her socks was white and the other pink. Her shoes were nearly worn through.

When the other detectives moved up behind Dino, someone was explaining how the telephone van had been reported stolen that morning.

When the meat wagon arrived and the coroner's men began unfolding the black body bag, Dino reached in and scooped Rawanda into his arms. He turned and waited until the bag was ready and then gently placed her into it.

Audubon Park

The stainless steel, two-and-a-half-inch .357 Magnum, usually worn in an ankle holster, was now strapped to LaStanza's right hip. He replaced the .38-caliber rounds with new semi-jacketed hollow-point .357 magnums, filling all four of his speed loaders with the same ammunition. Fuck regulations and fuck Harold Lemoni!

As Dino sat on a stool just inside the open doorway of the Hot Flash Bar, across Bourbon Street from Club Morocco, his eyes remained fixed on the sunny facade of Morocco's.

"Hey, Super Wop," Fel Jones called out from his own stool to the right of LaStanza, "if the windows start blowing up in our faces, I'm killing somebody this time."

Dino nodded, but his gaze never left Morocco's.

"I don't give a fuck if they got fifteen cops out there shooting," Fel continued, "I'm gonna shoot somebody."

Dino was still mute, his gaze moving up and down Bourbon Street, as it had all morning. He heard Fel but said nothing.

"You think those guys on the roofs can shoot?"

Faced with a direct question, Dino responded, "They're SWAT. They better know how." For a moment, he thought about the police snipers on either side of Bourbon Street. He hoped the sharp-shooters were well hidden. The chances of Lemoni just strolling in were slim, but if he spotted one of those snipers, he was gone. Harry was insane, not stupid.

"Talk to me, Super Wop," Fel said. "You been quiet all morning . . . too quiet. What's going on in that sneaky mind of yours?"

"Nothing. I'm keeping it blank so when I see Pus Face it won't be cluttered."

"If I did that, I'd fall asleep." Fel got off his stool and moved a couple of steps closer to LaStanza, careful to remain hidden in the shadows of the bar. "Hey, Super Wop, remember the sleep contest?"

For the first time that day, a smile almost came to Dino's face as he turned to Fel Jones.

On the dark face there was already a wide smile which said, "As I recall, I beat you bad."

"Ha! You lying *nigrolian*. The day ain't come when your black ass could out sleep *this* wop!"

"Yeah? Well, I still say you cheated. You brought a pillow!" Fel seemed happy just to have made him lighten up. If there was a way to make a partner laugh, Felicity Jones would find it. LaStanza's mind was temporarily distracted as he remembered a parti-cularly boring week on the midnight watch in which they had taken turns to see how long one could sleep during an eight-hour shift. Dino had won by cheat-ing. He had brought a pillow, a pair of sunglasses, and a large teddy bear.

LaStanza's distraction was momentary. In a mo-ment he was back at his watch. As calmly as he could, he awaited the inevitable.

When Mason dropped by shortly before dark, Dino was in the same position, seated at the stool in the Hot Flash. The lieutenant eased into the bar and took a stool between the two. "I got a schedule now for this task force," he declared. "We going on twelve-hour shifts." Holding back a yawn, he explained how the men were to work, how Dino and Fel were to take the day watch at Club Morocco, how Paul would take the day shift at the Louviers, how the Intelligence Division would cover the dungeon and the LaStanza home on North Bernadotte. "We got men round the clock at Jimson's, Porta's, and Badalamente's," Mason explained. "We're pretty thin at the rest of the LCN hangouts. I just hope this shit don't last."

"Fuckin' A," Fel echoed him.

"What about Koski?" Dino asked.

"We got somebody there too. Besides the sheriff's office."

Dino was content with his assignment. He'd spend his days at Club Morocco and each evening late into the night with Lizette, grabbing a nap and shower at the dungeon. He did not care how long it took.

When Lizette returned home from her first day of class, she found Paul Snowood still sitting on her front gallery. His portable police radio was at his feet, his coat tossed on the front porch swing, his tie wilted around his skinny neck. In his right hand was a styrofoam cup.

"Howdy, Princess," he greeted her with a nod. He also nodded at the uniformed officers who had been Lizette's shadow all day.

"Come on in," she told him as she walked past. She turned to the two patrolmen and told them to come also.

"They can't," Paul explained as he rose. "They gotta stay out here."

"Oh," Lizette stopped and told the patrolmen, "I'll send you some refreshments."

Over iced tea, in the middle of a listless conversation, Paul told Lizette, "I been worried about him ever since we found that little girl."

She could see the weariness in Paul's face, and the concern in his voice as he continued, "I thought he was gonna snap, being in that pressure cooker too long, but now I'm more worried. He's been so calm. Like he don't feel nothin' no more."

Lizette took over, "He's found something inside, a confidence."

"Is that what he told you?"

"He didn't tell me. I can see it."

"I don't know," Paul seemed to be thinking hard. "I think he's just holding it all in." He hesitated before adding, "and he just might blow up."

It made her feel a little better to see the concern in Dino's partner. She cupped her chin in her hands and said, "I thought you were mad at him."

"I was pissed. He's trying to out-dago these assholes. And people are gettin' hurt." He took a gulp of tea before adding, "Gettin' killed."

"Who's gettin' killed?" Dino asked as he entered the kitchen.

"Our beloved football team," Paul answered quickly. "Did you see that pre-season game?"

Dino moved over to Lizette and kissed her, then poured himself a tall glass of tea.

"I guess ole' Pus Face didn't ever show," Paul asked.

"No, just Mason." Then Dino took the next minute to explain the new shifts. When he finished, Paul got up, thanked Lizette for the tea, and started to leave. "The old lady's gonna be missing me, sooner or later." He waved, "I'll let myself out. See you in the morning."

But before Paul made it home, he caught a whodunit. Dino heard it on the radio and volunteered to help. "Naw," Paul snorted, "it's just an ole' dumped body." A moment later he added, "with some bullet holes."

"Any connection?"

"Can't tell," Paul answered, "but I doubt it. This one's shot in the back. Not to mention he's slightly Oriental."

Dino began to giggle until he was laughing so hard Lizette wondered when he would catch his breath. When he did, his eyes were watery. Then he began to cough and had to hold onto the counter to keep from falling. She reached over but could see he was simply in the throes of hysteria.

When he recovered sufficiently to speak, he explained, "Another murdered gook case! Paul *hates* gooks!"

The following day seemed extra long. While lying in wait in the Hot Flash Bar, Dino listened to Paul conducting his initial follow-up on his new case and yearned to be out helping his partner. He found many distractions that second day. His eyes and especially his mind constantly wandered from the front of Club Morocco. At least Fel kept up his end of the listless conversation.

When the relief shift was late, the time dragged so much that LaStanza was beginning to nod out until the relief detectives arrived. By the time he arrived at Exposition Boulevard, it was already dark.

Pulling up at the end of Garfield, he saw that the

Second District unit was empty. As he climbed out of his Chevy, Dino spotted a movement to his left. A car door swung open on a beat-up Oldsmobile and someone was inside. Dino's Magnum was already out.

"Hey! Hey! Candy Ass! What ya' doin'?" yelled Stan Smith as he stood up, stretching and grinning at LaStanza. Stan was all in black, a six-inch revolver on his hip.

"What are you doing here?" Dino asked, reholstering his Magnum.

"I'm guarding that house," Stan pointed to the Louviers. "In case some no-good greaseball, motherfucker shows his ugly face, because I'm gonna blow his brains all over Audubon Park."

There was the beginning of a beard on Stan's face. Dino asked, "How long you been doin' this?"

"Couple nights. We've been taking turns." Stan frowned at the marked unit. "We can't let the Second do all the work." He put an arm around Dino and shook him like a rag doll. "Now you can sleep at night. The boys from the Sixth are here. Your Princess is safe."

"What do you mean, taking turns?" Dino asked as he pulled away.

"Me and some of the other fellas from the Sixth. You remember the Sixth, don't you? Just hang a left at the Melpomene Projects."

Dino was shaking his head. "Well, come on in and get something to eat."

"I ate," Stan turned back to the Olds. "Go on in. I've got a greaseball to kill."

Dino found the two Second District men out in front of the Louviers. They were so bored they were taking turns playing hit man and target.

"Did you know Stan Smith's sitting on Garfield in

a beat-up Oldsmobile?" he asked Lizette when she let him in.

"They're everywhere," she nodded. "I bet there's one in the banana trees out back."

Her voice was strained. Once she opened up, Dino wondered when she would stop. Maybe it was better for her to get it out, so he just listened as she complained about the police escort and the men outside all night and the fact that her life just was not hers anymore. "I can't go anywhere. I can't even go to the store." She looked at him with angry eyes. "When is this gonna end?"

Dino stayed even later that night. They both fell asleep watching a Jimmy Stewart movie. Mr. Louvier woke them up with an even angrier look on his face.

It was after three in the morning when Dino climbed into the Chevy and started for home. Only he did *not* end up on North Murat Street . . . he wound up at the Café DuMonde.

Once he'd been awakened, Dino found his mind started toying with him, playing games with his case. "What if Lemoni didn't do it?" he asked himself. "Just because Karen Koski says he did it doesn't mean it's true. Just because it was probably his print on the murder weapon doesn't prove he pulled the trigger. Just because he kidnapped Rawanda and called doesn't prove he killed her, not positively . . . it could be Badalamente orchestrating the entire thing."

As Dino sat outside the café, his mind continued to unwind, like an old clock. "What if Lemoni didn't do it? In Homicide, few things are truly positive. What I need," Dino told himself as the first cup of coffee arrived, "is a confession. I need to make Harry admit it—no, not force him, but make him *want* to admit it. Then I can be positive." That was how a cop's mind worked at three-thirty in the morning.

This time Dino saw him coming. He saw the Hemingway face as it turned in to the Decatur Street side of the café, the shark eyes focusing on him. He felt him too, the needle pricking at the back of his neck. Like a hammerhead on the prowl, Badalamente weaved his way between the small tables until reaching the detective; sitting across from LaStanza. He snapped his fingers at the approaching waiter. "One black," he said.

When they were alone, Dino asked, "Come here often?" and immediately wished he had not spoken first. He should have let Baddie start.

"No," Badalamente smiled coldly, "but you do."

After the coffee arrived, Badalamente took a sip and then spoke, his eyes still looking down into his coffee. "I'm here for two reasons. First, to extend my daughter's apology. She says she was rude to you." The shark eyes looked up at Dino. "I think you were rude to her." His voice rose slightly. "I don't want you showing pictures of dead people to my daughter. *Capish?*"

"Si, signore."

"Good. In fact, I don't want you bothering her again."

Dino's voice rose slightly. "She's my victim's wife. I'll talk to her any time I want. *Capish?*"

Badalamente narrowed his eyes for a moment and then let his face relax. "My daughter told me the same thing."

"And what's the other reason you came?"

292

"I come to give you Harry."

"Nice of you." Dino liked the way his voice sounded, deep and solid. Maybe he was too tired to show his nerves.

"It's out of my hands now." Baddie raised both of his gnarled hands and played like Pontius Pilate, as if he was washing them. "I give Harry to you. You two deserve each other."

But Badalamente was not finished. "You and Harry are just alike."

Dino was tired of hearing how he was just like someone. "What is that supposed to mean?"

"You both have the eyes of a killer." The shark eyes were leering at Dino now, beginning to look luminous, like oily licorice.

After another sip of coffee, the signore added, "There's been enough sorrow at that pretty mansion on Exposition Boulevard, wouldn't you say so?"

"What's that supposed to mean?" LaStanza's voice rose again.

"It means Harry's insane. *Out of control.* You and me don't have to get crazy too. *Capish?*"

"A fuckin' *division* of scumbag Mafiosi couldn't get near my girl."

For the first time Dino felt he saw a hint of reaction on Badalamente's rocky face, a hint of annoyance. But the signore was quick to recover as he leaned forward and whispered, "I didn't mean her. I meant *you.*"

The needles were back, the size of ice picks. Dino caught his breath and said, "I guess this is where you give me the big kiss."

A craggy smile emerged on the Hemingway face. "If you're referring to the kiss of death, we don't do that anymore." Badalamente shrugged as he rose.

293

"We leave that to Hollywood. Anyway, it's not me who wants your ass. It's Harry. I just wanted to warn you."

"Why do I deserve the favor?"

The old Sicilian hesitated, then said, "Because my daughter asked me to." With that he turned to walk away. Dino's eyes followed the mane of white hair until it disappeared around the corner of the café.

"Who killa da chief?" Dino asked himself when he left the café. "Dagos," he answered himself. "Dagos."

Later, at the dungeon, while standing outside his front door, fumbling for his keys, Dino found his hands shaking. Then he heard something behind him. A car passed quietly as he stood like a stiff target in his doorway, holding his breath. The needle pricks were all over his body as he waited for the inevitable shotgun blast, as Baddie's words echoed in his memory: *I didn't mean her, I meant you.*

The car passed, but the blast never came.

The surveillance routine was switched the following day. As the case officer, Dino was placed with Mark to cruise, to supervise. Snowood was busy with his new Oriental whodunit. Maurice Ferdinand took LaStanza's place at the Hot Flash with an unhappy Felicity Jones.

"Where are we going?" Dino asked when Mark drove into Jefferson Parish.

"Got something to show you," was all Mark said until they pulled up at the Sheriff's office east bank lockup and then walked into the motor pool where, nestled in a corner under the causeway overpass, was Harry Lemoni's silver Seville. The car had been totaled. It no longer had a right side nor an engine block. "At about four this morning," Mark told Dino, "Harry cracked up into a telephone pole somewhere on Veterans' Highway."

Dino looked at his sergeant with pleading eyes, but Mark just shook his head. "No . . . the fuckhead got away clean."

LaStanza walked up to the Seville and wiped his shoe on the rear bumper. "Did they search it?"

"Their crime lab went through it all night," Mark explained. "They found some hairs, maybe fibers. Our lab will get together with theirs, and maybe we can come up with something."

Two more facts were now added to the case. Lemoni was still in town, and there was no need to look for the Seville. On their way back to the city, Dino's mind toyed with him again. "Just because we got the Seville doesn't prove Lemoni is still in town."

When Dino's phone rang at three in the morning, the last person he thought it would be was Gina. "It's just hard to believe it all," she told him.

"It's true."

"So," she said in a distant voice, "what are you going to do now?"

"Catch him."

"You mean *kill* him. Because that's what you'll have to do."

Dino did not answer. He waited as the pause in the conversation grew until Gina asked another question. "Have you spoken to my father?"

"As a matter of fact, yes."

"Did he tell you how much he couldn't stand my husband?"

"No. Was he supposed to?"

Gina's voice was stronger. "You don't get it, do you?"

"It's late," Dino answered, fighting back a yawn.

"My father knows all the right buttons to push."

"What's that supposed to mean?" he asked.

"First Harry. Now you."

"Are you trying to tell me your father pushed Harry's button and then . . ."

"Not exactly. But he certainly wants *you* to get Harry now, doesn't he?" Her voice was heavy with concern.

"What are you worried about?"

It surprised Dino when she answered, "You. I'm worried about you." She took a second to add, just before hanging up, *"You don't know Harry."*

Sleep did not come easily to Dino LaStanza that morning. He kept seeing the Gargoyle lying faceup on the St. Maurice Wharf, along with images of buttons being pushed by gnarled fingers, and a Hemingway face laughing, and then Harry's vicious face leering at him.

The first hint of autumn arrived in New Orleans at exactly seven that evening. Dino noticed because the humidity disappeared as a cool north breeze caused the temperature to drop into the sixties for the first time since April.

As the temperature outside dipped, Dino found himself sitting at his desk, talking on the phone.

"Maybe this weather will bring a change," Lizette was saying when Mark rushed into the squad room and shouted, "Dino, pick up line three!"

"What?" He put a hand over the mouthpiece.

"Lemoni's on line three!"

"Hold on," Dino told Lizette, punching the

296

"hold" button on his phone before punching line three. "Hello?"

"Hey, cocksucker." It was Lemoni all right. "Your girlfriend's got a *nice* body."

"What?" Dino answered in a low voice.

"Yeah. I liked that little striptease on the balcony the other night. Didn't know I was watching, did ya'?" Lemoni began laughing. Dino could not move, could not even speak.

But Harry was not finished. "I like the little red jumpsuit she's wearing tonight, too; think I'll go plant a big kiss on her filthy little pussy!" With that remark, Lemoni hung up.

Dino sat numb for several seconds, until he realized. . . .

He tried to keep the panic from his voice when he got back on the line. "Are you wearing a red jumpsuit tonight?"

"Yes."

"Who's with you? Who's there now?"

"My father," she answered hurriedly, picking up the urgency in her voice, "and two officers outside."

Dino turned to Mark, "Get those uniforms on the radio and tell them to get in the house with her. *Now!*"

He took a moment to calm himself before telling Lizette, "He just called. He knows what you're wearing tonight. I'll be right there."

Only one of the uniformed officers came in. The other stayed out on the front gallery, gun in hand. Lizette and her father waited with one of the policemen in the dining room. Lizette watched her father fidget nervously with the tablecloth.

Mark nearly set a land speed record from headquarters to Exposition Boulevard. Dino hung onto the dashboard all the way. But it still seemed like hours before they arrived. He radioed ahead for more units and tried not to think about Lemoni's ugly face watching Lizette stripping on her balcony. "He's been there watching," Dino told himself. "And he's there now!"

They took the corner of Calhoun and Garfield on two tires as Mark punched the brakes, sending the Chevy into a grinding halt at the end of Garfield. Lizette heard the screeching tires and moved toward the front of the house with her father and the patrolman close behind. She stopped in the foyer and peeked out at the park. The patrolman from the gallery was now standing just outside their front gate.

Dino saw one patrolman standing on Exposition Boulevard in front of the Louvier's. Instinctively, as he approached, he followed the patrolman's gaze out into the park and saw nothing but the oaks and a little fog in the darkness. When Dino and Mark stepped up, the officer shrugged and began to reholster his gun.

Lizette had started to open the front door when the shots rang out. The shock of the noise caused her to freeze with the door half opened.

Dino never heard the first shot, but when the patrolman fell next to him, he heard the successive shots and dived for the pavement. Off to his left he saw muzzle fire from behind an oak as more shots exploded. When they stopped, a shadow moved from behind the tree and started to run. Dino jumped up, Magnum in hand, and began running low and hard after the shadow.

Lizette saw Dino rise and start running down Exposition Boulevard. She tried to step out on the gallery, but her father grabbed her and pulled her back. She yanked away and managed to make it out on the porch as Dino disappeared into the darkness of the park. It was then she saw all the blood on Mark's hands as he was working on the patrolman. Mark's mouth was open, but it wasn't until the second patrolman reacted that she heard the screaming.

For a moment Dino lost sight of the shadow and slowed up just before tripping over a guide wire from a telephone pole alongside Exposition Boulevard, which sent him face-first into the dirt. When he looked up, he saw the shadow running again. In an instant he was up and running, following the shadow through the large oaks at the park's edge. When he lost the shadow again, he lunged for a tree. Several shots hit the tree a split second later.

When Lizette heard more gunfire, she pulled away from her father's renewed grip and moved to the side of the gallery.

"Where's Dino?" Mark was up and yelling.

Lizette's eyes met Mark's as she pointed in the direction of the gunfire. He began cursing and then started barking into his portable radio. She could hear him describing Dino, and the word *plainclothesman*. Behind Mark she could see the wounded officer sitting up, holding onto the second policeman. Beyond them fog shrouded in the park. Then she heard the low, distant wail of sirens.

There was no movement. Dino peeked out from behind his tree at the absolute stillness of Audubon Park. To his right he could see the glassy lagoon, its waters reflecting some light into the blackness. Staring straight ahead, he let his eyes roll into a soft focus, waiting for the slightest movement.

When there was a hint of movement next to a distant oak, Dino raised his hands, squeezed off a round, then bolted for the next tree. As he moved, he caught sight of the shadow again, running away. The shadow was moving fast, so fast it could not avoid the sliver of light that reached into the park from one of the streetlights of Exposition Boulevard. When the shadow ran through the light, Dino could make out a white streak of hair.

The new gunfire was different. Its echo boomed back to the Louvier house. Mark stopped yelling into his radio and looked back at Lizette. "That's Dino!" he screamed.

There was a gazebo ahead. Dino saw the streak of white hair run directly for it. Just before Lemoni ducked into the gazebo, Dino squeezed off another round, then jumped behind another oak.

As soon as his breath was back, LaStanza yelled, "Hey, Pus Face! *Fuck you!*"

Dino's answer came in the form of gunfire as Lemoni opened up from the gazebo, peppering the area around LaStanza. When the shots stopped, Dino peeked out again. "You can't shoot for *shit!*"

"Fuck you, cocksucker!"

And in an instant Lemoni was out and running again, away from the gazebo, still south between the lagoon and Exposition Boulevard. There was only one way for him to go, and that was Magazine Street. Dino followed, giving the gazebo a wide berth as he kept himself between Harry and Exposition Boulevard.

They took the wounded patrolman off in a police car as more police arrived. When Stan Smith ran up carrying a shotgun, he headed directly for the Louvier gallery. Lizette's father tried again to get her inside until she spoke for the first time since the shooting began, in a deep, firm voice, "I'm staying here." She moved her eyes from her father back to the park and added, "I've got to hear."

Stan positioned himself next to Lizette as her father tried to warn her that there could be more than one person out there. When Lizette would not answer, Stan did. He racked a round into the shotgun. "It'll take a division of greaseballs to get her now!"

They were silenced by more gunfire, by sharp cracks followed by loud, echoing booms. But in a moment it was silent again. Lizette reached over and touched Stan. "They sound different."

"The booming is a Magnum. Dino carries a Magnum."

Several more cracks were answered by a single boom and then quiet. Lizette stared blankly out at the park. They were too far away now, but her eyes remained fixed on the oaks and the fog that slithered between them.

Where the lagoon emptied into a wide pond, there was a large, elevated concrete pavilion with tall columns. Lemoni took this high ground to fire at the approaching detective, but Dino saw him first and stayed clear of the shots. Harry began to fire randomly.

As soon as Dino could find cover, he knelt behind another tree and reloaded before leveling his sights at the patch of white hair peeking out from behind one of the concrete columns. It was a long shot, but he managed to hit the column, which sent Lemoni scurrying off the pavilion, heading directly for Magazine Street.

Dino pursued him, pumping hard to keep up and thinking consciously for the first time. Lemoni was panicking. He could feel it. Random shots were made by a man who was scared.

As soon as Lemoni crossed Magazine, Dino saw just how panicky he was as he almost fell over as he

301

traversed the small neutral ground. Dino also got a good look at the dark automatic in Lemoni's hand before Harry disappeared into the darkness beyond the street.

Dino hesitated before crossing Magazine, waiting as a bus approached, timing it perfectly, taking a running start to cross as the bus passed. There was muzzle fire off to the right, but he made it across, tumbling onto the damp grass on the south side of the street.

"Missed again, Pus Face!"

"Fuck you, cocksucker."

"Is that all you think about, cocksucking?" Dino crawled forward, searching for a tree.

LaStanza's accusation was answered by more shots straight ahead. He could feel the grass strike his face as the slugs rained down around him. He fired a round himself, wildly, before rolling as fast as he could to his left into the deeper darkness of the park between Magazine and the Audubon Zoo.

When Lizette heard the lions roar, she told Stan, "King Kong will protect him now."

For the first time since assuming a position as her personal bodyguard, Stan looked back at her. *"What?"*

Lizette's voice was smooth and steady. "When he was a little boy, his brother used to tell him that King Kong lived at the zoo." She looked back at Stan and asked, "He never told you that?"

Her father was the next to speak. He told Mark that he thought Lizette was in shock. Mark moved up and tried to get her to sit down. She refused as she wrapped her arms around a railing of her front gallery, her eyes fixed on the park.

"None dared refuse," Lizette realized she was talking again.

"What?" Stan asked.

She turned and looked back at her father and said, *"Code duello.* Remember, Father?"

She could see anguish in father's eyes as her words registered. Lizette then looked at Stan and explained. "The Creole French started dueling here over two hundred years ago." Turning her eyes again to the park, she added, "when a gentleman was challenged, none dared refuse."

They quit bothering her after that. Not that her statement made much sense even to her. It was just a thought that came to her as she waited for the duel to end. They quit because she wasn't going to listen anyway.

Lizette continued staring as Mark continued with his radio, Stan with his guarding, and Lizette's father with his worrying that his daughter was in shock. She did not even notice the host of other policemen who continued arriving until Paul Snowood got there. She noticed only because he and Mark became involved in a shouting match on the gallery steps that stopped only when more gunfire echoed from the south.

There were several cracks, sounding more like firecrackers now, but they went unanswered by even a single boom. After an agonizing moment of quiet, more cracks sounded, followed by an even longer silence. Everyone in the gallery was motionless as the seconds ticked by until a boom sounded, like the mourning of a distant cannon.

Paul started running away from the mansion, down the boulevard, straight into the park, gun in hand. Mark yelled after him and cursed before getting back on his radio to give out Snowood's description.

They exchanged shots at the zoo fence, and Dino

thought he had hit Lemoni only to find himself ducking again from return fire. He had a clear shot at Lemoni when Harry reached the top of the fence, but in the darkness he must have missed. Now it was Dino's turn to scale the twelve-foot chain-link fence with the barbed wire on top. Lemoni could be lying in wait or could be running madly through the zoo, getting away.

Dino decided to try a running start, moving as fast as he could, giving Lemoni a moving target to hit. But there was no fast way to scale a fence, even with your Magnum holstered and both hands free. When he reached the top, he closed his eyes, just knowing it was coming. But the shots did not come until he was over the top, and then they came in rapid succession as he felt something strike the fence. He let go and fell to the ground. For unbearably long seconds he could do nothing. He had no breath. His lungs burned, and he could not breathe; and he knew it was coming now, he knew Lemoni was standing over him, taking aim. He closed his eyes and then felt a gasp of breath before he rolled again and stumbled away from the fence as more shots hit off to his right. The muzzle fire was close, but Lemoni's shots were erratic. "He's yanking his trigger," Dino told himself as he pulled out his Magnum and squeezed off a round that immediately silenced the shots.

LaStanza had to catch his breath. He found cover and reloaded again, slipping six more Magnums from another speed loader.

"The fucker must have a hundred clips with him," he told himself as he closed the cylinder. He looked out in the direction from where the last shots had come but could see nothing but blackness. Without consciously thinking of it, Dino's mind was telling him why they had been missing each other . . . adrenalin and running and shooting at random.

Off to Dino's left he heard something. Barking. Seals. He heard the barking at the sea-lion pool. And then he saw Lemoni heading for the pool: in the distance there was a streak of white hair running away from him.

Dino rose and began to lope in long, deliberate strides, straight for Lemoni, his breathing almost back to normal. And as he moved he told himself, "Ice in the veins. Ice in the veins." He knew that whoever was in control of himself first would triumph. And as he moved, he realized that he had to disregard the primeval instinct to survive. There would be no more ducking or hiding.

When Lemoni approached the sea lions, he veered off to the right. Dino followed in a direct line from tree to tree, hesitating only when he realized that the further they progressed, the lighter it was becoming. There were large lights around the sea-lion pool that cast a faint glow over the land.

Dino lost sight of Lemoni behind a tight row of magnolia trees, but continued forward anyway, fighting off the instinct to slow down.

Then he saw a sudden movement between the magnolias as Lemoni's red, panting face gleamed out at him, his gun pointed at Dino, who raised his own gun, cupping it in both hands, aiming carefully at the gleaming face. Lemoni's gun flashed as Dino's own gun recoiled from firing.

Fire. Fire was burning on Dino's neck. He grabbed the side of his neck with his left hand and felt wetness and knew he was hit. Gunshots burn.

Dino's mind ordered his eyes to focus, and when they did, he saw Lemoni still standing, but the gun

305

was no longer in his hand. Both of Lemoni's hands were at his throat, and the red face grimaced in pain. He heard a guttural sound, a gasping. Dino took a step forward and saw a dark stream of blood flowing between Lemoni's fingers.

Harry wavered a moment and then fell straight down. He came to rest in a sitting position, his back against one of the magnolias. Gasping for breath, his face contorted into a hideous mask of pain as he fought for air. When Dino moved closer, he could see blood gushing from Lemoni's throat as Harry's mouth opened wide in a useless attempt at breathing. Pus Face was gagging on his own blood.

LaStanza inched closer and with a steady hand placed the barrel of his Magnum inside Lemoni's gaping mouth. He cocked his Magnum and slowly squeezed the trigger. In the instant before the hammer fell, Dino saw stark fear in Harry Lemoni's ugly eyes.

"Kiss this," Dino said as the hammer fell, blowing Lemoni's insane brains over the base of the magnolia tree.

The silence was far worse than the sounds of gunfire. The shots had ended. Now there was only silence and the lingering minutes as everyone began to pay closer attention to the radio in Mark's hands.

The insectlike chatter on the radio made little sense to Lizette. Even the words she understood gave no hint as to what had happened. They were still looking.

Dino was beginning to feel weak. He sat against another magnolia and applied direct pressure to the left side of his neck. He did not think of firing into the air until some minutes later, when he thought he heard voices.

Closing his eyes for a second, Dino saw beyond a

306

dizzying fog something looking back at him; he saw Egyptian eyes.

He was about to pass out when Paul Snowood's face appeared in front of him talking excitedly into his radio. *"He's alive! I got him!"*

When Paul reached down to pick him up, LaStanza managed to tell him, "Hey, Country Ass. You're spitting brown shit all over me."

Lizette heard Paul's distinct voice over Mark's radio. Then she heard the sergeant ask, "What about the suspect?"

It took Paul a minute to respond. "He's 10-7."

Before Lizette could even ask, Stan started unloading his shotgun. "He's dead," Stan said, "Fuckin' asshole!"

Girod Street

Wherever he was, it was not Charity. The room had curtains. When Lizette moved over to him, Dino smiled weakly and said, "So, what's up?"

She laughed in relief, grabbed his hand, and squeezed.

"Where am I?"

"Ochsner," she answered, "Paul said it was closer."

He tried to nod, but his head hurt too much, only not as much as his right arm. There was a needle sticking in his arm, and he was having trouble breathing.

"Calm down now," the doctor told him. "You're going to be fine." For an instant Dino thought the doctor was Felicity Jones. The man could pass for Fel's brother. The doctor was writing on a clipboard and did not look up as he continued, "You won't even have much of a scar." When the doctor did look up, he addressed Dino but looked at Lizette. "You have what's commonly called a flesh wound, although you did lose a little too much blood." And with that the doctor turned to leave. "You'll be in your own room in a little while."

Dino looked around in confusion.

"You're still in intensive care," she told him as she began to touch his left arm with long, soft strokes and watched the injection take effect. It was not long before Dino's steady breathing eased him into a deep slumber.

When Dino woke later, his bleary eyes took a while to adjust in the dark room. Outside the window, he could see it was already night. He saw Lizette curled up in a chair on one side of his bed. His mother was in another. When he saw movement at the foot of his bed, he looked down at the smiling face of his dead brother. Joe winked at his little brother and began to move up the side of the bed. When Joe reached the top, he leaned down, kissed Dino's forehead, and whispered in their father's voice, "Get some sleep, son."

"Say, Wyatt," Paul called out as he entered Dino's room, "that was some good shootin'!" When Dino's mother looked over at him, Paul put a hand over his mouth, "Oops!"

"Go on," Captain LaStanza told him.

Paul looked sheepishly at Lizette before clearing his throat and continuing, "You did a real number on him, Wyatt." He had just returned from the autopsy.

"How many wounds?" asked Dino's father.

"Two, both fatal." Paul placed an index finger against his larynx and said, "One in the throat. One in the mouth." Looking down at his partner, he added with a chuckle, "The one in the mouth was a little close. Ol' Pus Face never looked better."

When Mark walked in a minute later, he was with

310

Millie Suzanne, who'd brought candy. Mark brought flowers. "Flowers are for dead people," Dino told his sergeant.

"You look in a mirror lately?" responded the large, grinning Napolitano face. Even Dino's mother smiled.

But as soon as Mason entered, the laughter exploded into a roar. The good lieutenant strolled into Dino's room wearing gangster glasses and a new sport coat. Mason owned exactly three sport coats, a maroon one, a blue one, and a kelly green one. He had one navy blue suit reserved for court. But on this day, he waltzed into LaStanza's room wearing a new tan sport coat, which caused Mark and Paul and Dino to roar so loud a nurse came rushing in.

"There are *sick* people here," the nurse scolded them.

"You telling *us?*" Paul answered.

Lizette watched the detectives joke around with Dino and watched his face light up with laughter. She was feeling so much better, she joined in. It did not even matter how sick the jokes were.

When it was time to go, Dino's father stepped forward, kissed his son on the forehead, and said, *"Mio leopardo piccolo,"* as he patted his son's cheek.

"What's that mean?" Paul asked.

"He called him his little Leopold," Mark said, causing Paul and Millie and even Mason to roar. But Lizette saw something in her boyfriend's eyes that kept her from laughing. When she saw the harsh look Dino's mother gave his father on their way out, she gave Dino an inquiring look.

"Actually," Dino corrected Mark, "he called me his little leopard." To which the roaring intensified.

"Leopard?" Paul yelled. "Ol' Wyatt's a *tiger*, at least!"

But Dino was not laughing. Lizette laid a hand on

his shoulder and asked, "What does it mean?"

He looked up at her and said, "A leopard, pound for pound nature's most efficient killing machine."

Mark and Millie began to applaud. Paul stomped his feet and howled. Only Mason and Lizette remained silent. There was a look of resignation in Dino's eyes. When the angry nurse came to clear the room, he asked if Mason and Lizette could stay a moment.

"Well, Wyatt," Paul added on his way out, "I gotta hand it to ya'. Ya' done better than Custer!"

Once they were alone, Dino asked Mason, "What about the patrolman?"

"He's fine. Caught one in the lung. But he'll be okay."

"What about Bogue Falaya?"

"What about it?"

"It's just . . ."

Mason shrugged, "There's no such thing as a perfect investigation. There's always some questions left unanswered." The lieutenant started to light up a cigarette then thought better of it, tucking it into his coat pocket as he added, "There's always more you can do. Then again, there comes a time to just stop and let it go."

He patted Dino's foot on his way out. "Get some rest."

"I guess I better be going too," Lizette said when the nurse returned again with an envelope for Dino and pointed to the wall clock, indicating that visiting hours were over.

The envelope bore no return address. Dino handed it to Lizette and asked her to open it. Inside the envelope was a holy card, a card of Our Lady of the Holy Rosary. On its back was written, "Cento Anni." It was signed "Gina."

312

Dino handed it back to Lizette. "It's from Gina Jimson."

"What does it mean?" she asked after reading it.

"It means a hundred years, may you live a hundred years." Then Dino pointed to the name. "And that means 'Gina.'"

She pinched him on his forearm and then gasped when he cringed. She had hit the spot where the intravenous had been. Dino closed one eye and squinted up at her. When she kissed him gently on the mouth, he pulled her back for more.

Before leaving, she told him that Karen Koski was at Ochsner now. "They moved her here for plastic surgery. I just thought you might want to know."

"Is he really dead?" Karen asked Dino when he stepped into her room. It was almost as dark in the room as it was outside. He could barely make her out.

"If I didn't kill him, the autopsy did."

"Good," she said, and then added, "What about you?"

"I'll live."

"That's *my* line," Karen snarled before clearing her throat and continuing, "Actually, the doctor says I'll be as good as new."

"Great." He could see some of the bandages were gone, but with her face in shadow, he could not see even her eyes.

"I was afraid," she said as the pause in the conversation grew, "that I would never be the same again." Her voice almost broke with the word *same*. But she recovered quickly and turned her head toward the window. "In New England the trees are all orange and red now."

"Must be beautiful."

313

"When they finish putting me back together," she said, "I'm going home. Back to Maine. And I hope I never see Spanish moss or another magnolia tree again." Moving her gaze back to LaStanza, she leaned forward slightly. He could see her eyes shining back at him. "I asked the doc if I'll be pretty, and you know what he told me?"

"No. What?"

"He says I'll be prettier. Can you imagine that?"

Dino could think of no response, so he said nothing. When he did not answer, she switched gears. "So, when are you getting out of here?"

"Tomorrow."

"Well, come back and see me when they finish. See how I turn out."

"It's a deal." He turned to leave, but stopped and added, "And when you get out, don't be a stranger." He smiled at her and, pretending to be punching numbers on a telephone, said, "You know my number."

When the entourage from the Sixth arrived, Dino knew it was time to leave. He was grateful Lizette was not present to witness the display. Led by Stan Smith and Felicity Jones, a host of semi-uniformed, semi-drunk, semi-moronic policemen entered LaStanza's room and took over, sitting all over his bed, flipping the channels on the television until they found a football game, eating the candy and even some of the flowers Mark had brought.

"See that!" Stan yelled when the New Orleans football team fumbled again. "I've seen this exact game before! Those sons-of-abitches have played this exact game six or seven times before."

Fel agreed, along with most of the others.

"Motherfuckers should be run out of town," some-one added.

"They should change their names to the Pussies," Stan yelled.

"Yeah, the New Orleans Pussies!" the mob agreed.

Stan was on a roll. "They could put a shitload of pubic hair on one side of their helmet and a trout on the other side."

"A trout?" someone asked.

"For the smell. That's what a pussy smells like, don't it?"

It was definitely time for LaStanza to leave.

When Captain LaStanza picked up Dino, he took his son for a ride downtown, parking on Girod Street, near Loyola Avenue. After turning off the ignition, the captain rolled down his window, looked around the bustling intersection, and spoke to his somewhat bewildered son. "When I was a rookie, they took us here to show us, telling us the old 'Who Killa Da Chief' story. This is where it happened," the captain added, "Girod and Basin Street, 1890."

"Hennessey," Dino said.

The captain looked back at his son and continued, "I just read a new book about it. Claims the Italians lynched after the trial just may have been innocent victims of an anti-Italian mob."

"Who did it?" Dino asked. "Arabs, Spaniards, don't tell me, the Irish?"

Captain LaStanza gave his son the same look he'd given him each and every time Dino had disap-pointed him, which was more often than Dino could remember. "Mafiosi did it," his father explained, as if he were talking to a child. "But not necessarily the ones they lynched."

"What are you trying to tell me?" Dino asked. He hated to have to figure out the secret meanings of things.

"Nothing. Except . . . well, it's been almost a hundred years, and they're still here. You can't get rid of them. Just like the roaches."

"Fuck 'em," Dino said.

"You just did, son. And they don't forget."

Dino refused to think about it. "So? Fuck 'em if they can't take a joke."

"*You'd* better not forget."

After a moment of tense silence, his father continued, "You know they'll have to do something. They'll have to respond in some way."

Dino nodded and looked back at his father with eyes narrowed and sharp. "I know."

When the captain started up the car again, Dino realized, "Wait a minute. Didn't you say Girod and Basin?"

"Yes."

"They don't intersect."

"Not anymore."

Dino looked around at the new sleek high-rises and at the towering Louisiana Superdome and sighed. "I wonder what Hennessey would think of all this."

"He'd probably blame it on the dagos."

"Take me to Exposition Boulevard," he told his father when they pulled away from Girod Street.

"Your momma's gonna be disappointed."

"I'll be by later. But I want to go to Exposition now."

Lizette was waiting for him in her white robe. "Are

316

we alone?" he asked as he wrapped one arm around her, slipping the other hand into the robe to feel her naked body.

She nodded, opening her mouth to kiss him. When their long French kiss ended, she asked, "Easy chair?"

"Easy chair."

She snuggled next to him, closed her eyes and whispered in his ear, "Hold me, Babe."

After a minute, she opened her eyes and saw that his eyes were open wide. "Are you all right?"

He nodded and looked down at her face. "Are *you* all right?"

She cuddled against him and closed her eyes once more. "Let's just snuggle."

When he started to remove her robe, her eyes snapped open. "Should you?" she asked, running a finger lightly over the bandage on the side of his neck.

Dino answered her by gently stroking her breast as his mouth sought out the soft spot on her neck just below her ear.

"You better take it easy," she warned him as her breathing grew deeper.

He did not take it easy. If there was one thing Dino LaStanza knew, you were only as good as your last case.

All Saints' Day

On All Saints' Day, special masses are held throughout New Orleans. After Mass, New Orleanians visit their little cities of the dead to lay flowers and wreaths against the sepulchers and the oven tombs of their ancestors. It is a time for cleaning the old tombs, whitewashing faded crypts, and sealing cracks in timeworn cement. All Saints' Day is the day to visit the dead.

When Dino LaStanza was a little boy, he truly believed that All Saints' Night brought forth the vampires of the Canal Cemeteries, who would once again prowl the southern night, along with the werewolves of City Park. All Saints' Night was the night for the dead to visit.

By All Saints' Day of that year, Detective Dino LaStanza had handled two more whodunits, solving each. He also handled three suicides, six killings, two misdemeanor murders, a sudden-infant-death case, and two accidental-death cases.

* * *

On All Saints' Night, Karen Koski left her mother's house in Maine and drove to a nearby Portland shopping center to buy a new pair of shoes. Her car was later found abandoned at the shopping center. There was no sign of foul play, although her disappearance was complete.

Two days later, a Portland detective called New Orleans Homicide for assistance in the disappearance of Karen Elizabeth Koski. Lieutenant Rob Mason forwarded the call to the case officer of the Thomas Jimson Murder. When the Portland detective advised LaStanza that Karen Koski had disappeared, Dino put the detective on hold, stood up from his desk, and kicked his trash can so hard it careened off the far wall. No one in the office seemed to even notice.